IN MY HEART

BETTE HAWKINS

BELLA
BOOKS
2019

Bella Books, Inc.
P.O. Box 10543
Tallahassee, FL 32302

Printed in the United States of America on acid-free paper.

First Bella Books Edition 2019

Editor: Medora MacDougall
Cover Designer: Judith Fellows

ISBN: 978-1-64247-061-1

Other Bella Books by Bette Hawkins

Like a Book
No More Pretending

Acknowledgment

Thanks to Bella Books and my wonderful editor Medora MacD. And thanks to my mother, who raised me on country music.

About the Author

Bette Hawkins is a social worker who hails from Melbourne, Australia. She lives with her long-term girlfriend and their very spoiled dog. In addition to writing, Bette's favorite pastimes include playing the guitar, watching films, cooking, and reading.

CHAPTER ONE

In the days when we spent all our time together, during the spring of 1958, Aunt May and I clung to certain rituals.

On Friday after we finished work, we climbed into May's car to travel along the dirt road to her house. This afternoon, she was letting me drive. She had taught me how and at first, she'd laughed at me from the passenger seat while I steered with white knuckles. By now I'd acquired her posture behind the wheel, loose and confident, the car an extension of my body.

I dreamed about Friday night from the moment I punched the clock on Monday morning. Though neither of us had much money to spare, May and I put great care into gathering provisions for our little parties. There was always something good to eat like deviled eggs, cherry tomatoes, roast beef with mustard, or sliced pork.

Though May's house only had a few rooms and paint flaked from its exterior, we treated it like a palace. We laid a fresh white cloth on the table and set the food out on her chipped plates.

We mixed gin and tonics and chilled a bottle of white wine in May's silver ice bucket.

After supper we sat on the front porch with full bellies, on kitchen chairs we dragged outside to cool ourselves down. May sipped her gin and tonic, rattling ice around in her glass so that it clinked against the edges.

"Alice, why don't you go on inside and get the guitar? Play me a song, will ya?"

My guitar was propped against the wall in the hallway. When I ran my fingertips over the smooth wood, it felt like the first time I'd touched it, when I'd discovered how it fit perfectly into my hands. The instrument spoke a language I picked up quickly, as though it was my native tongue. I'd developed thick callouses on the fingertips of my left hand and when I was bored I ran my thumb over them, testing their firmness.

I strummed an old song called "Grave in the Pines" while May sang with gusto, her voice made gravelly from cigarettes.

"Why don't you sing louder, Alice? You're like a little mouse!"

"I can't get it to sound the way I want."

"Who cares? It's like a stiff drink, it'll make you feel good!"

"I don't think Mama would approve of that idea, would she?"

May leaned back in her chair to look out at the stars. I played some chords, finding a pattern and repeating it. The edge of my thumb moved gently against the strings, the progression melancholy but pleasing. A melody suggested itself, and a song began to take shape.

"What's that you're playing? It's real pretty."

"Nothing. Just making it up."

"Just now? You could be famous one day. The next Kitty Wells. Just don't forget who bought you that guitar when it happens, will you now?"

I set the guitar down, laughing at her. The guitar had been a gift for my twenty-first birthday. I was twenty-five now, and I'd barely put the thing down since. When I peeled brown paper wrapping from the secondhand case, I was happy enough to cry.

She said that she was sure I'd be able to do something special with it. I'd been making up songs since I was a kid.

"I'll be famous when hell freezes over. I'm going to be stuck working at the phone company forever," I said.

"There's nothing wrong with that, is there? You'll be an old-timer like me. We can practically run the place together, keep everyone else in line," she said, smacking her lips after a sip of gin.

I plucked a couple of strings between my forefinger and thumb. "Sure, May. Sounds good to me."

"Stop being such a grouch. Now go and get the radio. Our country hour's gonna be on any minute. I don't want to miss the start."

"Okay," I said, the chair creaking underneath me as I stood.

May expected me to wait on her when I was at the house. I couldn't get too mad about her asking me to fetch things, not when she'd done so much for me. I was working in a cannery when a position at the telephone company came up, and she put in a good word for me with the manager. After I was hired as a gofer, running errands and making coffee, she showed me the ropes.

"Now don't talk to Evelyn, Mr. Clark's secretary. She's bad news and she'll only get you into trouble. Mr. White's girl is a good one though, she'll help you out. You need to put your head down and just learn for a while, act gracious to anyone who talks to you," May explained.

I heeded May's advice and after a couple of years, I moved up to work the switchboard alongside her. We passed our days working the lines, laughing together with the other girls. It bonded us so that May and I began to spend even more time together than we had before.

A lot of the time at May's it was just the two of us, but tonight when I came back outside with the radio there was a red car parked on the front lawn. Henry ambled up the stairs and took off his hat to greet me, revealing his almost-bald scalp. I looked away when he kissed May hello. Henry was nice enough, but I wondered how long he'd stick around.

"Go fix yourself a drink, Henry. You're just in time to listen to our show," May said.

She turned up the volume and the notes of the theme song rang out, making the speakers crackle. We'd been listening to Huck's Dixie Hour together for years. Only a handful of stations were in range of Greenville, but we could pick up a few from over in Mobile. Huck was the best; we loved his rapid-fire announcing.

"Welcome to the show, ladies and gentlemen! I've got a real treat for you tonight, a record that I just got into my hot little hands. It's by a group of sisters, a wholesome family band that I think you're all going to love if you don't already know them."

It was a number about loving a beau who lived too far away. I could pick out three voices bending together in harmony. May tapped her foot against the ground in time with the beat. The chorus played, and then there was a solo.

My arms broke out in goose bumps. That voice. It could make ships smash on the rocks, could make you weep with the beauty of it.

Henry came outside with a glass of beer, stomping along the floorboards. "Hey, May, you want a smoke?"

"Ssshhh!" I said.

Henry sparked a match on his shoe, then cupped his hands around May's to light her up. I closed my eyes and leaned against the back of my chair.

The song faded out. I got closer to the speakers, crouching up next to the radio.

"And that was the Stellar Sisters, with 'My Country Boy.' I may be a little late to the party, but I sure am glad I finally heard these gals, and I bet you are, too."

"Tell me all about your day, Henry. Alice and I had a boring old time at the office. I could use the excitement," May said, grabbing onto Henry's tie.

"I'm going to head on inside, play my guitar for a while," I said.

"All right. I can see your fingers itching. We'll come in a little later."

I pulled a chair up to the kitchen table, resting my guitar on my knee. The ballpoint pen and notebook I stored in my handbag were in front of me. I let the woman's voice play over in my mind. Though I wished I could listen to it again, its ghost was still with me.

The soloist had the voice of a caged bird, longing to take flight. The lonesome sound was searching for the right song.

I positioned my fingers into the shape of the chords I'd been playing earlier. I worked for a long time, adjusting the melody and playing until it flowed like a river. The lyrics needed filling in, but it could be the start of something good. I was going to call it "Do You Miss Me?"

When I was satisfied with what I had for now, I packed my guitar away, still humming my song.

The next day I walked into town to Stone Street Records, having decided that it wouldn't hurt to treat myself for once. Aside from the money I gave to my parents, I salted away every penny I earned. I'd been saving for a car since the day I started working.

I opened the door to the record store, hearing the bell chime as I walked in. The man behind the counter hurriedly dog-eared his paperback and stashed it under the counter. He was younger than the guy who usually served me, though there was a resemblance. Like the other man he was well-dressed, and I wondered if he was hot in his collared shirt and tie. The room was broken up into lanes by the wooden display cases housing records.

"Hello, ma'am," the clerk said, when I'd weaved around them to reach him.

"Hello. I was wondering if you had anything by a group called the Stellar Sisters?"

"The Stellar Sisters? I know those girls. I'm sure I've got a copy of 'My Country Boy.' Let me see."

He led me down one of the little lanes to the country section, then quickly flicked through the stack labeled "S."

"This group is great... Did you hear one of them left the group not too long ago? It's going to be a duo now, but there's nothing new out for them yet," he said, sliding the record out of the sleeve to check the label. "Not sure if they'll have the same sound."

"Oh? One of them left?" I asked.

"Dorothy. Great voice. She did a lot of the best solos with the Stellars… Did the solo on this one if I'm not mistaken. She's gone out on her own now. Going by the name of Dorothy Long."

"Do you have any of her records?" I asked.

"We sold them already, we only had a small batch. I bought one myself. You want me to order one in for you? I can have it in a few weeks," he said, moving back behind the counter to pick up a book.

"Sure," I said. I wrote my details on the slip he handed me before giving it back.

"You know, while you're waiting for that record, she's going to be playing out at Merle's in a couple of weeks. The honky-tonk just out of town? You could go on out there and see her if you wanted to."

"I might just do that," I said. "Thanks."

He scribbled down a note with the date, then tucked it into the paper bag with my purchase. Once it was inside, he folded down the top corner and sealed it neatly with his thumb, handing it to me with a grin. On the way home I walked faster than usual, clutching the bag against my side. Since the night before, the song was all I could think about.

"Do you mind if I use the record player today?" I asked Mama. I found her coming out of her room, finger combing her hair. It had turned from red to a rosy-blond shade with age, and I wondered if mine would be the same color one day.

"Aren't you coming to visit your grandparents?" Mama asked.

"I just got a new country record I want to listen to."

My parents only used their player to spin the handful of gospel records they owned. Sometimes we sat around to listen to them on Sunday evenings after dinner, Mama becoming misty-eyed.

"You can use it, but I don't know where you got your love of that stuff from. All that wailing and complaining about everything. At least it's not rock and roll music like that awful Buddy Holly, I suppose."

When she and Daddy were gone, I got on my back next to the player to listen to "My Country Boy." I'd wondered if I'd exaggerated something about the voice after I'd heard it, but it was just like I remembered.

I flipped the record to check out the B-side. The opening notes of a ballad rang out and then Dorothy sang the lead vocals. There was a throb of sadness in her voice, the kind that grants a contrary kind of pleasure with its pain. I held the cover against my chest, letting it run over me.

Afterward, I studied the photograph of the group on the cover. The three members stood in a row wearing identical red and white checked dresses, looking to be about the same age as me or a little older. They each had the same dark hair, but one of them had hair that was wavier than the others. I stared at the faces one after another, trying to guess which of the women was Dorothy.

It was impossible to tell. I drew the needle back and dropped it again.

On Monday mornings it was always hard for me to get going, but I liked being able to see May. We met in the breakroom to make coffee, then went to the switchboard to prepare for a day of taking calls. It was odd to sit in the room when it was still so quiet, the night shift girls on their way out, passing us with drowsy-looking eyes.

"How's that sister of mine?" May asked. "Was she mad that you didn't come home until Saturday again?"

"Of course not. She knows I was with my dear old Aunt May. I told her I was trying to bring you back to the Lord," I said, arranging headphones over my hair.

May swatted at me. "Don't you dare call me old. It's no joking matter, you know. She wouldn't be happy if she knew what we were up to. Especially if she knew there were men coming around. Even if it's just skinny old Henry."

"Well, she doesn't know, and she never will because you sure aren't going to tell her, are you?"

"I won't tell her anything about anything," May said. "I know she's never going to forgive me for getting divorced from Ernie, even if he was a dog who ran around on me all the time. She thinks I'm bringing shame on the family."

"It's coming up to nine. We'd better get ready," I said, avoiding the matter of being stuck between Mama and May. I slipped into my professional tone, my words even and sharp. I'd had to work at it, having always been the type of person who mumbled or trailed off.

"Good morning! Ladies, how y'all doing today?"

Frank came in to visit us at least once a day. For a time, I'd thought Frank was sweet on May. When I'd grumbled to May about him she'd accused me of being blind, saying that it was as plain on the nose on my face that it was me he was after.

I smiled genially at him, tucking my legs under the desk so he couldn't leer at them. "We're just fine, Frank, busy as usual, and how are you doing today?"

He hooked his meaty hands into his belt, his foot coming down on the empty chair next to me. A button was popped open on his plaid shirt, white skin standing out where his belly strained against it. "Just the same. So busy you wouldn't believe it. But I'm not here to talk about that. I'm here because I'm wondering…just when are you going to let me take you out, Alice?"

"Leave my baby niece alone, Frank. You need to beat it. You're going to get us both into trouble and not the kind of trouble you want. Shoo," May said, flapping her hand at him.

Frank cackled, slapping his knee. "You're just jealous I'm not asking you out, May. Don't worry, sweetheart. I'm always saying the pair of you could be sisters."

"Well, I'm only ten years older than Alice you know!"

It was something people always said about us. May and I had matching hazel eyes and reddish-brown hair, and we were both on the short side. She was fond of telling me how lucky I was to share her heart-shaped face and small frame. There was a greater likeness between us than the one I shared with my real sister, Francine.

"All right then," Frank said. "I'll get out of here, I guess. But I'm ready whenever you are, Alice."

"Don't hold your breath," I said, as soon as he was out of earshot.

May shoved me with her elbow. "I can't keep rescuing you, honey. One of these days you're going to have to go out with him or one of the other fellas. Just go out on a date or two. You don't have the marry the guy."

"I don't want to date Frank or anyone else who works here. Is there a rule in the company handbook that says I have to?"

"I don't know how any niece of mine got to be such a prude!"

A line lit up and I leapt to answer it. "Alice speaking, how may I direct your call?"

When I was done May was on a call herself. I waited for her to finish, knowing that by the time she was done the subject of men would be forgotten.

"Hey, I was thinking. Maybe we could go out soon? Have some fun?"

May's face brightened, a loose line clutched between her fingertips. "You want to go out?"

"Sure. I was thinking about going to Merle's."

"The honky-tonk?"

"That's right. I heard there's a good singer playing out there in a couple of weeks."

"Maybe," she said doubtfully. It was hard to pry her away from home sometimes, where she could have her radio and mix her own drinks.

"I was thinking you could bring Henry and see if he has a friend he might like to bring, too?"

"I thought you didn't like his friends?"

"Maybe he has one I haven't met yet."

"That sounds like a good time to me! I'll talk to him about it when I see him tomorrow night."

"That'd be swell. You go on and do that."

I faced the switchboard, trying to ignore the way she smiled proudly at me from my peripheral vision.

On the night of Dorothy Long's show, I waited for my date to come and get me. When Mama answered the door, his deep voice was followed by Mama's laughter.

I took one last look in the mirror and wondered if I should do something different with my hair, but it was too late for that. I hadn't been to the salon for a long time; it was long and hung in a simple style around my face. I'd always hated having red hair, because I had the light freckles dusted over my nose to match. I checked my lipstick, then straightened the hem of my only good dress. It was soft blue, gathering in at the waist with a full skirt. Mama sewed it for me for a dance a few years back, and I'd hardly worn it since.

In the living room, my date was sitting on the sofa between my folks. It was strange seeing how young he looked next to them, like just a boy. Daddy's beard was salt-and-pepper; I doubted my date would even be able to grow one.

"Good evening, ma'am," the boy said, hat in his hands as he stood up. "I'm Tommy."

"Nice to meet you, Tommy. I'm Alice."

"Pleased to meet you," he said, with a shrewd scan up and down my figure.

I would try very hard to like him. Perhaps May was right when she said I never gave anyone a fighting chance. At least Tommy was close to my age, when Henry had introduced me to much older friends in the past.

Tommy walked me out to Henry's red Pontiac, idling in the driveway. Henry and May sat in front, and Henry capped his flask when we walked up to the car. Tommy held the door open for me so that I could get into the backseat, then ran around to the other side to slide in next to me.

"Good evening, young Alice, and may I say you are looking lovely this evening. As I told Tommy he is the luckiest man in town," Henry said, looking over the back of the seat at me.

"Not as lucky as you. Stop that smooth talk and get to driving," May said. "We've got a show to catch. You didn't tell

Shirley I was in the car, did you, Alice? She'll be mad at me for not saying hello."

"Of course, I told her!"

"Christ," May said.

"Do you go to this place much?" Tommy asked.

"When there's someone good playing. I haven't been down there for a while," I said.

Tommy nodded politely, then hunched forward to talk to Henry. I listened to them, thinking about Dorothy Long. I couldn't wait to hear her sing or to finally see what she looked like. My Stellar Sisters record had been on constant rotation during the past few weeks.

When we arrived at Merle's, Tommy helped me out of the car with a clammy palm. I discreetly wiped my hand on my dress, May and I following behind our dates as we walked toward the entrance of the honky-tonk.

It was heaving with people, who pushed up against one another while they danced. The dusty wooden floorboards shook with movement, the air thick with smoke around us. I raised myself onto my tiptoes to peer over all the heads in the crowd. There was a small stage in the corner, raised slightly over the room.

There wasn't a girl up there though, not yet.

"What can we get you ladies to drink?" Henry asked, yelling over the music.

"I'll have a soda, thanks. Lemonade," I said.

"Gin and tonic for me. Let's get ourselves a seat," May said, pointing over to the tables in the corner.

We fought our way over to them and I sat next to her. May shook her head and gestured across to the other side of the table. "What are you doing, girl? Get over there so Tommy can sit next to you."

"Excuse me, I wasn't thinking."

My new position was better, because now I was facing the stage. I drummed my fingers against the checked tablecloth along to the music. May leaned across the table. "So, what do you think of him?"

"Who? Oh, Tommy? He's really…nice?"

May nodded enthusiastically as the men came back. Tommy pushed a frosted glass of lemonade across to me.

"So, how do you fellas know each other? Henry here, he likes to keep everything a mystery. He's under the impression that it makes him charming," May said.

"Well, I'll solve that mystery for you at last," Henry said.

"What is it, are you two joining the space race together or something? You'd think it was something top secret, from the way you carry on," May said.

"Work," Henry said, tipping his head across to Tommy. "This guy comes into the store all the time and we got to talking one day."

"And you ladies work together, don't you?" Tommy asked.

I let May answer for me while I looked past her toward the stage. The music died out, and the room filled with chattering voices. A double bass and a guitar were being carried out. Three men in suits stood there, one of them lifting the guitar and adjusting the strap over his shoulder. Another perched on a stool behind the drum kit, smirking at the others as he twirled a stick in his fingers.

Where was she? I craned my neck and checked around, wondering if there was still another band to come before her.

Finally, a woman in a red dress walked across the stage.

This was the woman with the golden vocal cords. Even from back here in the dark I could see that there was a spark about her, a specialness that she vibrated with.

When Dorothy opened her mouth to sing, the conversation at our table stopped. Henry and May twisted toward her, and I leaned forward. Dorothy's voice was rich velvet, like smoke curling around us.

When the song ended Henry stuck his fingers into his mouth to whistle. The sound, long and low, pierced through the crowd.

"What a singer, dang!" Henry said. "Glad you dragged us all down here tonight, Alice."

"I'm pleased you're enjoying it. Excuse me, I'm going the powder room," I said, not meeting May's eye. I didn't want her to offer to come with me.

The area right in front of the stage was impossible to see from our table, obscured by the audience. The next song was another ballad, and most of the people on the dance floor were coupled up to waltz. I watched them for a while before I turned to the stage.

Dorothy's eyes were closed, displaying her long thick lashes. Her head was inclined toward the silver ball of the microphone, a hand curled around it. Coral pink lipstick painted her full lips and the lights caught her shoulder-length hair, making her waves shine underneath them.

No matter how high the notes were, and regardless of how much she was belting them out, it appeared to not cost her any effort. For her, singing seemed to be as natural as talking. I could write something special for that voice. Even if she never knew about it, there would be a song from my pen that was just for her.

Dorothy opened her eyes. They were a missing puzzle piece, bringing her face together. Her eyes were large and brown, sweeping over the crowd with a curious hint of sadness.

For a song and the next, I watched the guitarist's fingers. When I got home, I would play the parts I could remember.

Between songs, the drummer put down his sticks to roll up the sleeves of his shirt and wipe sweat from his forehead. Dorothy leaned down and picked up a glass of water that stood by her feet. All around me the crowd buzzed, returning to talking and laughing, the band forgotten for now.

Dorothy set the glass down and conferred with the double bass player. When she turned back to the crowd, her gaze came to rest on me. I looked away as soon as our eyes met. The band launched into a faster-paced tune, the drums and the double bass chugging along like a train.

I started at a tap on my shoulder, spinning around to see May standing behind me. "Where have you been all this time?

We were looking for you, the boys want to get up and dance. I thought you said you were going to the ladies' room?"

"I did go. I was just passing back this way and I wanted to hear the music better."

"Well, come on now. They're waiting for us at the table. Hurry," she said, tugging at my wrist.

Tommy led me out to the dance floor, while Henry did the same with May. I positioned my hand on Tommy's shoulder, looking past him toward the stage as often as I could. When the show was over we broke apart. Tommy's cheeks were flushed, dark patches showing on his shirt from sweat.

I sought out Dorothy one last time, catching a glimpse of her back as she exited the stage to the crowd's applause.

The night air was cool on my skin when we walked outside. People milled around, soaking up the music spilling from the open windows.

Henry took a pull from his flask and winced before offering it to Tommy.

"Well, what do you say we all go out to May's place, have a few more drinks?" Henry said.

"I told my mother I'd be home by eleven," I replied.

May slapped my arm. "You fool. Why didn't you tell her you were staying at my place tonight?"

"Sorry. That's why I was only drinking soda."

"You're a good girl, not like your aunt, huh, Alice?" Henry said. "Come on, we'll run you on home."

When we arrived, Tommy walked me up to the door. I turned around, stepping back from him. "Thank you for this evening. I had a lovely night."

"Me too," he said, leaning toward me.

"My mom is probably watching from over there," I said, pointing to a window.

He laughed and put his hat on. "Well then, I'd best be on my way. Don't want your father coming out here with a shotgun or anything. You enjoy the rest of your night."

"Thanks. And thanks for this evening, I had a nice time."

I waved goodbye to Henry and May, who stuck their hands out of the open windows of the car to wave back. Stepping inside, I smiled to myself.

I'd done it. I'd seen her, and she was extraordinary.

CHAPTER TWO

No matter how special a night is, life goes on just as it did before you had it. After I found Dorothy I returned to my routine of working and helping Mama out around the house.

Yet inside, I was different. I'd never exchanged more than a look with Dorothy Long, but I was altered by hearing her sing. Inexplicably, it made me sure of myself and of what I might do.

The first thing I did with that feeling was take another look at the song I'd written after I'd first heard the Stellar Sisters. I worked on "Do You Miss Me?", crossing out lines and scribbling new ones until I'd worn down the jagged edges. I copied it neatly into a notebook, writing lyrics with chords notated above. That was all I knew how to do, and I remembered melodies by heart.

Soon afterward, a fresh idea sprang into my mind. It developed into a song about a woman losing her husband in wartime, and I called it "He Won't Come Home." I was thinking about a friend of my brother's who'd died in Korea. The story had always haunted me. At work I jotted down an idea for a song about hearing tragic news on the telephone. I rhymed lines to myself in lulls between calls, and the song was halfway done by the time I got home. I wrote feverishly, composing during every spare moment I could snatch for myself. I discarded as many ideas as I kept, ruthless about what was good and what wasn't good enough.

A week after the night at Merle's, on a bright Saturday morning, I returned to the record store.

"You're here again! Good morning. I'm Bill, by the way," the clerk said, sticking his hand out. It took a beat to figure out what he wanted from me; a man had never offered to shake my hand before.

"Pleased to meet you. I'm Alice. I was wondering if my Dorothy Long record had arrived?"

"Oh yes, I have it. Did you get on down to the honky-tonk to see her?" Bill asked, taking my record from a shelf behind him and handing it to me.

"I did. It was wonderful," I replied, surprised that he'd remembered the detail.

That day I played my record several times, both for the pleasure of listening to it and to study Dorothy's range. I wanted to mold my ideas to that voice.

As I sought out inspiration for my writing, my obsession with music mushroomed, spreading toward different artists. I'd always loved country music, but now it became a subject for me to research and master. In the evenings I scrolled through the stations on my dad's transistor radio, seeking out programs to find new acts when I was supposed to be sleeping. I had to sneak it out of its place in the living room. Its sole purpose was for Dad to listen to the nightly newscasts, muttering about the Communists all the while.

I acquired more records, not caring for once that I was supposed to be saving money. Bill took an interest in helping me build my collection. Each time I went to the store, Bill showed me the new arrivals he'd kept aside for me, and we listened to them on the player he kept in the shop.

"See, this is Don Gibson. Do you like this one?" he asked.

"I do. I've never heard him before."

"He used to play in a band called Sons of the Soil."

"That sounds a little familiar… How do you know so much about music, Bill? Is it just from working here?"

"Always had an interest. I've been playing music since I was a little kid. I took piano lessons. I have one at my house. I'm no Jerry Lee Lewis, but I do okay," Bill said, putting his fingers on the counter to mime playing.

"You like Jerry Lee Lewis?"

"Sure! I like everything. Rock, rhythm and blues. Classical, too."

My new friend lived and breathed music, and I was rapidly discovering that I did, too.

On Friday night I fell asleep on May's sofa. I dragged myself home in the morning with my head pounding and cotton in my mouth. When I got there, I showered and dressed in my faded black pedal pushers. Mama and I beat the rugs and swept and mopped the floor, until every surface in the house was sparkling clean. Daddy mowed the lawn and trimmed the bushes, and soon the outside of our place looked just as neat as the inside.

Mama and I prepared roast chicken with beans and scalloped potatoes. My specialty was fresh baked rolls, and together we made pecan pie for dessert. Mama had taught me to make a perfect crust when I was barely a teenager.

While supper was warming in the oven, my brothers and sister arrived with their spouses. They swarmed into the house like ants, talking rowdily to one another as they came in. The kids stayed outside to play on the porch while the adults gathered in the kitchen and living room, prying open bottles of soda.

"How are you doing at work, Alice?" my sister-in-law asked. Janice always dressed well, even for our regular Saturday night gatherings. Tonight, she wore a poodle skirt with a light pink blouse. My oldest brother stood sideways to us, but he was listening. I knew what he thought about women who worked.

"It's just fine, thanks," I said.

There was a thump from the hall. My nephew John had knocked over a lamp and he reached out a skinny arm to right it, then sprinted away.

"Slow down! No running in the house!" Mama said.

"That's great. It's so nice that you earn a little money to help out your folks," Janice said. Her ponytail curled perfectly at the end. Once after she'd been at the salon she asked me to touch her hair, and it was as soft as it looked. I always wondered how Janice ended up with a man like my brother. Though he wasn't yet forty he looked much older, potbellied and red-nosed.

We gathered at the table to eat, everyone talking over one another to demand that plates be passed around. Now and then one of the kids came over to their parents to nag or tug at a leg, before being banished back to the card table set up for them nearby.

Gus shoveled food onto his plate, almost emptying out the dish of scalloped potatoes as he scraped the spoon along the bottom.

"These are good, Mom," he said, brushing cream from the corner of his mouth.

"Your little sister made those."

"I'd say she'd make someone a good wife, but I don't think she'll ever leave this house."

"You never know. Alice had a date with a young man a while ago, didn't you, Alice?" Mama's eyes shone as she looked across the table at me. I turned my attention back to my plate, tearing open my roll.

"Well that's marvelous, Alice. Do you have plans to see him again?" Janice asked.

The faces of everyone at the table were turned toward me. "Sure. Soon."

What would they think if they knew that Tommy had told Henry he'd like to see me again, but I'd refused? May kept trying to talk to me about it at work, but I cut her off every time.

"Well, maybe some feller will finally marry you, and you can give Mama some more grandchildren," my sister Francine said.

I looked over at the kids' table. One of my nephews was pouring milk onto his sister's plate while she bawled. "I think she has enough."

Janice, Francine, Mama, and I cleared the table while my brothers went out to the porch to smoke. After we were done,

Mama and I made coffee and carried mugs into the living room. My niece Norma clambered up onto my lap, asking me to plait her hair.

"Alice! Be a doll and get us the guitar? We want to sing a few songs," my brother Buddy yelled to me from the front door. His cheeks were flushed, and a lock of hair hung over his eye.

I patted Norma's hair and gently pushed her off my lap, then went to my room to fetch my guitar. As I handed it to Buddy, I hesitated. "Just don't break a string like you did the last time, okay?"

"Yeah, yeah," he said. He stubbed his cigarette out under his boot and grabbed the neck from me.

I sat on the stairs with my hands underneath my thighs. Buddy played "Will The Circle Be Unbroken," and Francine's husband Joe joined in. Buddy fumbled the chord changes, squinting down at his thick fingers. The rest of the family drifted outside, though my parents didn't join us. They didn't like the bawdy combination of booze and music, but they never tried to stop us.

Buddy passed the guitar to Gus, who played an old gospel song we'd all grown up listening to.

"Why don't you play us a song now, Alice?" Janice said when he was finished.

I shook my head and pulled my legs up toward my chest. Gus played another song, and I watched mosquitos buzzing around the naked bulb hanging above the porch. I'd play tomorrow evening while my folks were out visiting my grandparents.

When it was late, and the house had emptied out, I got into bed and turned off my lamp. It was a hot night, my nightgown sticking to the sweat on the back of my legs as I moved. I clutched Daddy's transistor radio, throwing the top sheet back to lay on the thin cotton. I switched on the radio and turned the volume down. One song gave way to the next and then Dorothy Long's lush voice was casting its spell, low in my ear. It was a ballad called "Stay for Me."

These last months, I'd followed her career closely. A few stations had picked up her songs since I'd seen her play at

Merle's. Bill liked her almost much as I did, and we listened to her all the time at the record store.

Though I was happy for Dorothy's growing success, I had the feeling, a puzzling one, that I was sharing her with the world. It didn't seem possible that all the people who were buying her records understood her music or that they could connect with her in the special way I did. Even Bill, who said she might be on her way to becoming one of the best girl singers around, wasn't quite as awed by her as I was.

I hadn't told a soul that I'd been writing for her. It was crazy, but I was acting as though one day I'd be able to walk right up to her and hand her a tune. Each night when I was trying to sleep, desperate to shake off the mundane day, I'd soak myself in fantasy about what she'd say to me about this song or that one. She became a collaborator, eager to give me ideas and have me shape them for her.

I wished I'd written "Stay for Me." I wanted to fashion songs that could give someone a lump in their throat like this song did for me, even if it was about feelings I'd never had. I'd come close with a girl called Sandra when I was in high school. But I knew that it wasn't what most people thought of when they were thinking about love.

I turned off the radio, lowering it to the floor next to the bed. Curling up on my side, I thought of Dorothy's eyes that night at the honky-tonk. For the briefest of moments, they'd looked right into me.

The following Saturday morning I went to Stone Street to talk to Bill about his newest batch of 45s. There were boys walking up and down the aisles, play fighting with one another. They were dressed in blue jeans and T-shirts, all three of them sporting greaser-styled hair. Bill raised his voice so that I could hear him, but after a while he got tired of it. One of the boys knocked a stack of records from a pile, ignoring them when they dropped on the floor.

A dark-haired boy glanced at me, trying to catch my eye. I focused on the small pile of records Bill had laid out for me.

"You guys want to get a soda or something?" the dark-haired boy said.

"Nah! I told you, I want to get some records."

"You ain't even looking, you germ."

Bill stared at them, brushing his hand over his hair to smooth his palm over the neat part. "Say guys, do you think if you're not real interested in buying you could take it outside?"

The dark-haired boy had pulled a friend into a headlock, ruffling his hair, but he released him now. "It's a free country, ain't it? We'll look at your music when we're ready."

Bill shoved his hands into his pockets and leaned forward. "That's right, sir, it's a free country, but this is my store. I'm asking you to leave."

The boy glanced around at his friends. One of them shrugged, sleepy-eyed. "Well, that's just fine by us. We don't wanna be in a store run by a damn sissy anyway."

The sleepy-eyed boy spat on the ground, and they ran outside shouting and laughing. Bill shuffled through the pile of records, color spreading up to his face from the beet red at the back of his neck.

"What a bunch of hoods. You handled them well, Bill."

"Thanks. I should go and clean that mess up, but first listen to this. I think you'll like this one."

He dropped the needle, conjuring the bright sound of a fiddle.

"You know my taste so well. This is really good."

"Thought you'd enjoy it. The fiddler played on some Stellar Sisters tracks. Oh, that reminds me. These were dropped off yesterday afternoon. I didn't get the chance to put them out yet," Bill said, leaning down to gather a stack of bright orange flyers from behind the counter, handing me one.

"Oh. Dorothy Long's playing soon?"

"Uh-huh, your absolute favorite. I know you've been waiting to see her sing again."

It was at a hall over in Mobile. I'd have to either convince May to go with me or borrow her car for the night. I bit my lip and clutched the pamphlet between my fingers. What if I couldn't get her to agree to it? She still wasn't happy with me for giving Tommy the slip.

"Thanks, Bill."

"You're welcome. I was thinking I might go myself. Singers like her don't come along too often. I want to be able to say I saw her when she gets really big."

"I don't suppose we could go together, do you? I'm still saving for that car and I can't think of how else I'd get there."

"Well, sure. I'd be happy to drive you. It's only a couple of hours or so. We'll take snacks, listen to music on the way. How about that?" he asked, smiling so that the gap between his teeth showed.

"That sounds wonderful. Thank you."

We went back to listening to the player. It was a long time since I'd made a good friend, and I'd never had one who was a boy.

On the night of the concert Bill showed up early to pick me up, dressed in a light V-neck sweater with a collared shirt underneath.

"Good evening, Mr. Johnson," Bill said, shaking my father's hand. "Mrs. Johnson, it's lovely to meet you."

My parents each looked at Bill and then at one another. All I'd said to them was that I was going out with someone, and I realized now that they must have thought that it would be Tommy who would be coming to the house.

"Well…Would you like to come and sit in the living room for a moment?" Mama asked.

"So," Bill said, relaxing onto the sofa. "Alice tells me that you both enjoy gospel music?"

"That's right. We have a few records of that kind," Daddy replied.

"Well, my father is a big fan of it. We have the best collection of religious music in the state, he's made sure of it. We do a big mail order business. Send them all over the country," Bill said, waving his hand expansively.

"Is that so?" Daddy asked.

"You're welcome to come down to the store any time and take a look."

"We should be going," I said.

The interior of Bill's green and brown wagon was immaculate, and a lemon-scented freshener hung from the rearview mirror. When I got my car, I was going to take care of it like this.

"Thanks again for taking me tonight," I said.

"It's no problem. Hey, I brought a thermos of coffee. You want a cup?"

"Great idea!" I said, retrieving the thermos and tin cups from where Bill had stowed them on the floor. I poured us each a cup, handing him his so that he could drink it one-handed. "Do you go to Mobile very often?"

"I do. I like driving over to go to the pictures and things like that."

"What kind do you see?"

"All kinds! I love foreign movies if I can find them, old film noirs, anything really. I like Cary Grant, he's always good. What do you like?"

"I don't know. I'd like to see more."

"Well, what do you like to do with your time, aside from listening to records all day long?" Bill said, handing me his cup so that he could make a turn. "I know you like playing the guitar. Did you always do that?"

"No, I only got the guitar a few years ago. I did always like singing, though."

"I'd love to hear you play sometime."

"Sure. Hey, Bill…" I said.

His blue eyes darted away from the road for a moment. "Is there something wrong, Alice?"

"No, not really. I just hope you didn't think I was being forward or anything like that, when I asked you to take me to the show."

He tapped short square fingernails on the steering wheel. He looked toward me again, for as long as it was safe to, then he stared back out at the road. "I don't really care about that stuff. I mean, I don't care how girls are supposed to behave or about boys and girls and all that. Do you know what I'm saying?"

I looked straight ahead too. I'd never heard anybody talk like that before. "That's certainly okay with me. I don't think I care about all that stuff either."

Bill's toothy smile flashed again and he smacked the steering wheel. "Well, Alice, I do believe that you and I are going to get along just fine."

As we drove into Mobile, the bright lights all around us gave me a lift. I'd never gone there just for fun, though Mama and I took the bus at Christmas time every year to do our shopping. I gave a little whoop out of the window, Bill laughing as the wind blew through my hair.

When we were inside the hall we dove into the sea of people, the crowd jostling us as we rushed to get good seats. We ended up toward the middle and halfway back. I sat on the edge of my red velvet seat, leaning forward and biting a nail. I tried to sit up taller to see over the man in front of me.

"Can you see okay?" Bill asked.

"Sure," I said. "It's all right."

"Here, switch," he said, and when we swapped seats I could see much better.

The support act, a pair of brothers who sang in perfect harmony, seemed to go on forever. The crowd's applause was muted, as though they were as impatient to see Dorothy as I was.

At last the curtain went up to reveal Dorothy standing in the middle of the stage in a red sequined evening gown. There were murmurs all around us about how lovely she looked, her dress sparkling under the lights.

"Good evening, Mobile. Well, I can't tell you how happy I am to see all of you. This is a lovely hall and you are one good-looking crowd. Hey, house, turn on the lights out there so I can see them better? Yep, just like I thought, a crowd of handsome guys and beauty queens."

The audience rippled with laughter.

"Okay, that's enough. Turn them off or I'm not going to be able to concentrate with all those lookers out there. I'm going to begin with a song called 'Stay for Me,' that's out right now."

The hall lent a more relaxed tone, making this show different to the one that I'd seen at the honky-tonk. Because there was no dancing, I could sit and focus only on how lovely Dorothy sounded. When she hit the notes of the chorus, chills ran up my spine and I closed my eyes.

The lights came up for intermission, waking me from my dream state.

"Want to go out and stretch our legs?" Bill said.

"Sure."

As we walked out to the lobby along with the rest of the crowd, a long line was building against the wall.

"What do you think that line's for?" Bill said.

I searched the front of it. "It's the guitar player! I guess he's selling records or something?"

"You're such a fan, you should go over there," Bill said, gently pushing my shoulder.

"No, I couldn't. I already have it, anyway," I said, staring at the guitarist. His brown hair was slicked back, giving him a more rock'n'roll look than I would have expected.

"Get another one, and ask him to sign it! If you want to talk to him you should just go and do it. What have you got to lose?"

"What would I say to him?" I said.

"Whatever you want! Tell him you appreciate their music or something. Look, if it makes you feel better I won't watch. I'll go and get us both a soda, how would you like that?"

This might be my only chance to meet someone in the band, and I knew I had to do it. "That would be great. Thanks."

"I'll meet you back in the hall. I'll try to snag seats in the same area."

As I stood at the back of the line, my heart hammered. Maybe I should just lie and tell Bill they'd run out of records. I tried to think of what I was going to say when I reached the front, but I hadn't figured anything out by the time I got there.

I'd never been this close to a musician before. The guitarist's strong jaw was clean shaven, and his black jacket was accented with red stripes so that it matched Dorothy's dress. I stared at him until he grinned at me, pointing toward the stack of records in front of him. "You gonna buy one? I can sign it for you."

"Yes, please."

"So, are you from around here?" he said, uncapping his black marker.

"Oh no, I live about a couple of hours away. Drove up for the show."

"That's nice. What's your name? I'll make it out to you."

"Alice."

"Lovely name, Alice," he said, scribbling across the cover of the record.

"I'm such a fan of the band. I love your picking. It's been wonderful to see it in person tonight."

"Well, that's awfully kind of you, thanks," he said, sliding the record across the table to me.

"Will Dorothy be signing records tonight as well?"

"Nah, I don't think so," he said, leaning an elbow on the back of his chair. Despite the line of people waiting behind me, he wasn't in a hurry.

"Oh," I said. "I'd love to meet her sometime. You see, it's just that I write music, and I wish there was some way for me to play my songs for her. It's not that I think they're that great, I'd just love to have a chance someday…"

"You write songs, huh?"

"I'm sorry, I didn't mean to say all that. I'm just a really big fan, is all."

"Forget it. Don't meet a lot of girl songwriters. It's interesting," he said, head inclined as he studied me.

"Well, you have now," I said.

He cracked another smile. "You know what, Alice? I'd love to hear your songs. We're going to be having a little party back at the hotel after the show. Why don't you come by?"

"I don't know… My friend might want to head right back to town…"

"Well, if you do want to, come on down to the Waldon. Dorothy splashed out on a big old suite down there. Seven thirty-three. Say Dirk said it was okay for you to be there."

"Okay, thanks," I said softly. Behind me, people grumbled at the way I was holding up the line. It wasn't long before the show was due to start again. "Bye, Dirk."

I worked my way back to our seats, finding Bill sitting close to where we'd been before. How could I convince him to stick around after the show? Bill was open-minded, but still I could imagine what he might think of me wanting to hang out with a bunch of musicians.

"Did you meet him? How was it?" Bill asked.

"It was lovely. But you're going to think this is real strange. He invited me to spend time with the band at their hotel."

"Well, that is strange," he said, eyes narrowing. "What did he mean by that?"

"I wouldn't go or anything. I mean, I know we've got to drive back. But I don't think he meant it like that. I told him about my songs, and he was interested in them. It would be a party, not just him there."

"Oh, I see. Well, I don't have anywhere to be back home, do you? It's Friday night! In fact, there's a bar I wanted to go to later, but I could only go by myself," Bill said, not meeting my eye.

"So, you think I could go to the party then?" I said. "Do you think it would be okay for me to go on my own?"

Bill put his fingers under his chin. "Hmm. I'll tell you what. Why don't I come with you to this party, check things out? If it all seems okay, I'll take off and then come back to get you a couple of hours later."

"Really?" I said, my voice squeaking.

"Really. Your folks won't mind if I get you home late, though, will they?"

They'd pitch a fit, but it was more than worth it. "Don't worry, it'll be fine."

For the rest of the show, I tried to imagine what would happen when I got to the hotel. What if Dirk was just inviting me as some kind of joke? It was hard to believe that anyone would really want to hear my songs. Still, just being in the same room as Dorothy was enough to make going there worthwhile and was enough to make my stomach flutter.

After the concert, Bill and I stopped in at a diner to have cheeseburgers and chocolate shakes. We wanted to be sure the band would have ample time to get to the hotel before we showed up.

There was valet parking at the Waldon, and Bill tipped the driver as we stepped out of the car. When we got into the lobby, I stared around at the high ceilings and marble floors. When my family travelled, we huddled up, sharing beds in relatives' houses.

Bill strode over to the elevator and gave instructions to the operator while I followed behind. "We're going to the seventh floor."

As we walked down the hall approaching the room, music and the murmur of voices grew louder.

I grabbed Bill's forearm. "You know what, maybe this isn't such a good idea? We don't know these people at all. Maybe we should just go? I'll wait in the car when you go to your bar. I don't mind at all."

Bill turned and looked down at me. "You know, I reckon if we don't go in there tonight you're going to regret it. As soon as we get in the car, you'll wish you did."

"This is kind of crazy, though, don't you think?"

"That's why it's fun. Come on now, what have you got to lose?" Bill pointed to the gold numbers on the door. "See that, he gave you the number, didn't he? He wanted you to come."

"Maybe...."

"You know what? I dare you."

I drew in a deep breath and walked forward, knocking on the door and looking back at Bill. "Anyone in my family will tell you, I don't back away from a dare."

The door opened, and a man stood there who wasn't much taller than I was. After a moment I recognized his sandy-blond hair, cut into a flat-top. It was the drummer in Dorothy's band.

"Don't know you pair," he said, eying us slack-jawed.

Dirk came up behind him, slapping him on the back. "Let 'em in, Jackie boy, I invited them. Come on in, welcome. I'm Dirk."

"Hi, I'm Bill."

Bill and Dirk's hands pumped up and down as they shook.

"Glad you came, Alice! What can I get you to drink?"

"I guess...I'll have a glass of wine or something?"

"I'm fine, thanks," Bill said.

When Dirk walked away, I gathered the courage to look around. Ricky Nelson's version of "I'm Walkin'" drifted over the room from a radio in the corner. People were scattered around the suite, sitting in the chairs against the window or on the cream-colored carpet. The duo of brothers who'd played before Dorothy stood in a corner, one of them so intoxicated he was leaning on the other. From where we stood, I could see into the bedroom with its red velvet curtains. Two people sat cross-legged on the queen-sized bed, facing one another and talking.

I couldn't see Dorothy. Was she even going to be here?

As I searched for her a door opened, and she walked into the room.

Dorothy stalked over to the coffee table, less than ten feet away from me, and picked up a highball glass. Her sequined dress had been replaced by a simpler one. It was red too, but in a lighter shade, and there was a silk scarf knotted around her neck. Jack had moved to join her, standing at her side.

Dorothy held her glass, glancing around at the faces of her guests. Finally, her gaze settled on mine.

When we made eye contact, her expression was blank. This might be the only chance I had to be near her. I wanted to be seen by her, in the way that I'd always wanted to be seen by someone.

When she looked away at last, she talked to Jack. As she spoke to him, he stared right at me.

"She's real pretty up close, isn't she?" Bill said.

"I guess so," I said.

Off the stage, she still had that special vibration about her. From here I could see the fine arch of her brows, the dimple in her cheek showing when she talked. Her teeth were white and even. I'd never seen anyone so beautiful.

"Here ya go, Miss Alice," Dirk said, handing me a wine glass.

"Thank you, Dirk."

Dirk stood in front of me with his glass of whiskey. "So now, tell me about your songwriting. What do you write?"

"Country songs, of course," I said. Dorothy and Jack were still talking, and she gestured with her glass in hand.

"Tell me who you like to listen to. Aside from us, of course."

"Oh, lots of things. I enjoy Hank Williams."

Dirk put his hands together in prayer. "God rest his soul. He was the best. Who else?"

"Kitty Wells, the Carter Family. I like Johnny Cash, too."

"We have a few things in common, Alice!" Dirk looked down at his empty glass. "Say, I've drank this a little fast. I'd better go and get another. Just a moment."

Bill leaned toward me. "I can stick around if you need me, but would you be okay if I took off? These people seem okay, don't you think?"

"Sure. It seems all right," I replied. I wanted him to stay, but he was already doing so much for me.

"I'll be back in two hours on the nose, I promise."

I watched him go over to the door, and Dirk was back at my side a few moments later.

"What's it like, playing professionally?" I asked. "It must make for such an interesting life."

He cocked his head, considering. "Sure. Lot more work than you'd think. Sometimes you think you're going to be playing to a big crowd and you end up in some dive with five people. But you know, I wouldn't change it. Like you said yourself, it's an interesting life."

"It doesn't sound so bad at all."

"You seem like you'd like to try it yourself sometime. Hey, why don't we go into the bedroom? I can tell everyone to clear out of there, and my guitar is right downstairs. I'd like to hear one of your songs," Dirk said.

"Oh, I don't know. Listen, I was rambling when we talked before, and it's not really like me. I mean, I'm not sure about this."

"I only mentioned the bedroom because it'll be quieter in there. If it eases your mind, we'll leave the door open. I'm a happily married man," he said, hand on his chest.

I took a big gulp of air, remembering what Bill had said about the regrets I might have after I left. "Okay. I'll do it. I'll play for you. Thank you."

CHAPTER THREE

Dirk's was the most beautiful guitar I'd ever seen, its black body shining and perfectly shaped. When I took it in my hands and strummed a chord, a pure tone rang out. If I had a guitar that sounded as good as this one did, I'd never want to put it down.

I sipped from my wine glass to moisten my dry mouth. Aside from May and Henry, I'd never played the guitar in front of anyone. I had to play my best song, the one I'd worked over so much that the kinks were ironed out. It had to be "Do You Miss Me?"

I could only perform with my eyes closed. At first my voice shook, so I pictured my own bedroom around me. I saw the single bed in the corner and my record collection in its crate, sitting in the middle of the rug. By the time I mouthed the second verse, my voice was clear.

When it was done, I slowly opened my eyes.

"Play that again," Dorothy said, leaning against the doorframe. She stepped into the room and closed the door behind her, muffling clinking glasses and voices.

I looked at Dirk. How long had she been standing there?

Dorothy sat on the edge of the bed expectantly, crossing one leg over the other. Her feet were bare, her toes painted with glossy red polish that matched her dress.

This time I kept my eyes open but trained on the guitar, watching the movement of my hand on its neck. Dorothy made a circling motion with her finger, asking me to play it yet again.

At the chorus Dorothy raised her voice with mine. I stopped singing, awed by the fact that words I'd written were falling from her mouth. As the chorus ended she fell silent. I sat dumbly with my fingers resting on the frets of the guitar, worrying the strings under my hand.

"Well, and where did you come from?" she asked, her voice just as tuneful as it was when she sang.

"I was at the show earlier tonight. It was really wonderful. I enjoyed it a lot."

"I met her when I was signing, and we got to chatting about her songs. What can I say, I had a feeling about her," Dirk said, tapping his temple with a finger. "My intuition, you know."

"You wrote that song all by yourself?" Dorothy asked.

"Yes."

"Is that the only song you've written? I mean, do you have more?"

"No, I've written several," I said, speaking like I did when I was on the phone at work, my chin subtly thrust out.

"Can you play another please?" she asked, eyebrows raised.

"Of course. This one is called 'Message for You.'"

When I played the opening riff, Dirk and Dorothy exchanged a look. At the conclusion of the song, Dirk clapped. Although Dorothy didn't join him, she was nodding deliberately.

"Alice, these songs of yours are really good. Have you played them for anyone else?" Dirk asked.

"No, not really."

"Your playing is excellent too. Who taught you how to play guitar?" Dorothy said.

"Nobody. I taught myself."

"And you're saying you have more songs, aside from the couple you've played for us right now?" Dirk said.

"A dozen or so that I'm happy with. And I can always write more."

At that, the two of them looked at one another again.

"Do you have a recording of these songs? A demo?" Dorothy said.

When I shook my head, Dorothy stood and went to the desk, searching the drawers. While she rummaged around for the hotel stationery, she looked back at me. "Can you write music? The notes I mean, so that we could read all the songs you've written?"

"No. I mean, I know chord names but I can't transcribe the melody. I'm pretty sure I know someone who can, though. My friend Bill, the man who was here with me earlier."

"Good. Now I'm not making any promises, I want to be very clear about that. But I'm going to write down an address for you, and I want you to work with this friend and get what you have down on paper. Put together a little package of songs and send them to me so that I can show them to our manager. Of course, you'll need to let me know how to get in touch with you."

Dorothy's long fingers gripped the pen as she scrawled across the page in large handwriting. As she wrote I noticed the simple gold band on her wedding ring finger. She covered her mouth to stifle a yawn. Tearing off the sheet of paper, she held it out, walking toward me. As she came closer I saw how much taller than me she was.

I reached for it uncertainly. "I don't want to seem ungrateful or anything, I'm really, truly honored you'd want to see them, but wouldn't it be silly of me to just send them off to someone like that? I mean, if you like them…"

Dorothy cocked an eyebrow. "Smart girl."

"Like I said, I really don't mean to seem ungrateful."

Dorothy came still closer, sticking out her hand and looking me in the eye. "We don't know one another, Alice, but you have my word. Anyone will tell you I know how to keep it."

I reached out and placed my hand in hers. Her palm was warm and soft, her dark eyes staring into mine. "Okay."

"Now listen, I'll be passing back through town again in about a month. We always pull a good crowd here. If you can have your songs done and sent to me before then, I'll meet you right here in this hotel and we can work something out. Would you like that? Do you want other people to perform your songs?"

I already trusted her. "I do. I don't write them for myself. I want other people to play them."

"Well, I do believe you'll get your wish, one way or the other," Dorothy said, releasing my hand. For the first time since she entered the room, a smile spread across her face.

"I hope so," I said.

The guitar still lay across my lap, and I held it out to Dirk. Dorothy yawned behind her hand again, and I stood up, folding the piece of paper.

"Thank you very much for inviting me, Dirk," I said. "And to both of you for listening to me play. I should be going."

"It was nice to meet you. Shall I call you a cab?" Dorothy asked.

"That's all right, thank you. My friend will be picking me up."

"Your boyfriend?" she said.

"Just a friend. He drove me here."

"Have a pleasant drive home then," she said. "Dirk, can you help me get rid of all these people? I know they just got here, but I'm exhausted."

I took the elevator to the lobby to wait for Bill, rocking back and forth on my feet. The last hour wouldn't be real until I'd told him all about it.

"How was your night?" I asked when he came to collect me, grasping the precious piece of paper as I got into the car.

"Never mind my night. How was yours? What happened?"

As soon as I described the conversation between Dorothy and me, Bill jumped in. "I'd love to help you. It'd be an honor to have some small part in all this."

He slapped his thigh. "I can't believe it! Can you believe it?"

"No, I can't. It feels like a dream. When I wake up in the morning, I'm not going to know if any of this really happened."

"It's like something out of a movie, you getting discovered like this!"

"Let's not get ahead of ourselves. This might not go anywhere."

"It will. I'm sure of it."

Though I had a whole month for transcribing, I was eager to deliver the songs to Dorothy as soon as possible. For two weeks, I drove over to Bill's small weatherboard house on the edge of town almost every day after work. Bill made pots of coffee and sweet iced tea, and I brought over bread and leftover meat to make sandwiches.

One by one, I played my songs for him on the guitar and sang while he sat at the piano with a pencil behind his ear. Slowly the songs turned into black marks on pages as he matched the notes up. Each time we were done with a song I completed the painstaking work of writing it out again neatly so that I'd have more than one copy.

When I was ready, I sat at Bill's dining table and gathered the sheets of paper, tying the stack together with brown string. All together there were fourteen compositions.

"I can't believe they're all done," I said.

"I can't believe how good they are!" Bill replied. "I'm telling you, you have something special here."

"I couldn't have done it without you. Now help me. What should I write on the front page here? Should I write a note to her?" I asked, smoothing my hand over the paper. It was exhilarating to think that Dorothy's hand was going to touch it soon.

"Maybe just a little something. Oh, you should write the names of all the songs down on a list for her, like the title page in a book. It'll make it look professional."

"I like that."

I wrote them as straight as I could, then penned my phone number at the bottom, checking it over twice to make sure the numbers were correct. At the post office my palms sweated, my skin so slick that I fretted it would dampen the pages. My whole life was wrapped up in that little stack of paper.

I was still going to May's on Friday nights, though I hadn't told her anything about meeting Dorothy. I couldn't face it if things didn't work out and I had to tell everyone that I'd failed.

One evening, we were sitting out on the front porch when a car pulled up out front. It wasn't Henry's Pontiac, but the outline of Henry's hat was clear.

"That's Henry, but whose car is that?" I asked. "Is he with someone?"

May squinted out into the dark, trying to see past the lights. "I don't think so, but that's definitely him. Must be a loaner."

Henry opened the door and stepped out, leaning up against the car showily, pushing his hat back on his forehead with a finger. He held out a hand and swept it over the body of the car. "What do you think, ladies?"

"Whose car is that?" May asked.

Henry pointed at me. "It's hers for three hundred bucks if she wants it. I've been keeping my eyes peeled for a good deal. I borrowed it to bring it over and show it to you."

I ran over to him. I didn't know a lot about cars, but as it gleamed under the porch light it looked to me like it had been well taken care of. I ran my fingers over the smooth green paint, solid cool chrome under my hand.

"What do you think, Henry? Do you think it's a good car?"

"Wouldn't have showed it to you otherwise. It's a '41 Studebaker Champion. She's old, but she's got a great engine. The man I got it off inherited it from his mom. She barely drove the thing, but he helped her take care of it."

May sucked on her cigarette and shrugged. "Henry don't know much, but he knows cars. He knows better than to swindle my favorite niece anyhow."

"Tell your friend I said yes. Can I sit in it please?"

Henry opened the door and stood aside, dangling the keys in front of me. When I got behind the wheel I knew it had to be mine. I ran my hands around the steering wheel and bounced up and down on the upholstery. I turned the key in the ignition just to feel the vehicle shuddering to life underneath me. I rolled down the window, and Henry put his hand on the roof, looking down at me. "You'll take it?"

"Thank you so much, Henry. I'll go to the bank in the morning."

I couldn't believe that I finally owned my own car, something I'd been dreaming about for years. I'd always imagined getting out on the highway by myself, flying past the fields out of town. I'd roll down the windows and lay my foot heavily on the pedal, watching the road disappear underneath me. It was just like I'd imagined it would be, the joy of it helping me get through the long weeks of waiting for Dorothy. I loved everything about it, even going to the gas station. It made me feel grown up to watch while the attendant pumped gas, chatting to them while they worked.

As the date of Dorothy's return to Mobile drew nearer, I spent more time at home waiting for her call. When the phone finally rang, I was working on a pie crust, forking butter into a bowl of flour.

"Don't answer that!" I said.

I wiped my hands on my apron furiously, but Mama had already picked it up. "Yes, she's here. Who did you say was calling?"

Mama held the receiver out to me, cupping her other hand over it. "A lady says her name's Dorothy, for you?"

"Thank you." I took the phone and stretched the cord, moving partly out of the kitchen and into the next room. "Hello, this is Alice?"

"Hello, Alice. It's Dorothy Long speaking. How are you doing?"

"I'm very well, thank you. How are you?" I asked, squeezing my eyes shut and gripping the receiver.

"We liked your songs very much," she said. "Very much."

"Thank you."

"We'd like to meet with you. Will you be available this coming Saturday afternoon? We're going to be playing a show in the evening, but we'd like to see you at the hotel before that."

"I'm free, yes," I said, scrambling to find something to write with.

"We've reserved the same suite as last time, that's number seven thirty-three. Could you be there at three o'clock?"

"Sure. That sounds fine."

"Who was that answering your phone?" Dorothy asked.

"Oh? That was my mother."

"You live with your parents? You're not married, then? You don't have children?"

"No, I'm not married or anything like that." I moved enough to see that my mother had taken over making the pie crust. She'd formed my dough into a ball, and I was sure that she was overworking it.

"What do you do then, Alice? Do you work?"

"Yes, I have a job. I work at the telephone company."

"Okay. Well, I'll be seeing you on Saturday."

The line clicked, and when I hung up the phone I jumped up and down where Mama couldn't see me.

I was too nervous to go to Mobile on my own. Bill was good company during the drive, trying to distract me, talking while I barely listened. He was the only person I trusted enough to tell what was going on. Mama and Daddy hadn't been happy that I was missing family dinner, but when I told Mama that I was going out with Bill she'd smiled and told me to have a good time.

We pulled up to a movie house, so I could let Bill out.

"Enjoy your movie," I said.

"Enjoy your meeting! Can't wait to hear how it went."

I drove to the hotel and gave my keys to the valet, grateful that I'd seen Bill do this, otherwise I wouldn't know how to navigate it all. I strode into the lobby and found a restroom to freshen up. What if my dreams had to end when I went up to that suite? What if she'd summoned me here to say thanks, but no thanks? I brushed my hair, then went to the elevator.

Dorothy answered the door on the first knock. I hadn't seen her dressed casually before; she wore blue jeans and a green blouse. Her skin was scrubbed clean of makeup, and she somehow looked even prettier without it. I hoped my own makeup wasn't too thick. I'd worn my good blue dress.

"Alice, thank you for coming," she said, standing aside.

"Thank you for inviting me here." I clutched my bag, looking around the suite. Dorothy gestured toward one of the chairs under a window, and I sat down, pulling it in jerky movements up to the small round table. I laid my hands in my lap.

"Can I get you a drink?" When I shook my head, she poured a glass of water for herself and sat across from me in the other chair.

"I'll cut right to the chase. Alice, we'd like to record your songs."

"That's wonderful," I said, my shoulders loosening. "I'm honored."

She looked away after a moment while I composed myself. "They really are great songs. We've all been wondering where you've been hiding yourself."

"Where I've been hiding?"

"It's just… Your songs seem to have come out fully formed, like you're an old hand at this."

"I'm anything but an old hand."

"I'm starting to understand that," she said kindly. "There's something else I'd like to ask you."

"Yes?"

Dorothy ran a finger around the rim of her glass. "The reason I asked about the circumstances of your life, and whether you have children, is because Dirk and I were very impressed by your playing and singing, as well."

"Thank you very much, that's so kind of you," I said quickly, too nervous to connect the dots.

"We want to explore the idea of you joining us, as a member of the touring band. If you think you might be interested, I'll have the rest of the guys come in and meet with you. We'd like to have you play a song or two for everyone. This is the kind of decision we would usually make together. What do you think of that idea?"

I gaped at her. My greatest hope had been that I would leave the hotel knowing that they were going to buy my songs from me.

"Have you any interest in joining a band?"

"I'm not sure. I thank you very much for even suggesting it. It's just…"

How could I tell her I didn't feel nearly up to the task? Playing with Bill was the first time I'd performed alongside another person and even then it was only for transcribing.

"The thing is, Alice, you could go into publishing and be very successful. A lot of people would want your songs. But it can be a hard business. You might get taken advantage of, among other things."

"I really don't know much about any of this."

"If you decide you don't want to join, I'd be happy to talk through some things with you. Give you some advice. But I want you to consider this carefully first. There are some things we'd have to talk about. But my main concern with anyone in the band is that I only hire good people. And my instincts tell me that you're good."

"I'm not really sure that I'm what you're looking for. I have no experience at all."

Dorothy tapped her finger on the table between us. "Maybe not, but you have talent, and that's a much harder thing to find. We've played your songs, and they fit us like a glove. You've written them without ever playing with us. We want to see what you can do when you're actually part of this group."

"I've listened to your music a lot."

"Can you see then that if you were to play with us, your songs could fit us even better? We could work on them together. I'm not really a writer, but I have some ideas. I feel like you might be able to help me."

I stared out of the window, across at the red brick building next door. "I'd like to try out, then."

Dorothy smiled and nodded once, as though it was all settled. "Well, okay then. Alice, there is just one thing, and I hope you'll understand why I'm bringing it up now."

"Of course, what is it?"

"As I said I have a good feeling about you, but it's different for a woman in this industry. I need to know that you can behave in a way that's respectable. Responsible."

"I'm not that type of girl. You wouldn't need to worry about anything with me."

"I'm glad to hear it," she said. When she looked intently at me, I had the strange feeling that she was seeing me more than other people did. Still, she couldn't know why it was that she wouldn't have to worry. In that moment, I made a promise to myself that she would never find out.

"Thank you for the opportunity. There is a problem, though. I can't play, because I didn't bring my guitar."

"That's quite all right. You can play Dirk's again. I'll call them over now."

When she rose to make the call, I admired the long line of her and the shape of her hip. Even when she was doing something as mundane as picking up the telephone, her movements were graceful.

Soon the band was spilling into the room, smiling or looking curiously at me as they came in. There was a tall, bulky man with them that I didn't recognize.

"How you doin', Alice?" Dirk said. "I believe you met ornery old Jack here, but you didn't meet Errol."

"Hi, Errol. You're the double bass player?"

"The one and only. Hello, Alice," Errol said, and I liked him right away. He had light brown hair and his nose was squashed as though it had been broken, but his eyes were gentle.

The big man stepped forward, his black cowboy hat shiny and crisp. Nobody I knew would ever wear a hat that looked like it hadn't been worn before.

"This here's my husband, Earl," Dorothy said. "He manages us."

"Hello, Earl, pleased to meet you," I said. He smiled, the toothpick stuck in the corner of his mouth poking out. I'd known that she was married, but he wasn't the kind of man I'd pictured her with. He was much older than her and I didn't think he was at all handsome. His face was stubbly, and curly chest hair showed from the top of his shirt.

Dirk held out his guitar and I sat back down in my chair. I pulled at the neckline of my dress.

"Do you need a glass of water?" Dorothy asked.

I took the glass from her and sipped it in between tuning the guitar. Dirk tipped his head toward me, the fact that he was rooting for me easing my nerves, but only slightly. I looked back at him, then over to Dorothy. My mind emptied into a blank space.

"Can you play 'Do You Miss Me?', please?" Dorothy said.

The room was quiet aside from the steady tap of Dirk's foot beating the ground, in time with my playing. When I was finished I cleared my throat and reached for my glass again, shakily taking a gulp of water.

"Thank you. Play that again. Now I'm going to harmonize with you, and we'll see how that sounds," Dorothy said.

As her voice tangled in with mine, I noticed how much better it made me. It elevated a sound that I'd always thought of as too deep and dull.

"Now just do some picking," Dirk said, leaning forward and signaling toward the guitar. "Have some fun with it."

I was warmed up by now. My fingers flew over the fretboard in a sequence I picked when I was practicing and wanted to move fast only for the pleasure of it. Errol nodded approvingly toward Dirk, spurring me to play even faster.

"We really liked 'In Any Small Town.' Can you play that one for us?" Dorothy asked.

This time Jack, Errol, and Dirk joined at the chorus, and the words I'd labored over in my bedroom shaped themselves into something real.

"In any small town there's a girl like you/Longing for love that's sweet and true/Who winds up lost and feeling blue/I'll tell you what you've got to do."

Earl moved forward from his place, leaning on the wall. "Thank you, Alice, that was great. Would you mind stepping into that room for a moment, so we can have ourselves a little meeting?"

"Of course."

Earl led me to the bedroom, then shut the door behind me. I pressed my ear to the polished wood, hearing only muffled voices. I paced across the room, my glance darting toward the door every few seconds. A tan leather suitcase lay on the bed, clothes spilling out of it. There was a black silk nightgown sticking out from under the pillow. I could never imagine owning something like that. My face grew warm, thinking about Dorothy wearing it to bed each night.

When I'd played, they all seemed impressed. Despite not wanting to get my hopes up, I was sure they were going to ask me to join them. I couldn't wait to tell Bill, but it was so crazy I didn't know how I was going to tell anyone else in my life. I might as well be telling them that I was running off to join the circus.

The door sprang open and Earl held it, Dorothy at his side. There was a quiet eagerness about the way she looked at me and I knew as soon as I saw her that I'd been right. They were asking me to go with them.

"Sit down?" Earl said, gesturing toward the beige sofa, and he sat across from me. Dorothy sat next to him. "Well, Dorothy and Dirk said you were good, and we're mighty impressed by what we've seen here today. What do you think about coming on board?"

"I'm honored. It would be wonderful."

"Well, then, this is going to be great," Earl said, adjusting his hat. I looked at Dorothy and her lips curved into a smile, showing her dimple.

"When does it happen?" I asked. "I mean, what happens now?"

"We were thinking that if you said yes, it might be a good idea for you to come on up to Nashville. Is a month long enough for you to get your affairs in order? We'll be finished this tour by then. But then we're going to head right out on the road again, after a little while anyway. We're still trying to get my name out there, so we're doing lots of dates," Dorothy said.

"Yes, ma'am. I think a month is plenty of time."

"Great. Well, you'll come on down and rehearse with us to work out the new set list. You'll stay at my place, like all the boys do when we're working on a tour. I've got a big place, with a nice big rehearsal room." Dorothy looked at me, her head tilted. "Is there something the matter, Alice?"

"No, not really. I'm just thinking, my guitar is not so good. I might need a bit more time to save some money, so I can get a better one."

"Is that it?" Dorothy said. "We'll get you a guitar when you come. Earl will arrange everything. We'll cover your fare to get to us."

"I'd like to bring my car, if that's all right?"

"Of course. Now listen, we'll have to sit down some time and sort out all the business. You'll get a cut of the take when we're on tour, and then we'll work out a contract to stipulate songwriting royalties and such. Does that sound okay to you?" Earl said.

"Sure, that sounds fine," I said.

"I think this calls for a celebration," Dirk said, clapping his hands together. "Let's all have us a drink."

Dirk poured out glasses of whiskey. He brought one over to me and sat down on the arm of the sofa. I wanted to throw my arms around him. If not for him, I wouldn't be here.

"So, Alice, I would be honored if you'd let me help you choose your guitar. What do you think?"

"I'd appreciate that. I'd like to get one like yours, only maybe a different color."

He picked up the guitar, laying the base of it on the ground and spinning it around by the neck. "I can see why, she's a beauty. And I can see you with one of these. It fits you just right."

"I can't wait!" I said.

"You going to come down and watch the show tonight?"

"I was planning on it, yes."

"Great. You can watch us from the side of the stage."

Dorothy was on the other side of the room, talking with Earl. I wanted so much to be the one at her side. I wondered about so many things, like how she came to be a singer. It was strange to think that I'd have plenty of opportunities to ask her questions, though I didn't know how I would ever overcome my shyness with her.

That night I was close enough to the band to be hit by a drop of Errol's sweat as he moved around. I stared out at the audience, unable to see much of the people under the bright lights of the stage. From this angle, I could absorb Dorothy's profile and see the way the slight prominence of her nose added to her beauty.

As I listened to her sharing anecdotes to get the crowd going, it struck me that she was like two different people. When she was standing up there joking around you'd never guess how serious she could seem. Dirk was different when he played too, so focused that it almost made him mean-looking. It was impossible to believe that soon I'd have my own stage persona, and people might even wonder what I was really like.

The thought sent a shiver of excitement through me, and I mouthed the words as Dorothy sang.

CHAPTER FOUR

I steered into Dorothy's driveway, the property surrounded by lush green fields. The large house was white with green shutters and a rust-colored roof. An oak tree out front stretched its long branches across the sky, and on the porch there was a bench seat and a rocking chair. I could imagine sitting there to view the sun coming up or going down; it looked like an ideal spot for it.

I got out of my car, stretching my arms over my head and rubbing my eyes. It was late afternoon and I'd been driving since before dawn, determined to make the trip in a day so there'd be no need to stay anywhere overnight. On the way I'd eaten egg salad sandwiches, stopping only to use restrooms at roadhouses. When I closed my eyes, I could still see the white stripe on the road in front of me.

Dorothy came out onto the porch and a little white dog with brown spots ran up beside her. Dorothy looked fresh and pretty in navy blue high-waisted shorts, the buttons and cuffs on her white blouse matching her shorts. When I smiled at her, the corners of my mouth trembled with nerves.

"Hey there, Alice," she said. She leaned forward to kiss my cheek, slinging an arm around my shoulders. Her lips were soft on my skin, a floral scent wrapping itself around me.

"Hello," I said.

Dorothy drew back, her gaze sweeping me up and down. "You found the place all right?"

"Yes, thank you, your directions were very useful."

"Good. I'm awful glad to see you. I was worried that you might change your mind or your folks might have a problem with it or something."

A lump rose in my throat at memories from the last week. I'd faced only disbelief and anger at home. Daddy was mainly silent, but I caught him staring at me like he didn't know who I was. Mama had followed me around the house, railing at me.

"What have we ever done to make you want to run away from your family like this? How can you choose to do such a useless, frivolous thing with your life?"

The night before, our goodbyes had been stiff. They hadn't risen from bed to see me off.

At the office, I hadn't told anyone but May what I was doing. She was excited for me, but she was puzzled by how sudden it was and she seemed a little worried for me too. It made me understand that however much she'd always encouraged my dreams, she had never wanted them to become reality.

Dorothy's dog jumped at me and I leaned down to it, patting its scruffy fur. It panted up at me with its tongue hanging out.

"That's Scout, he won't bite you," she said.

"Hi, Scout," I said softly.

"Earl! Come and help Alice with her things," Dorothy called out.

Earl yelled hello at me as he came outside. I looked away as he lifted the beat-up suitcases out. Having no luggage of my own, I'd asked my brother Buddy to borrow his. After buying my car I didn't have much in the way of savings left.

"How was your trip?" Earl asked.

"It was fine, thank you."

"Awfully nice car you have. If you want to give me your keys, I'll move it into the garage," he said, standing with the handle of a case in each hand like they didn't weigh a thing.

"Come on in, I'll show you around," Dorothy said.

I followed Dorothy, gazing around at the wall-to-wall carpeting and the fireplace in the living room. A fuzzy-looking blanket was thrown over the back of the sofa, and there were framed photos lining an oak sideboard. The house felt cozy everywhere we went.

"You have a lovely home," I said.

"Thanks, Alice. What I really want to show you, though, is the rehearsal room," she said, leading me to a far corner of the house. She threw open the door with a flourish to reveal it to me. The space was furnished with sofas, ashtrays set upon tables, a bar, guitar amplifiers, and a drum kit. The walls were lined with photographs of the band and framed records. The carpeting was thicker here, I guessed to muffle the sound.

"What do you think? It was one of the first things we set up, soon as we moved in."

I paced around, running my palm over the varnished wood of the bar. In the mirror behind it, Dorothy's reflection was watching me. "It's just swell. I can't wait to play in here."

"Glad you like it! Come, I'll show you to your bedroom," she said.

Dorothy shifted from foot to foot while she watched me take it in. It was small but neat, with a chest of drawers, a closet, and a bed. "I know it's not much…but do you think you'll be comfortable here?"

"Of course, it's all I need," I said. "You mentioned that the band would be staying here, too?" It would soothe my nerves to have Dirk around to talk to. He was so unselfconscious that he brought me out of myself.

Dorothy shook her head. "The boys will be here tomorrow. Didn't I mention, I asked you to come a day early? I thought we could spend a little time getting to know one another. Come, so

I can introduce you to my mother-in-law. She lives here with us."

As Dorothy moved down the hall, I stared at her shapely legs under her shorts. A woman, white-haired and stooped, stood at the kitchen counter. Putting down the spoon she was using to mix batter, she smiled at me kindly. "Welcome. You must be Alice. I'm Sally."

"Pleasure to meet you."

"You too, honey. I'm glad you're here in time for supper. I'm frying up some chicken."

"That sounds wonderful. I'll go and wash up," I said.

In the washroom, I brushed my hair and washed my face, staring at myself in the mirror. It was a relief to have some time to gather myself. My expression showed how off balance I felt, just to be near her. Being around Dorothy was like sliding into the pages of a book you'd been reading to meet a favorite character. Or it was like walking up to the screen at the movies to admire a beautiful actress and then passing into the film and becoming a part of that fantasy world. I wondered if Dorothy would transform into a real person.

I went to my room to quickly change into fresh clothes. Though I'd wanted a few moments to myself, I couldn't wait to return to Dorothy's company.

When I got back my plate was piled high with chicken, creamy mashed potatoes, greens, and corn on the cob. Steam rose from my biscuit when I broke it open, and I melted butter onto it.

"So, tell me about your people, Alice," Sally asked, ladling gravy over her mashed potatoes.

"She's had a long day of driving..." Dorothy said.

"I don't mind at all. I've got four brothers and a sister. I'm the youngest."

"Oh, the baby! And do you all look the same? You all have that lovely auburn hair?" Sally said.

"Thank you. Just my mama. I take after her. I look a lot like my Aunt May, too."

I took another bite of the fragrant chicken, perfectly crispy and juicy. After a day of eating behind the wheel of my car, this was heaven.

"You said you had a job at the phone company?" Dorothy asked.

"Yes. I was there for three years. For the last while I was working the switchboard," I said, though I didn't feel as proud of it as I'd used to. In contrast with the life Dorothy led, it was pretty dull.

"And you liked it?"

"I worked with my aunt, so it was never lonely."

"That sounds great. You know, I've never even had a real job," Dorothy said, chin propped on her hand.

Along with Dorothy and Sally, I helped clear dishes from the table. We washed and dried them, working mainly in silence, though Sally hummed quietly. When Dorothy moved past me to put the plates away, she brushed against me, putting a hand on my hip to steady herself as she reached for the cupboard.

"All right then," Sally said. "I'm going to go and relax with some needlepoint in the living room."

"I'll join you, Mom. I'm going to read the paper," Earl said, from the kitchen table.

"I might go off to bed. I'm beat from the drive," I said.

"Oh...I was hoping we could have a little talk before everyone else arrived. If you're too tired, maybe we can talk in the morning?" Dorothy said.

"I can stay up a little longer."

Dorothy smiled at me. "I'll get us some iced tea and then let's go out on the porch."

We sat together on the bench seat, Dorothy close enough that I could feel the warmth of her skin. I studied Dorothy's thighs from the corner of my eye, eying how supple but firm they looked. I sipped my sugary tea, wondering what Dorothy wanted to talk to me about.

"So, there are some things I wanted to get out of the way. This band is like a family, and it only works that way because there's a few things we understand about each other and about how things need to go."

"Yes?" I said. There was nothing she could ask for that I wouldn't want to give. I'd do anything I could to make this a success.

"First of all, Earl and I are very private people. You might see or hear things about us. The band knows not to gossip with people they meet along the road. Do you understand?"

"I understand," I replied. I couldn't imagine what kind of things she was talking about. Still, I had always been sensitive to what people said and thought about me. Maybe this was like that. Dorothy liked for people to mind their own business.

Dorothy had been resting her hands on her knees, but now she lifted them, scratching her nail against her palm. "Good. Now the other thing is, and don't get me wrong. I'm real glad to have another woman here. But we have to talk about the fact that things can be hard for a girl in this business."

"Of course. I remember what you said before. I won't do anything to embarrass anyone," I said.

We turned our faces toward one another, just for a moment, before Dorothy's gaze ran down my front. I was what Mama called well-developed for my frame, and I'd always been careful to not show my bosom off. I put my hand on my chest when she looked away, making sure that I'd done up the top button of my blouse.

"It's not you that I'm worried about, Alice, not exactly. You're a pretty girl. There are a lot of people out there who'll try and take advantage of you. If one of the guys in my band ever did anything I could just toss them out. Not that they would, understand. Earl and I chose them for a reason. But I can't control all the other people you're going to meet. Club owners, booking people, other musicians…I couldn't bear to think I was putting you in harm's way or anything like that."

As she spoke I shifted against the seat. Was being around Dorothy going to be like spending time with Aunt May, who treated me like a little kid? I was sure that Dorothy was only a couple of years older than me. I wanted her to treat me as an equal, even if she was married and therefore more mature than I was.

"I'll be fine. I've been around enough to know what to do."

Dorothy put her hand on mine, too briefly. "I'm sure you can handle yourself. I'm not saying you can't. But I'm married, and that affords me a kind of protection that you don't have. I just want to make sure you know you can come to me if anything happens, okay? If anyone bothers you, you just talk to me about it."

"Okay. I'll talk to you. I promise."

"Good. And don't you worry, I'll set them right. I can be mean as an old snake when I want to be. I think everyone's a little scared of me," she laughed.

I laughed with her. I couldn't imagine how anyone could ever think she was mean.

"I want to thank you again for giving me this chance," I said. Just yesterday I'd been at our little house, ignored by my parents and in a town where nobody ever thought I'd amount to much. I'd never met anyone, not even Aunt May or Bill, who'd showed as much faith in me as Dorothy had.

"Just remember I'm not giving you anything. You're bringing something into this yourself. You're here because of your own work."

"I know, but still. I'll work hard, do everything I can. I won't let you down."

Dorothy patted my knee. "I'm glad to hear it, because we'll work you hard. You can be sure of that. It's not all glitz and glamor out on the road."

"It's got to be better than where I've been."

I thought of Greenville with its few main streets, with the folks who stared at any strangers who dared to come into town. People looked down on Bill, just because he wasn't like other men. But Dirk had shook his hand and looked him in the eye, and none of these people thought I was strange because I wasn't married yet.

Dorothy's hand stilled, and then she rose to walk across the porch. She gripped the railing in front of her, looking out into the dark. Her silhouette showed the curves of her hips, the way they flared out from her small waist. Every movement she made invited me to look at her; I couldn't seem to stop.

"Sometimes, it can get lonely out there. You might be more homesick than you've ever been in your life. A lot of the time, touring is just being tired and dirty and wishing you were somewhere else. You need to understand that the big fancy hotel we were in when we met isn't usual for us. Sometimes we treat ourselves, but we're not rich. We're going to be staying in a lot of dumps to save money. I hope that hotel hasn't given you a false idea of what we are."

"I'm not really the fancy hotel type. I don't mind at all."

"Good. The most important thing to know is that you might find that something you think you really want isn't what you want at all."

When she turned around, I was surprised to see her smiling in the moonlight. "But what I just said is only half of it. You'll also have the best times you've ever had in your life. You might be so tired you can hardly see straight, but you'll be doing something a lot of people wish they could. You won't be living that nine-to-five life that I can already tell you hated even when you're nice about it. You'll get to see the country and have a whole lot of adventures while you're doing it."

"Well, now you're talking," I said, a smile slowly breaking across my face.

"I can't wait to show it to you."

"Me neither," I said, our gazes meeting across the porch. I wished she would come and sit close to me again.

"There's a lot to do. Dirk said he wants to take you shopping for that new guitar tomorrow, then we'll start rehearsing. How does that sound to you?"

"That sounds wonderful."

"You're still worried about something. What is it?"

I picked at the hem of my skirt. I wanted to act confident, but something about the way we talked in the dark opened me up. "I guess there's just a big part of me that doesn't even know if I can do this. If I can measure up. I'm a little scared this won't work out."

Dorothy shook her head. "Don't worry yourself about any of that. We've got almost a whole month to get you ready and we're going to pour everything into that. Anytime someone new joins a band you've got to work out the chemistry. It's nothing that hasn't been done before."

"Thank you, Dorothy," I said, trying out the sound of her name. Until now, I'd been scared to address her by it.

"Okay now, I'm going to go to bed. Do you have everything you need?"

"I do, thank you."

She smiled at me again before she walked inside. I sat holding my glass, staring into nothing for a while. Dorothy had warned me about being homesick on the road, but I was already there. I thought of Mama and Daddy, who'd be in bed by now. They would have eaten alone, talking at the table even less than they did when I was there. Mama would have cleaned up all by herself. I wished I could call them to say good night, but they were too mad at me for that right now, and I'd only wake them.

My first morning at Dorothy's house, I stared up at the unfamiliar ceiling, taking a moment to remember where I was. When I checked the time on a grandfather clock in the hallway, I saw that it was still early. I washed and dressed, then wandered around the silent house as I tried to get my bearings. Soon I heard footsteps, moving around the kitchen.

"Good morning, Alice, I'm making coffee. Can I get you a cup?" Sally asked.

"I'd love one, thank you. Can I help with something?"

"You're a guest, sit down," she said, pulling out one of the stools that rested under the counter.

"I insist."

"Well then, you can help me with mixing up batter for pancakes. We're going to have bacon and eggs to go with them."

After breakfast I helped clean up, then I went back to my room. I took my clothes out of their cases and hung them in the wardrobe or folded them into dresser drawers. It went a small way toward making me feel at home.

At noon, Dorothy called out to me from the hall that the boys were arriving and that Sally was about to serve dinner. I helped set the table while Errol, Dirk, and Jack carried their things inside. There were echoes of home in the way we gathered around the table, the guys slapping one another on the back or shaking hands before digging into their meals.

"Well, Alice, why waste any time at all? Shall we go into town and get that guitar, so you can have it for when we start rehearsing this afternoon?" Dirk said, wiping his chin with his napkin.

"Sure! Thanks, Dirk," I said.

After my long drive the day before, it was a relief to settle onto the passenger seat and watch Dirk behind the wheel.

"Bit hard to leave home I got to say. I have a wife and two kids back home," he said, when we were on the road.

"How old are they?"

"They're five and three. A little boy and a little girl."

"You must miss them something awful when you're away?"

"Sure, I miss them a lot. But you know, I'm providing for them all, starting to make a little money out of all this. We live with my wife Winnie's folks, but if we keep going the way we are I can give the kids a good future. And I drive home to see them as often as I can."

I trailed behind Dirk as he opened the door to the music store, gazing around us as we entered so that I almost bumped into him. We didn't have anything like this back home. The space was crammed full of guitars, banjos, and violins, in so many shapes and sizes it was hard for my eye to settle on any one thing.

A man approached us, white-bearded and with tan cowboy boots on his feet. "Mr. Shelby, nice to see you, friend. Who are you playing with these days?"

"You too, Mr. Williams. I'm playing with Dorothy Long. We're working on some new material right now," Dirk said.

"Oh, wonderful. Someone told me a while back that Jack Miller had joined up with her. Sounds like she's put together a mighty good group."

"Indeed, she has," Dirk said, winking at me. "We're in the market for an acoustic. Can you show me a couple?"

Mr. Williams summoned another clerk and they carried over a guitar each, holding them out in front of themselves. My attention was caught by the one Mr. Williams displayed. The red around the edges bled into an orange center, set off nicely by a white pick guard. The pearly accents on the fretboard gleamed under the light.

"I like that one," I said.

"That's cherry sunburst," Mr. Williams explained. "She'd make a great choice, Mr. Shelby."

"It's not for me, it's for her," Dirk said, a lopsided grin on his face.

"Oh. Well. Here you go, ma'am. Would you like to try it out?"

I beamed when we got back into Dirk's car, unable to believe that the precious guitar in the trunk belonged to me. I couldn't wait to be alone with it. I'd told Dorothy before we left that I was going to pay her back as soon as I could, but she said she wouldn't hear of it.

When we arrived at the house I raced to my bedroom, opening the guitar case like it was a present at Christmas time. I sat on my bed to familiarize myself with its shape. It was bigger than what I was used to, making it feel quite different in my arms. I loved the tone of it, pure as Dirk's but all mine.

After I'd played through almost all the new songs I'd written, there was a knock at the door. Dorothy poked her head inside.

"Hey, Alice, sorry to interrupt."

My skirt had ridden up and I quickly pulled it down, crossing my legs. "That's all right."

"The guys are all gathering in the rehearsal space. Are you ready to come and join us?"

"Sure," I said, standing up with the neck of the guitar in hand.

"What a lovely choice! It suits you," she said. I smiled shyly back at her.

"Lead the way," she said, standing to the side so that I could walk in front of her.

"Woo-eee!" Errol said. "That's a nice one, Alice."

"Thanks," I said.

Dorothy motioned to a stool that was set up not far from the drum kit. "You're welcome to sit to play if it makes you more comfortable, especially while we're finding our feet."

I perched on the stool. Jack rolled his sticks across the skin of the snare drum, warming up. Errol played scales on his bass, and Dirk was tuning his guitar. I tuned my own for something to do, though it was already pitch perfect.

Dirk walked over to me, strumming an open chord. "So, I was thinking, Alice, to start with you can play rhythm on most tracks and I'll play lead. I had a lot of ideas when Dorothy showed me your songs, played around with some solos a little bit. Is that okay with you?"

"Of course, it is," I agreed. Aside from some riffs and picking patterns I'd worked out, playing the chords for my songs was all I knew how to do. I hadn't thought much about what other guitar parts would sound like. I had so much to learn.

"Good. Now don't worry, I don't want you to think I'm taking over. I know what you can do, and you'll get plenty of chances to do solos."

"I'm not worried! But thanks."

"Good. It's going to be great to have a second guitar. Will be real good to get a bit more texture in our sound. A little more twang."

Dorothy joined us, hands on her hips. "Earl helped out with arrangements for the rhythm section, and we practiced a little bit toward the end of our last tour. We need to tighten everything up, but the bare bones are all there. So, we can just launch into one of the songs when you're ready. Once we're all square I want to work on adding some harmonies and so on."

"Sounds good," I said. Taking everything in was overwhelming, but I just had to play the songs I knew so well and take it one step at a time.

"Okay. How about 'In Any Small Town'? Let's start with that one," Dorothy said.

Jack counted us in and I managed to hold my own. I'd spent so much time listening to the music and taking it apart that it wasn't too difficult for me to play in time and make smooth transitions. If I focused on my part and tried to not worry too much, it worked out okay.

Dorothy held up her hand and everyone quieted. "Alice, you sound real good. You were just a beat behind us during the bridge. Can we try that again?"

I frowned, going over it in my mind to work out what I'd been doing wrong. Dorothy approached, standing close to me. I glanced around at the boys, but they were either talking to one another or noodling around on their instruments. "It's okay, don't worry. This is the first run through, and you're getting it much better than I would have expected already. Okay?"

She put a hand on my shoulder while I looked up at her. She smiled reassuringly at me, her touch lingering until I dipped my head at her. The second time, it was almost perfect.

"Okay, let's take a little break," she said, going over to the bar to pick up a glass of water. Though I could hear the guys joking around, I didn't join in. I sat and played the chords from "In Any Small Town" over again quickly, making sure I had it down.

"How 'bout 'Do You Miss Me?' I'd like to do that one next," Dorothy said, striding back to her place in front of the band.

"This one's her favorite, I can tell," Dirk said, leaning close to me like he was sharing a secret. I looked down at the ground and smiled because it was my favorite too. Hearing her sing it was the fulfillment of all those wishes I'd held tight, alone in my bed.

Dorothy crooned the opening lines so sweetly that my hair stood on end. "You've been gone/For so long/I just don't know/ How to be strong…"

It enraptured me to hear my words wrapped in that voice. The effect was amplified by the fact that she was a scant few feet away, her voice raw with longing. I closed my eyes when she hit a high note and when I opened them, she met my stare until the song was finished. There was the hint of a smile on her lips, and I nodded as I strummed the last chord.

The ensuing long silence ended when Dorothy broke eye contact to look around at everyone. "I think that's going to be the show stopper. What do you boys think?"

"I don't know," Jack said, spinning a stick around in his fingers. "Not sure if it's us? I think we should speed it up. It's got a good sound, but it could have a whole different tone if we wanted."

"You always want to speed everything up," Errol said, shaking his head.

"So do you," Dirk said, pointing at him. "I like it the way it is, but we could give it a try, I guess. Jack's right every once in a while."

"Okay, count us in how you want to do it then, Jack," Dorothy said.

It took a couple of bars to find the beat, but I got there eventually, the rhythm section moving along quickly beneath us. Dorothy changed her approach to the song, singing loosely and carelessly, and it wasn't the song that I'd written anymore. When we were finished, Dorothy looked around again to see our reactions.

"Boy, that'll get them up dancing!" Jack said, kicking the bass drum and hitting a cymbal sharply.

"It's good. But I like it much better as a ballad. No contest," Dorothy said.

"It's nice as a ballad, but I think it has crossover potential if we do it with more of a rock beat, maybe tweak the melody. That's what you keep saying you want?" Jack said. "To cross over."

"What do you think, Alice?" Dorothy asked.

Jack's eyebrows were raised, sticks poised. I'd liked it much better slow too, and for me there was no comparison. The fast pace diluted the emotion of the lyrics and took away everything about the song that made it special. But these guys were professional musicians and knew much better than I did what would be good for a performance.

"I like both versions," I said finally.

As Dorothy turned away from me I caught the slight downturn of her mouth. I'd given the wrong answer.

"We'll come back to that," she said. "What's next? Can we do 'He Won't Come Home?'"

We practiced for a couple of hours, breaking every twenty minutes for people to have a smoke or get a drink of water. Time passed quickly, my mind clearing of everything other than what I was creating with my hands. We were running through the opening of "In Any Small Town" again when the band slowed then stopped, Dorothy holding up a hand.

"Hey, Sally," Dorothy said. "Are we being too loud?"

"You're always too loud! You have been in here for hours. It's almost supper time. It's quarter of an hour away," Sally said.

"All right, boys…and Alice. Excuse me, I'm going to have to break that habit. Thanks everyone. We'll pick this up tomorrow. Alice, can you stay a moment?" Dorothy asked.

Steeling myself against the criticism I was certain was coming my way, I stood up, leaning my guitar against the nearby wall. Whatever it was, I'd take it with grace and promise to do better. I'd practice all night, every night to please her.

"Let's you and I have a little walk before we eat," Dorothy said. "You haven't even had a good look around the yard yet, have you?"

"No, not really."

I shadowed Dorothy until we were outside, watching the sway of her hips under her dress. The setting sun painted an array of stunning oranges, pinks, and reds across the sky. Dorothy guided me toward the fence line so we could walk along it and I was conscious of her close beside me, bumping against me with her arm now and then.

"We got these guys so we could have fresh eggs," she said as we passed the mesh fencing around a chicken coop. "I come out here in the mornings and look for them. It's the little things in life, isn't it? The things that make you happy, I mean? You wouldn't believe how good it makes me feel when I find a bunch."

"Was there something you wanted to talk to me about?"

Dorothy rested her hand on my lower back, dropping it when I started. "I'm sure you've figured by now, I'm a straight shooter. If I've got something on my mind I like to say it. So now tell me, what did you really think of what Jack was trying to do with 'Do You Miss Me?' Did you like it sped up like he was trying to make it?"

"Both versions were good?"

"Alice. Do you want to think about that answer again? Really think about it, I mean?" she leaned against the gnarled wooden fence. I stood beside her, my elbows resting on it. The next house over was so far away I had to strain to see it.

"Okay, well, I guess I thought it lost something when we did it sped up. It was just…very different. Good, but different. It just wasn't how I thought of that song being when I wrote it."

Dorothy nodded eagerly. "I thought that might be how you felt. Listen, there's nothing wrong with having different opinions. We thrash things out as a group and there are no hard feelings. When I ask for your opinion, you need to give an honest answer. Doesn't matter if you're disagreeing with me, I just want to hear what you think. Do you understand?"

"I do. I'm sorry. It's just kind of hard. You guys are a band and you know one another so well, and I'm just coming in, all brand new. I'm trying to feel my way along," I said, wringing my hands lightly.

She touched my back again, and this time I didn't flinch. "Of course, I understand that. This is a good group, but they're still men. And especially in this business, men will always think they know best. Hell, Jack will try to speed every song up because he just likes to hit it hard. It doesn't mean anything. You've got good musical instincts. That's why you're here."

"Thank you, Dorothy."

"I invited you into this band to be a full member. I didn't just want a good-looking girl to stand behind me to look nice on stage. You got that?"

Now her hand made small circles on my back, brushing against me.

"I…I got it," I said.

"Good. Now let's go in there and eat."

There was another feast ready at the table. We gratefully tucked in to the steaming hot plates of pork chops and vegetables. Earl, who'd made himself scarce while we practiced, sat at the head of the table.

"How was your first rehearsal, Alice?" he asked.

"It was fine thanks. I had a great time," I said, spearing green beans with my fork.

"Oh, that reminds me, guys. Alice and I were having a little chat about the song we were talking about earlier," Dorothy said, winking at me.

I swallowed rapidly, forcing the beans down. "That's right. On second thought, I think I like the slower version of 'Do You Miss Me?' after all."

"I think you're right, Alice. I say we play it how we did the first time. Let's have another run through of it tomorrow. I'd like to try some things out," Dirk said.

I hoped that Jack wouldn't feel we were ganging up on him. He was gnawing on a piece of meat, gripping the pork chop between his fingers. "All right, gang, if you think so."

"Why would you try speed that song up anyway? It's a lovely ballad," Earl said, holding his glass up with conviction.

"All right, no need to rub salt in my wounds," Jack said, and everyone laughed. Dorothy winked at me once more, and I grinned at her.

I couldn't wait until the next day, when I'd be able to do it all over again.

CHAPTER FIVE

By the end of the first week we'd worked up a rough set, but Dorothy said there was still a lot of work to do. We weren't as tight as we should be, and there was some tinkering to be done with the arrangements. The five of us ran through the songs again and again, making alterations here and there.

"Can we play the second verse again, please? I'm thinking about something," I said.

"Of course, we can. Take it away, guys," Dorothy said.

I took a pencil from behind my ear and scribbled down notes. "That line's been bothering me. I think this one might be better."

Dorothy took the paper and read it over. "You're right. This is better, I like this."

"And Jack, can we maybe speed it up just a little bit?"

Jack threw me a cheerful salute. "You know you don't have to ask me twice. What do you think of this?"

"Not that fast!" Errol said. "Take it down a little bit."

Jack held up his sticks. "C'mon, stop screwing around, would ya?"

"I'm not!"

"Guys. Stop. Jack, the new tempo you were doing was good. Errol, just try it please. Let's run through the whole song. Okay?" Dorothy said, holding her hands up.

Dorothy faced me with her eyebrows lifted, and I raised my chin at her. She spun back around to the group. "Okay, everyone, it sounds good. But there's a bit of a problem with your singing, Alice."

Blood rushed to my face. "I'm sorry. Am I off-key or something?"

Dorothy stabbed a finger in the air, but she was smiling at me too. "No. The problem is that I can't hear you! It seems like you're trying to sing real quiet, almost like you don't want anyone to hear you."

Now that I knew I was calling more attention to myself by being so quiet, I raised my voice. It was liberating to open my mouth and sing properly, and my voice melted into the rest of the group's. Dorothy called, and we responded, and it was a sweet release for me.

When we weren't rehearsing, I spent a lot of time in the kitchen alongside Sally. I typically approached her first thing to help her prepare breakfast and then did any other work she wanted to put me to. Together we made pies, baked cookies, plucked chickens for dinner, and put sauces on the stove to simmer.

Today she'd asked me to chop onions and crush garlic. She was working on a big stew for supper that she planned to serve with homemade bread. I loved listening to Sally's stories about the children she'd raised and her husband, who'd passed a few years back.

"So I was happy when Earl and Dorothy asked if I wanted to move in with them. I'd been pretty lonely, rambling around in the big house all by myself. All my kids grown," she said, chopping carrot with a practiced hand.

"I can imagine. Have you been living here with them for long?" I asked, my eyes watering heavily. The onion I was chopping was a bad one.

"Not so long, just since they bought this place. They didn't want strangers in the house, and Earl knows how much I love cooking and gardening and such. This place is like my idea of heaven. It's not work for me to help them out."

"It must be nice, for all of you."

"Oh, it is. I love the company."

I was washing my hands when I heard Dorothy's voice behind me. "Alice, are you finished helping Sally? I was wondering if you wanted to come out with me."

"Sure," I said, rushing to wipe my hands on a dish towel. Dorothy's hair was pulled back into a ponytail, highlighting the porcelain skin of her cheek and jaw.

We went out to the yard, the grass dewy under our bare feet. The mornings she asked me to come with her were my favorites. She linked an arm through mine while we strolled around.

"Let's see if we have anything today," Dorothy said, speaking for the first time in a while. Contrary to her usual manner, Dorothy was a little quiet in the mornings. We went into the coop, poking around. I pushed some grass aside, finding two smooth round eggs.

"Hey, they do have something for us!"

Dorothy rushed over, taking them from my hands, her skin brushing against mine. "Good find! Should we go and feed Scout now?"

Afternoons were reserved for rehearsing, but we always retired after supper. Some nights we gathered in the living room to talk or listen to the radio. Unlike my family, Dorothy and Earl had a television set, and we watched newscasts and comedy or variety shows. Everyone liked *Name That Tune*, and we fell over one another to guess the songs first.

Other times, the guys wanted to sit outside to drink whiskey and talk. The first time it happened they invited me, but I felt strange about being the only woman out there, with Sally and

Dorothy having each declined. I was sitting on the sofa with a novel in my hands when Dorothy bent down toward me.

"Would you like to come with me while I take Scout out for a walk?"

"I'd love to," I said.

As we walked away from the guys on the porch, their laughter receded. It was dusk, the yard smelling of freshly cut grass.

"It's so nice to have a girl to spend time with," Dorothy said, taking my hand and squeezing it.

"It's very nice to be here," I said.

"I don't like to drink alcohol too much. It's hell on the vocal chords. I try to drink lots of tea before we go on tour. Why don't I make us a pot when we get back?"

"That sounds nice," I said. Scout drew us across the yard. I looked down at our feet, watching them move in time with one another.

"Have things been going well so far for you with the group?"

"Yes. I'm enjoying myself, a lot."

"You don't miss your family too much?"

"Of course, I miss them but…this is like a dream come true for me."

There was a sideways glance at me, a step closer. "I'm glad. I want you to be happy here."

Dorothy went to the kitchen when we got back inside. I sat on the sofa again and took up my novel. Bookshelves were everywhere in Dorothy's house, giving me access to so many stories that I could pull from their homes and lose myself in. I'd found one I'd never heard of called *A Tree Grows In Brooklyn*, and I couldn't put it down.

I was immersed in its world when I became aware that Dorothy was smiling down at me. I started, putting my hand on my chest. "Excuse me! I didn't realize you were there."

"That's okay. You look like you're enjoying that," Dorothy said, setting our tea cups on the coffee table. When I moved to put my book down, her hand came to my shoulder. "Please, don't stop for me. I'm going to flip through a magazine myself."

I watched her bend in her graceful way to pick up a magazine with Marilyn Monroe on the cover before she joined me on the sofa. She sat close to me and we each sipped from our teacups quietly.

"I really like this book. I wish I could go to New York," I said.

"It's wonderful, isn't it? I hope we'll get to play there someday," Dorothy replied, turning the page of her *Look* magazine without looking at it.

"Have you ever visited?"

"I have. I went there by myself when I was twenty-one or so. Just wanted to see it."

I couldn't imagine doing anything so brave at that age. I could barely imagine doing it now. "Tell me all about it."

Dorothy put her magazine aside, eyes lighting up. "Well, it's not like anywhere else. You've never seen so many people rushing around, and you better get out of their way! It's fascinating though. There are all kinds of people there." I leaned toward Dorothy, hungry for her stories, wanting to understand all the things that she'd seen.

That night when I returned to my room I took my guitar from its case. The house was quiet around me, so my fingers were soft on the strings and I muted the sound with my palm. We had more than enough songs for a full set, yet I couldn't seem to stop writing.

I was looking forward to composing with Dorothy someday, but during the time I'd been at the house she hadn't mentioned it again. Though we weren't collaborating directly, being around her inspired me. I put down a couple of lines about a young girl going to the big city. Eventually I cast that idea aside to focus on the song that I'd been spending most of my time on. Since I'd discovered how much Dorothy loved "Do You Miss Me?" it had been my goal to write something she might like even more.

Dorothy had sat so near to me on the sofa tonight. I was high on how she'd lavished me with all her attention. I teased out lyrics by putting down what I felt and then working backward, carefully obscuring who the song was about. The plump red lips, golden voice, and wavy hair were erased and replaced with descriptions of an imaginary man. I retained Dorothy's soulful brown eyes, trying to capture the depths I saw in them.

I was dreaming up another melancholy tune, slow and laced with yearning.

Two weeks into our rehearsal time, Dorothy pulled me aside after a big breakfast of grits, eggs, sausage, and biscuits. I was sure I was going to be ten pounds heavier once we got on the road.

"Do you have any plans for the next couple of hours?" Dorothy asked.

"I was just going to help Sally bake a pie for this evening," I replied, leaning against the wall and looking up at her. She was smiling down at me, standing close. "But if there's something else I'm sure she can spare me."

"We'll have a talk with her and make sure it's okay. I thought perhaps we could go into town to see about getting you some clothes," she said, putting a hand on the wall beside me.

I glanced down at myself before looking back at Dorothy. My dress was simple, the plaid patterned cloth faded with age. It had been handed down from Francine. I'd never cared much about what I wore, if I looked neat and clean.

"I was planning on going to get some new clothes once I started making some money."

"Oh no, I didn't mean it like that at all," Dorothy said, her face falling. "Excuse me. I meant clothes for performing in. I want to take you to meet my seamstress, Gene. If we want your outfits to be ready by the time we head off again, it's important we get it all started now. Gene is quick, but not that quick!"

I broke into a grin. Now that Dorothy brought it up, I recalled that when the band was performing, they dressed alike. If Dorothy wore a fancy red dress, then the band wore black suits with trim and red ties.

"What will I be wearing?" I asked.

"I was thinking we could get you dresses that are made with similar fabrics to mine, but in a different style. So that you blend in with the group, but we look different at the same time. What do you think?"

"I think that sounds great. Shall I drive?"

"You'll have to drive, honey. I don't have a license!'

I bent my head. She'd never called me "honey" before.

When we were in the car, Dorothy reclined against the passenger seat, sinking into the leather upholstery. It was the first time I'd had the opportunity to drive since my arrival, and it thrilled me when the engine throbbed underneath us. The feeling made me cocky, and I hummed to myself as I checked the mirrors before backing out of the garage.

"Who taught you to drive?" Dorothy asked.

"My Aunt May," I replied.

"Well, she did a mighty fine job. You look very comfortable behind the wheel," she said, pointing me in the direction I needed to go as we came to a crossroads. Her other arm was laid across the back of the seat, her hand resting not far from my shoulder.

Reaching forward, she twisted on the car radio. It was halfway through a news story, and in a moment I realized that the announcer was talking about another university being integrated. When he started talking about protests, Dorothy clucked her tongue and quickly twisted the dial until soft music played. Back home, I'd learned a long time ago that it was best for me to keep my opinions about all that stuff to myself, seeing as it only caused fights.

"I don't know why folks can't just live and let live. We're all the same on the inside," she said.

"That's exactly what I think."

When I said it she touched my shoulder for a moment.

"Do you mind if I ask why you don't drive? Did you just never learn?"

"You can ask me anything you like, I don't mind! To be honest, I really like being a passenger, looking out the window while the world goes by. Plus, I never really saw the need. Earl drives."

Throughout our conversations so far, she'd never once broached the subject of her marriage. I had no idea how long she and Earl had been together. They reminded me of my parents, quiet companions to one another, even if my father would never defer to my mother like Earl did with Dorothy. My parents never fought, and I couldn't imagine Dorothy and Earl raising their voices either. And as with my parents, I preferred to think that Earl and Dorothy's marriage was a chaste one.

"Have you and Earl been married for a long time?"

"Not really. Only about eight months. We married around the time I decided to strike out on my own."

"Were you together for a long time before that?"

"Not really," she said again. She stared out of the window.

"When you left the Stellar Sisters, you mean? They put out some great music when you were with them."

When I changed the subject, she turned back toward me. "Thank you. I'm proud of what we did together. When I left it was only because I wanted to go in another direction, but we're all very close. There's no hard feelings or anything like that."

"That's good to hear. It would be a shame if anyone was unhappy about it."

"Well, we're family, we've got to support one another. We've sung together all our lives. Still do when we get together, matter of fact. What about your family? What was it like back home?"

"Oh, you know…big family…"

"They must be awful proud of you."

My eyes watered, but I kept my voice steady. "They're not all that impressed with what I'm doing, if you want to know the truth."

"Family certainly has a way of keeping you humble, doesn't it?" Dorothy said, so gently my eyes welled up even more.

"You could say that. I guess we're all very different people. For one thing my sister doesn't work, and Mama never did either. They think I should be married by now instead of working or joining a band like this."

"I see. And are you the only one in your family who likes music?" she asked.

"Some of my brothers play the guitar, but they're not as interested in it as I am. I'm the only one who writes music. And my parents are quite against it if you want to know the truth."

There was a long silence, Dorothy looking out of the window again. "Then you're even more special, aren't you?"

I tucked it away to think about later. Nobody had ever called me that before.

Dorothy talked on. "You know, it takes a lot for a woman to go out and do something nobody expects. It means we end up having to be braver than anyone. That's what true strength is all about. If men had to do what we have to do, I can guarantee you they'd fold like a deck of cards."

"Well, now, my folks would certainly be worried if they knew I was hanging around with someone who talks like that!"

"Oh, well! I won't tell them," Dorothy said, and we both giggled. It was quiet for a moment, then she started singing. I knew right away it was "Purple People Eater." May loved it and turned up the radio whenever it came on.

"That song is so silly!" I said.

"But it's fun! Come on, sing it with me!" she said. When I refused, she only sang more raucously, going back to the beginning. "Come on!"

"I don't know the words."

"The hell you don't. Sing it!"

Our voices were loud, spilling out of windows that we rolled down so that the wind could whip through our hair. By the time we got to Nashville, I couldn't stop smiling.

"I love your voice," Dorothy said as she gestured toward where I should park.

It was hard to love singing so much and to not be so great at it. I figured she was complimenting me just to be nice. "I know it's not that good. It's too deep. I wish I could sing more like you."

Dorothy rubbed her fingers along my forearm. "I mean it. It's unique. You should be proud of it."

"Thanks," I said.

"It's just over there," Dorothy said. There was a shop front with "Gene's Tailoring" painted on the glass. Together we entered the small store bursting with colorful fabrics, mannequins, and rows upon rows of garments.

"This is Gene. Gene, this is Alice. The friend that I called you about," Dorothy said.

Gene nodded, appraising me over the rim of her glasses. She was an older woman, a hooked nose perched on her thin face. "Hello there, Alice. I hear you're joining the band. Are you Dorothy's back-up singer?"

"No, ma'am, I play the guitar," I said.

"A guitarist, huh? And what are we going to do with you?"

"I was thinking we could put her in the same fabrics as my dresses but have them made in different cuts. I don't want us to wear exactly the same dresses, like we did in the Stellar Sisters. Do you think that would work out all right?" Dorothy said.

"I think that's a fine idea," Gene said, turning to me with her head tilted. "You two have different shapes. Dorothy's tall and a bit straight up and down, you see, so she looks good in a pencil type skirt. We need to figure out what would work on you, Alice. Now let's see…"

Gene went to a rack and rifled through it, mumbling to herself as she pulled out dresses. Eventually she came across a blue one with a sash around the middle. "Let's try this cut on you. You're skinny, but you have a good bust on you and hips. We want to emphasize your waist."

Taking the dress from her, I stepped into the small fitting room. There was a long mirror in a bronze frame, and I held the gown up against myself for a moment before undressing.

"How's Earl doing?" Gene asked.

"He's very well, thank you. And your family? How are the kids?"

I tried to tie the sash myself, but I wasn't sure whether it was supposed to be done at the front or back, and in the end, I gave up. I couldn't do the zip all the way up, either. I examined myself in the mirror once more. I was drab looking, especially with my hair hanging loose and no makeup on, but the dress was gorgeous. I'd never worn anything as fine.

Pulling the curtain open, I stepped outside and waited for them to finish their conversation. Finally, they turned to look at me.

"I wasn't sure what to do with this," I said, gesturing helplessly toward the sash.

Dorothy's eyes were on my body, and I cleared my throat, tugging at the sash again. Her hand was on her neck, the corner of her mouth was raised in a smile.

"Ha! See, my eye never fails me. I nearly always get it right on the first try," Gene said.

"Here, let me help you," Dorothy said.

She stepped behind me and slowly drew the zip up, then tied the sash at my front. She was close enough that I could feel her breath, light against my skin. When she was finished, she put her hand on my shoulder.

"There," she said. Then she moved to stand next to Gene.

"It's perfect, I reckon. What do you think, Dorothy? Do you think I'm right?"

"I agree, it's perfect," Dorothy said, clasping her hands together under her chin.

Gene circled me, eyes narrowed under her glasses. "Now, Dorothy, do you want me to do a few dresses in this cut? A red one, gingham one, and so on? Or do you want a couple of different cuts like what you have?"

"No, this is the cut. They should all be just exactly like that. Is that okay with you, Alice? You're comfortable in that one?"

"Yes, it's fine."

"Good. You are one easy customer. Go on in and get changed, then I'll measure you up," Gene said.

Gene unzipped the very top of the dress for me and pulled on the sash, untying the bow. Gene started talking as soon as I was out of sight, as though I couldn't hear everything she said from behind the curtain. "Golly, Dorothy, if you don't mind me saying so, aren't you worried about having a girl like that in your band? She'll upstage you!"

"Oh, come now, I don't mind that. I knew what I was getting when I hired her," Dorothy said, more quietly than Gene.

I stared at the curtains, wondering if I'd heard her right.

When I emerged Dorothy was in the corner, sitting on a stool. Gene asked me to step behind a partition in the corner of the room, telling me to strip down to my underwear. I felt like a doll as I lifted my arms and turned when she asked me to.

"And I don't know what I'm going to do with her. She won't listen to one word I say," Gene said.

"That sounds so difficult. What happens when you try to pull her into line?" Dorothy asked.

"Not much. Next thing you know, she's going to be pregnant or something like that, and then I don't know what we'll do. I wish I could get her on that new pill I heard about that stops you having babies. If I could find a doctor to give it to us, I would."

"You'll work it out, Gene. I'm sure of it," Dorothy said firmly.

"I better. Well, we're all done here. When did you say you need them?" Gene said, winding up her measuring tape.

"In a couple of weeks. That's when we head out for the tour. You're sure I've given you enough time?"

"It's not long, but you're my favorite customer. I won't let you down."

"Wonderful. Thank you. We'll see you later."

"Shall we drive back now?" I asked, holding up my keys. I loved driving Dorothy around and being able to do something for her that she couldn't do for herself.

"I don't know. I think we have time to do something else while we're in town. I don't feel like rushing back home just yet. Is there anything you need to do here? Any stores you need to go to?"

"Not really," I replied. "But it sounds like a nice idea. I haven't seen much of the area. I'm happy to stay."

"I have an idea! Why don't we go to the pictures? We might be a little late getting back home for dinner, but it'd be worth it. I hardly ever get to go."

"That would be wonderful. Me neither!"

We drove around until we found a movie house. Together we walked toward it, reading the names on the marquee. Throughout my childhood my father had railed against movies and their immorality. He was always saying that Hollywood was full of reds. Even as an adult, purchasing a movie ticket made me feel like I was doing something I shouldn't be, something forbidden and fun.

"Look, that one has Elizabeth Taylor in it," I said, so excited that I forgot my self-consciousness and took Dorothy's arm. Though she'd taken my arm many times, I'd never returned it. "*Cat on a Hot Tin Roof*, it sounds interesting."

"Oh, let's see that. She's such a beautiful woman, those eyes! She's a great actress too," Dorothy said, resting her hand on my upper arm.

We sat in the theatre, armed with popcorn and sodas. As the lights went down I childishly kicked my feet, so happy I was ready to burst. There was a newsreel about something called NASA, but I was really only pretending to be interested in it. When Dorothy smiled across at me, her face was lovely by the screen's flickering light.

All my dates with men had been forced and strange, performances in shows where I didn't understand my role. Now, for the first time, I was full of the excitement you were supposed to feel when you were sharing a thing you liked with someone special.

I wished I could lean over and kiss Dorothy's lips. As I was trying to imagine what it might feel like, Dorothy moved even closer to me, her arm pressing against mine. When she touched me I always felt it low, in a place I didn't let myself think about very often. I knew she didn't mean anything by it, but it teased me with closeness, making me want her even more.

Maybe it was something about sitting with her in the dark, but I was suddenly struck with the most terrible guilt. The wrongness of my feelings overwhelmed me.

I'd been thinking about her this way since we met, and I'd been allowing myself to enjoy it. Because of Sandra, the girl from high school, I'd always known that these feelings were possible for me. But I'd imagined that at some point they'd go away, that I'd grow up and grow out of them. I wasn't like Bill, who didn't seem to be at all troubled by his nature.

I put my hand on my stomach.

"Alice? What's wrong? Are you ill?" Dorothy said, looking at where my hand lay.

"Nothing. Just feeling a little sick," I whispered.

When she touched my forehead, I closed my eyes. "You're kind of warm! We can leave and take some air. I really don't mind about the movie, we can see it some other time."

"No, no, please. I'm all right. I'm sure I'll feel better soon. I'll just sit here and rest."

"I suppose that will give you plenty of time to get better before you have to drive. This is one of those times I wish I'd gotten my darn license. I could drive you home."

"I'm truly okay. I'll just go to the ladies' room and freshen up. That will make me feel better."

Once I'd splashed my face with water, I looked in the mirror, gripping the edge of the basin in front of me. Though my reflection looked back at me gravely, I was reassured. Regardless of what was going on inside of me, I looked just like any normal girl. There was no way to tell what lay inside of me, no way of anyone guessing how queer my thoughts were.

I returned to my seat feeling better. So much so, that I didn't feel too awful when Dorothy reached over and placed her hand on my knee. "Are you sure you don't need to leave?"

"I'm fine," I said, laying my hand tentatively on hers.

That night after supper I excused myself from the table and took my guitar out onto the porch. Everyone else was setting up for the night in the living room. The trip home from the movies had been a quiet one, and I'd hidden behind my supposed sickness to put some space between Dorothy and me.

I placed my notebook next to me on the seat. It was remarkable that I'd felt physically ill at the movie house, all because of what was going on in my mind. It afforded meaning to a term I'd only thought I understood before.

I was lovesick.

I opened the notebook and found the new song I'd been writing about my feelings for Dorothy. It didn't have a name yet, and I scanned over the lines, frowning as I looked at them with fresh eyes. When I read something I'd written a while earlier, the distance made things so much clearer. I crossed many of the words out, angry at the girl who'd been so brazen about her emotions. Even with the way I'd tried to disguise my intent, it might be obvious to anyone who the song was about.

I strummed the guitar and set about building back up what I'd just torn down.

I could exorcise feelings through music if I tried hard enough. Sadness became less scary when I organized it into a tune. There were so many songs about longing for a person that you couldn't have, but I didn't know if there were any songs about a woman pining after another woman or a man for a man.

I played and sang, noting my progress on the paper next to me. I marked down words that spoke of secrets, concealed depths of feelings deep as the ocean. The title came to me easily, and I knew it should be called "In My Heart." Once I was done, I was relieved that I'd found the balance I'd wanted to. It was one hundred percent personal to me, capturing everything I felt, but like the best songs it could be about anything.

I'd played it through for a third time, reassuring myself that the message was disguised enough, when someone cleared their throat purposefully.

"Dirk! You scared the life out of me."

"Sorry, darlin'. You're working on something new, aren't you?" he said, stepping further out on the porch.

"Yep. How much of it did you hear?"

"Not much, just the end," he said. He pulled a cigarette packet out of his front pocket and tapped out a smoke. "Enough to know you might have something. Why don't you play it again, so I can give it a good listen?"

"I don't know if it's ready. It's really new…"

"Never mind that. I think we're past that by now, don't you reckon?" he said, lighting up and folding himself onto the seat next to me. "It's the perfect moment for a special song. Please, play it for me."

When I was finished, the ash on Dirk's cigarette had grown long, spilling unnoticed onto the ground in front of us. In the silence he finally drew his cigarette to his mouth, inhaling and then blowing out the smoke leisurely.

"Alice. That was haunting. Just…haunting. Can I go in and get the others? They should hear this."

"It could always wait until tomorrow."

"You know it's too good to wait until tomorrow! Some of them might have gone to bed, but I'm going to gather up whoever I can."

"Okay. But why would people have gone to bed already?"

A mouthful of smoke shot out as Dirk coughed, the spluttering turning to laughter. "You don't even realize you've been out here for hours, do you? It's late as hell! Sit tight, I'll be back in a moment."

When he returned, it was only Dorothy who walked behind him. She was in her nightgown, wearing her silk robe and slippers.

"Oh, Dorothy, you should go to bed. It's not important. Dirk shouldn't have told you to come!"

"I wouldn't dream of going to bed at a time like this. Dirk tells me you've got a masterpiece I need to hear immediately," she said.

"No, really, I think it's too late for all of this."

"I'm only kidding you. I'd love to hear it. It's never too late for a good tune. I don't mind a whit what time it is."

Sitting down in the rocking chair off to the side of the bench seat, she crossed her legs and leaned forward. When she moved, it placed her in the path of a shaft of light from the hall, as though a spotlight was shining on her.

To her, I sang all the things I couldn't say.

Each time I glanced at her I could only see her staring down at the floor, concentrating. She was as still as Dirk had been. Finally, as I strummed the final chords, she looked up at me.

"I don't know what to say," she said, wiping a tear from under her eye.

"I know, Dottie," Dirk said. "It's a special one, isn't it?"

She dragged the chair closer to me, gazing into my eyes. "Please, teach it to me."

CHAPTER SIX

"In My Heart" became the new Dorothy Long Band's first true collaboration. For the next week, we conjured up the song together piece by piece. Those days were even more precious to me than the others. While we were striving for the common goal of perfecting the song, we were completely in tune with one another. We barely spoke about anything other than the music. Instead we concentrated only on creating something vital, laboring until the parts knitted together perfectly.

We decided that the opening would be sung a cappella. The first line, "You have me lovesick," pierced the silence in a plaintive cry. The accompaniment then swelled up until it met Dorothy for the chorus. By the time the arrangement was set in place, I was prouder of it than of anything I'd ever done. We agreed that it was to be the final number of our new show.

For the first time since we started rehearsing, Dorothy brought Earl into the space. Though I'd never forgotten that it was his house, it struck me as an intrusion. Earl was disrupting a balance wrought with time and toil that he could never understand.

"I've been telling Earl I think we have our next single," Dorothy said, standing close beside him.

Earl took the detective novel he'd been reading and lay it on the ground at his side. He sat cross-legged, resting his chin on the heel of his palm, a toothpick poking from the corner of his mouth. As he stared up at us he chewed it, his face a mask of childlike wonder that made me feel terrible for not wanting him there.

During the performance, the only thing that Earl moved was his eyes as they scanned from one of us to another. When it was complete he slapped his palms together firmly, he and Dorothy beaming at each other. Dorothy had allowed me to feel like it was she and I who made decisions about songs. Now I understood that all along, it was Earl who possessed the power of the final say.

"Wow! That's going to knock everyone's socks off. We should test it on the road for sure. I reckon it'll bring the house down," Earl said.

"Alice wrote it," Dorothy said. When she gazed at me with a soft smile on her lips, some of my jealousy over Earl fell away.

"I had the idea, but everyone contributed."

"You're our secret weapon, Alice. I can't wait for everyone to hear these songs," Dorothy said.

"When do I get to hear the full show?" Earl said, taking the toothpick from his mouth. "You've been keeping it to yourselves pretty good until now."

"End of the week, we'll play it for you," Dorothy said. "What do you think, gang? We'll do a run through for Earl, then have ourselves a party to celebrate. After that, everyone can have a few days off to spend with their nearest and dearest before we get out there. Earl will be nailing down final details for the tour."

"Sounds good to me, boss," Dirk said.

"Sure," I said.

Earl and Dorothy shared a quick hug, something they'd never done before in my presence. Sometimes at night I lay stiffly with sheets pulled up to my chin, brooding about the fact that they shared a bed. The image of him kissing her, of his thick body lying on top of hers, made me seethe with an envy I had no right to.

"All right then, that's that. Let's hang it up until tomorrow," Dorothy said.

The next day, we dug into polishing our set. The songs had been molded into their final versions, and the only thing left to do was to play them repeatedly to ensure quality. We switched around the order of the songs, and Dorothy ran ideas past us about how she was going to introduce them.

On Friday afternoon when we'd rehearsed the complete set three times in succession, Dorothy stood in front of us. She was breathless from belting out the final song. "I think we're ready. It's time to play a show for Earl."

Once again Earl was an enraptured audience for us, nodding along to the beat. Afterward he paced across the room, gesturing like he couldn't sit still any longer. "That was rock solid. So tight, so well done. Wonderful work, all of you. Now tell me, are you ready to play the best set of shows we've ever done?"

"Yeah!" Dirk yelled.

"You bet! We're ready to go," Jack said.

"Then I'd say we're ready to let loose tonight! You've all worked so hard and I want to thank you properly. Earl has been out picking up enough liquor for us all to get drunker than a poet on payday," Dorothy said.

The gathering began in the backyard, near a barbeque pit Earl had dug into the earth. Card tables had been set up with liquor bottles covering the surface. Earl had also stocked ice chests full with sodas, bottles of champagne, and cans of beer. May would love a party like this and I wished she was here.

"Did I hear something about a party?" Sally said, walking outside with her hands up in the air.

"Get a drink, ol' girl," Dirk said, and Sally pulled a face at him.

"I want to make a little speech!" Dorothy said, gripping the neck of a champagne bottle. Her light blue sundress was decorated with flowers, and she looked so gorgeous I couldn't take my eyes from her. The halter neck revealed beautifully shaped shoulders.

"All right now, I want to toast to Alice, for being the newest member of this here band. And I want to thank you for all your hard work over the past few weeks and all of you fellas for making her welcome. You guys are the best band in the world, and Earl, you're the best manager and booking agent any band could have."

"Hear, hear!" Errol said.

The champagne bottle burst open with a loud pop, the liquid bubbling over Dorothy's fist.

"To the band!" she said, taking a sip right out of the bottle.

We spread out on the lawn, chatting to one another and drinking as the sun went down. Sally brought around plates stacked with brisket, coleslaw, and potato salad.

The rub on the brisket was divine, and I sat next to Dirk licking the flavor from my fingers. "I'm going to miss Sally's cooking so much when we go."

"Oh, I know," Dirk said, talking through a mouthful. "But there'll be plenty to keep us occupied out there. Trust me, we've met so many great people on tour. You're going to meet everyone you ever dreamed of."

"I can't wait! Are people usually nice?"

"Mostly. Some of the guys are really full of themselves, though."

"That's a shame. I'd hate to stop liking some of the people I listen to."

Dirk tipped his head back, upending his beer can and shaking it into his mouth to get every drop. "Alice, maybe I shouldn't talk to you about this, but you're practically one of the guys now. I got to say, you wouldn't believe what some of the married men get up to on the road with women who definitely aren't their wives. Some of those guys are just bad news."

"I can imagine."

"None of us, though. There's a lot of nonsense Dorothy wouldn't hold with. She runs a tight ship. You know, I must be getting a little tipsy if I'm telling you this, but…" Dirk looked down at his empty beer can, as if blaming it for his loose lips.

"Go on now, I'm not a shrinking violet. You can tell me whatever you want," I said, tipsy myself.

"Okay," Dirk said, leaning toward me. "I really wonder about those two."

"What do you mean?"

"Well, I wonder about Earl and Dorothy. Their relationship is a little…different. Their marriage isn't exactly what you'd call normal. You noticed that?"

"Not normal how?" I whispered.

Right now, Earl stood talking to Dorothy, stomach hanging over his belt. How could any man run around when he was married to a woman like Dorothy? Still, even with my limited experience I was aware that for some people what they had at home had nothing to do with it. May and I had talked about that kind of man a lot and that kind of woman too.

Dirk wiped drops of beer from his chin with his sleeve, his mouth and eyes going wide for a second. "All right, I guess I might as well say it. You're gonna find out soon enough. Just promise you won't say I said anything to Dorothy. I love that woman, the last thing I want is for her to be mad at me."

"Scout's honor," I said, holding up a hand. "I won't say a thing, it's between you and me."

"Well, they just seem more like friends than a married couple, which is strange considering they haven't been married for a year. Winnie and I acted crazy about each other when we first got married. Still do sometimes."

"I guess they do seem kind of like friends. I just figured that's how they like to act around other people, though? It's proper."

"Darlin', it's not just that. How many married couples you know been together such a short time but who don't even sleep in the same room?"

"They don't?" I asked. I remembered that when Dorothy had shown me around the house, I hadn't been anywhere near her bedroom.

"No, and it's not like they're old or nothing. Earl even has his own entrance to his room, so he can come and go without disturbing anyone. He goes out sometimes at night, don't know where, but other women might have something to do with it. I've seen him when I was out in the yard, having a smoke."

"That's crazy!" I said.

"Mmm hmm. It's funny how she wouldn't tolerate it with us, but she must know what's going on in her own backyard. And when we travel? Even though it must cost 'em a lot of money, they don't even share a room out there half the time."

"Huh," I sipped my drink and looked over at Dorothy and Earl. They looked to be deep in conversation with one another, Earl gesturing with a plate in his other hand.

"Anyway, remember what I told you, all right? Don't say anything," Dirk said.

I mimed a zipping motion in front of my mouth. "You got it. Not a word."

"Good, now excuse me, doll. I'm going to talk to Errol."

Sally was by herself, on the grass with her plate resting on her lap. I got up and walked over to her and eased myself down next to her. "How are you doing, Sally?"

"I'm good. But you know I've been thinking about how much I'm going to miss you. Nobody's going to be around to help me out, which wouldn't normally bother me, but you've been so great."

"Oh, thank you, Sally, I've always been glad to help," I said. I wished so badly that she was coming with us. Sally was nicer to me than my own mother had ever been.

Dorothy had moved to sit across from me, next to Jack. Her face was upturned to the sun, bathed in light so that her hair shone like a halo. Seeing her joking and laughing with Jack filled me with nostalgia. I was already missing treasured time that would never come again.

"Excuse me, Sally. I'm going to go and fix myself another one," I said.

At the drinks table, I filled a cup with ice and poured gin and tonic over it. As I was garnishing it with a wedge of lime, Dorothy stood next to me.

"What's that you're drinking?"

"This? It's a gin and tonic," I said. "I used to drink them all the time at May's place."

"Would you mind terribly if I tried it? I've been having champagne, but I think I might like something different," she said, holding out her hand.

I passed the sweating glass to her and she drew it up to her mouth, her full lips closing around the rim. She raised her eyebrows and looked appreciatively at the drink before handing it back.

"That's so refreshing. I never tried one before, I'm not sure why now."

"Shall I make you one?" I said, reaching for the gin bottle.

"If you don't mind, that would be wonderful."

"Here you go," I said, our gazes locking as she accepted the drink from me.

"Thank you. Come sit with me?"

Dorothy led me away from the group. Her sundress was cut low, showing the pale skin of her upper back. She sat down, sweeping her dress underneath her.

"Hey, can you hold this for a moment, please?" she asked, raising her glass up to me. When I took it, she slipped her shoes from her feet. "Here, now give me both of those glasses, so you can take yours off too."

I kicked my shoes off, feeling the dense green grass underneath my feet.

"I just love being close to the earth like this, don't you?" she said, wriggling her toes in the grass as I sat down next to her.

"I never really thought about it," I said. "But it's very nice."

"So. How do you feel about going on tour so soon?"

I watched Earl and Jack horsing around while Sally walked around talking to everyone, probably to offer them more food. "Um, excited, nervous, scared, overjoyed. I'd say I switch pretty often between all of those things."

Dorothy laughed, pulling her legs out from underneath her so that she sat with them straight out in front of us. I mirrored her pose. "I've been doing this for a while, but I still feel like that before every tour. Just like you described it."

"You do? You don't just…I don't know, get used to it or something?"

"Not really. It's always a little different. Don't forget, it's only been just me out front for a little while. I'm used to doing everything with my sisters, not being out front all the time like I am now."

"That's hard to believe sometimes. That the band is so new. You really are like a family, you seem so comfortable."

"Oh, well, that's because I've known most of these guys for a long time," Dorothy said, pointing to each of them in turn. "I met Dirk in high school, not that I finished school. Jack played with the Stellar Sisters, and they weren't too happy about me poaching him, believe me. Errol played with another band the Stellars used to knock around with. I handpicked these guys, because I knew it would work out. Knew we'd all be a good team."

"You chose well then. They're great musicians."

"Not just that, they're great people. I chose pretty wisely with you, too, I reckon," she said. Dorothy inched her foot over, kicking me. I kicked back, and afterward neither of us moved our feet so that our bare skin remained against one another's.

"It still feels like a dream sometimes, you know? I never thought I'd be doing anything like this. Did you always know that you were going to be a singer?" I asked.

She put her drink down and put her hands behind her, leaning back so that her curves showed under her sundress. "I did, from when I was a little girl. I never could imagine doing anything else. If I couldn't sing, I'd want to die."

"You really feel like that? It's that important to you?"

Her nose crinkled up. "You don't think I'm just being dramatic, do you? Alice, it's the same for you. Anyone can see that. You're not meant for anything else."

I sipped my drink, looking away from her. I might have survived living back at home, working in the office, but I'd never been as happy as I was right now. "Maybe so, maybe so."

"I've been wanting to ask you something," Dorothy said, her voice low. "But I'm not sure if I should."

I leaned so that my head was nearer to hers. "I'm sure I won't mind."

Now she rubbed her foot against mine, so faintly that it was difficult to know if she meant to do it. I couldn't concentrate on anything but the sensation of her skin against mine and the way it excited me.

"Is there anybody special, back home? Someone that's waiting for you?"

"There's nobody like that."

"No? Then who are all your songs about? Someone from before, an old flame or something?"

"My songs aren't about anyone in particular. I just dream them up," I said. I took my foot away and sat cross-legged, pulling out blades of grass.

"Okay. I was just thinking that if those songs were about someone back home, they'd be lucky is all."

I was still staring at her when she held up her empty glass and shook it from side to side. "I think it's time for a refill. What do you think?"

The sun dipped down, and the party went on. I was lingering at the drinks table when Sally came down the steps on her way back from the kitchen, stumbling as she started across the lawn.

Earl helped her stay upright, grabbing her by the arm. "Whoa there, Mom. Are you okay?"

"I'm just fine, but I'm too old for all this nonsense. I'm taking myself off to bed," Sally said.

"Let's move this party inside so we can listen to some records!" Dirk said.

We piled into the rehearsal room. The large open space with its bar was a perfect setting for a party. Dirk lay back on one of the sofas, and Earl and Jack lolled on the floor beside it. Errol beat out a clunky rhythm at the drum set.

"Errol! Sally just said she wanted to go to bed. Shouldn't you be quiet?" I asked.

"Don't be a wet rag. She's over the other side of the house," he said.

"Okay, okay. Maybe I should go to bed like Sally."

"No, don't go!" Dorothy said, grabbing my arm. "I was hoping you'd make me another one of those gin and tonics?"

"Oh, well, how could I refuse?" I said gallantly.

I mixed at the bar while Dirk rifled through a box of records. He pulled out an album by the Ink Spots and dropped the sleeve onto the ground. Bill loved the Ink Spots; he'd played their records for me in the store. They were so beautiful they gave me chills, in the same way that Dorothy's vocals did. Jack stared at nothing, a cigarette stuck to his bottom lip, but soon even he started to click his fingers along with the melody.

"I didn't know you all liked other kinds of music. Aside from country, I mean," I said.

"Why wouldn't we? If it's good, you should listen to it, simple as that," Dorothy said.

"I agree," I said.

"Who wants to play poker?" Dirk said. "With real money, of course."

"Deal me in," Jack said, rubbing his hands together. Errol left the drum kit, and Earl joined them. They arranged themselves in a circle on the floor and Dirk expertly shuffled a deck of cards.

"That's the way, Jackie boy. You want to join us, Alice?" Dirk asked.

"No, thank you. Maybe I'll just watch."

Dorothy rolled her eyes. "They do this all the time. They'll be playing 'til sunrise. Fellas, don't expect me to step in if anyone cheats or loses too much money. I'm not getting involved."

"It's good luck," Dirk said, throwing cards down in front of each player. "Like you said, we do it every time. If we don't, we'll have a bad tour."

"Whatever you need to tell yourself, friend. Alice, how about another drink?" Dorothy asked.

The guys barely spoke unless it was to announce whether they wanted to check, call, or fold. Jack wobbled drunkenly in his seat, but he was holding his hand steady and seemed to be winning. After a while of watching, my eyes began to droop.

"This is making me tired too. Let's go to the sofa and talk," Dorothy said.

We stepped over stray glasses, sinking down on the sofa on the opposite side of the room. I shifted around to get comfortable on the hard springs and Dorothy leaned up against the sofa's arm, her legs folded to her side. She twirled hair around a finger, and I wondered if it was the alcohol that caused her to fix her eye on me so strongly.

"Do you like this music?" she asked.

"I do. There's so much music I do like."

She poked my arm. "You're a dreamy little one, aren't you?"

"Dreaming is usually better than real life, isn't it?"

"That depends," Dorothy said.

"What on?" I asked.

"How much things go the way you want them to go," she said. Her brown eyes remained trained on me, studying my face and laying me bare.

"I suppose you're right. I don't know, really."

She trailed her finger down my arm. "I just want to make sure you're happy. You might find out when we go out there that things don't go the way you want them to."

"Why are you always doing that?"

"Doing what?" she said, flinching subtly.

"Warning me, worrying about me. You've given me this opportunity. You don't have to look after me on top of it all."

When she avoided my eye, adjusting her dress underneath her, I wished I hadn't said it.

"I didn't mean to make you uncomfortable."

"You're not making me uncomfortable. Just trust me. I'm very happy here."

"It's a little hard to tell what you're thinking most of the time. Do you know that?"

"No. I don't."

"Well, you are a mysterious creature, Alice."

I couldn't believe that she devoted any time at all to wondering what I thought. "I don't think so. Usually I'm just mulling over what we're doing, dreaming up new ideas. That kind of thing."

"I think the inside of your brain would be a very interesting place," she said, tapping her head.

"I don't really know any different now, do I? It's the only one I've ever been inside of," I said. She laughed, a tinkling sweet sound. I loved the way she looked at me when I made her laugh.

"Can you two quiet down over there? I can't concentrate," Errol said, pushing hair out of his eye. The four of them sat mutely, contemplating their hands.

"Errol's losing, in case you can't tell," Dirk said from the side of his mouth.

"Heaven forbid we should interrupt your precious poker game!" Dorothy said, jumping up to glare at them.

"Shhhh!" Errol said.

"This is my house, you know," Dorothy said, but she was smiling, and I guessed that she wasn't all that angry. "Come on, Alice, let's go somewhere else."

"Sorry, ladies," Dirk said.

"See, this is why I'm especially glad that you're around, Alice," Dorothy said. "These men have no manners at all."

I let her take my hand. Focused only on our intertwined fingers, I didn't care where we were going. We were outside, and then she was taking me past the porch and down the steps, then at last we were in the yard. All around us were the dark shapes of the fence, Dirk's car, the oak tree ancient and tall.

"What are we doing out here?" I said, looking up at the moon. It was almost full.

Dorothy dropped my hand and I wanted to grab it again. She bent down, slipping off her shoes once more. "Don't you love being outside, on a night like tonight?"

The moon cast a glow over the yard. I could hear dogs barking far off in the distance, but here there was only the rustling of the leaves on the trees. After a few moments Dorothy laid down.

"What are you doing?" I said. She really was very drunk. Maybe I should suggest that she get herself to bed.

"I'm enjoying the night. Enjoying the moon. C'mon, get down here beside me. Trust me, there's nothing more beautiful than the sky out here. Look at those stars."

I got onto my back, and she wriggled toward me until our shoulders were touching. The sky was black, with shining points of light stretched out above us. I stared up at it, my mouth opened slightly. "You're right. It really is beautiful."

"I've done this since I was a little girl. Nature is such a wonderful thing, you've got to get out and really appreciate it. That's what I think, anyway."

Whenever my parents talked about nature it was because it was God's creation. For me it was just *there*, not something I thought about too much either way. I liked seeing things through her eyes. Dorothy sang one of the songs we were listening to inside. No matter how many times I heard it, her voice melted me.

"That sounds so lovely," I said. "You sing it so well, maybe we should put a version of it in the act."

"Listen to you, always working. I just like it. Some things should just be for appreciating."

"Okay."

"Don't get sore."

She poked me again and I caught her fingers. "I'm not *sore*. I just really like the way it sounds when you sing it, that's all."

The volume went up, Dorothy flinging her arms about where she lay. It was so silly I laughed, until she got up to continue the performance on her feet. After a while it was strange lying down when she wasn't, and I stood too.

"I feel like dancing," Dorothy said, holding out a hand. "Come on, don't look so scared. I'm not gonna bite you. I can hardly go in and interrupt the guys so someone will dance with me. They'd kill me!"

I stepped closer to her, brushing my hair behind my ears. I could do it. It was just a dance. "We don't have any music, though."

"Nonsense. We can make our own music. C'mon, put your hand on my shoulder."

Dorothy rested one of her hands on my waist. She pulled me close to her, and when her body was against mine I was grateful for the fact that she couldn't see my face.

We moved together, our bodies swaying as one in the dark. She gently put her hand on the back of my head, encouraging me to relax against her. My head fit perfectly in the crook of her neck. Finally, I slackened against her, holding back the sigh that threatened to spill from my mouth.

I'd never felt anything like what it was to be in her arms, like a precious thing she was cradling. I closed my eyes, following her lead. I could feel the vibration of her voice against my cheek, the sound close to my ear.

Soon there was only silence while we moved. I didn't know why people thought men and women fit so well together, not when you could have this. Her breasts were pressed against mine, and I adored the way she smelled. There was her perfume and the slight tang of sweat.

When she stopped moving, I clung to her, my hand tight against her shoulder. Dorothy gently rubbed my back, her hand sliding against me. I felt her breathe in deeply against my chest. I could stand here all night, with her hands on me.

My arms were empty a moment later when she stepped back. She put her hand on the back of her neck. I wished I could see her eyes better.

"Well…I think it's time I went to bed," she said.

"Me too. Are you going to go on in and say good night to everyone?"

"I don't think so. I know what they're like once they get going on poker. They're not going to notice if I'm around or not."

"I'm just going to stay out here for another minute. Look at the stars."

"Okay," she said. "Good night, Alice."

I watched her go, my disappointment bottomless. I'd never wanted to follow anyone so much in my life. I wrapped my arms around myself as I looked at the sky.

CHAPTER SEVEN

The next morning I awoke with my limbs twisted in sheets and my dress bunched up around my waist. I'd fallen into bed without undressing or brushing my teeth, overcome by the alcohol and dancing with Dorothy and the whole night. At least I'd had enough sense to take my shoes off; they were tossed on the floor beside the bed.

The days between now and the tour stretched out before me. I had no idea what I was supposed to do with my time now that we weren't rehearsing. I wanted to stay in bed and nurse my hangover, but I forced myself to sit up and put my feet on the floor. Mama always said that it was rude to sleep in when you were a guest in someone's house.

As I padded down the hall I glanced at the wooden grandfather clock. It was only six. I supposed that I'd find Sally beginning her usual morning preparations, especially when she'd gone to bed so much earlier than the rest of us.

When I got to the kitchen Dorothy stood at the sink with her back to me, drinking water in big gulps. The cream silk robe she wore was belted at the waist, accentuating her shape.

"Good morning."

Dorothy spun around. "Lord! You scared me half to death!"

"I'm sorry," I said.

Still catching her breath, she placed a hand on her chest, drawing the edges of her robe together more securely. "Never mind. It's so early I wasn't expecting to find anyone up. And you're already dressed too! I have one hell of a hangover. How about you?"

"I'm tired, but other than that I'm not feeling too poorly."

"I haven't drunk so much booze in an awful long time. I've never been too good at holding my liquor, you can ask any of the boys," she said, her speech rapid.

Dorothy turned to place her glass in the sink, moving her hand around at first as though she wasn't sure what to do with it. When she turned back toward me, she crossed her arms. My eyes dropped to her chest, the neckline of her robe revealing alluring cleavage. I wondered what her skin would feel like under my fingers.

"Anyway, I just got out of bed to get myself some water. I was parched. I'm going to go back to bed," she said, already moving past me. "I need to sleep this off properly. You should drink some water too. It's good for a hangover."

"Okay. I will."

I should have told her to sleep well or done anything other than just stand there as she left. I slowly approached the sink to get myself some water. I picked up the glass that she'd been using and ran my finger around the rim.

The next days were as empty as I'd feared they might be. Dirk, Jack, and Errol left to return to their own houses or to visit friends and family. As the only member of the band who didn't have anywhere close enough to drive to easily, I had no choice but to stay.

At first, I hoped that the house being almost empty might mean I'd be able to spend more time with Dorothy. It became clear to me immediately that it wasn't going to happen. Dorothy became a ghost, slipping in and out of her bedroom so quietly that I never knew for sure where she was. She came into the kitchen to make tea while I was helping Sally, but aside from that I rarely saw her.

Earl spent a lot of time on the phone, set up at the dining table with papers fanned out in front of him. "I'm telling you, we're not doing a show for that amount of money. Do you know how many folks she's going to bring into your place? How many drinks you're going to sell 'cos of us?"

When I wasn't with Sally I stayed in my room, writing letters for everyone back home and reading on my bed. On the second day after the house had emptied out of people, I drove into town to wander around the streets.

In a drugstore I scanned a row of old pulp novels, enticed by the bright colors of the cover art. It was amazing to think that I could take home any book I wanted. I'd always been told that books like these would rot my brain, filling it with ideas a girl shouldn't have. I'd never dream of buying them back home, because I didn't trust my parents to stay out of my things.

My gaze fell on a cover I couldn't take my eyes from. Two women were in a near embrace, one woman standing with her hands on the other's shoulders. The title, *Strange Sins*, was written across the cover in lurid red text. The blurb promised a tale of desire that would shock me. Heart racing, I found two detective mysteries and sandwiched my prize in between them. When I walked up to the counter, I clutched the bundle in my hands trying to look nonchalant.

That night I read *Strange Sins* from cover to cover. I huddled under the quilt, ready to hide it if anyone came to the door. The novel's tragic ending made my eyes prick with tears. Was that the kind of life that lay ahead of me?

I paged back through the novel. There were sections that made me feel some of the thrill that Dorothy did, and I read those parts again. Though it was against everything I'd ever been taught, I was starting to want to chase those urges, to let them run hot through me.

When I switched off my light, I rolled over in bed and imagined a happy ending for the two girls in *Strange Sins*. Didn't they deserve it, as much as anyone else did? The idea of it made me smile into the dark.

The next morning I found Sally in the kitchen, already working on making a cake.

"Good morning, sweetheart. How are you?" she asked, cracking an egg into a bowl.

"Hey, Sally, do you think I could help you with something today?"

"I told you yesterday, you're supposed to be resting," she said, picking up a whisk.

"I've never been good at resting. I'd really like to help. You're going to have the place all to yourself to run soon. There must be something we can do."

"All right, then. Get into some work clothes and meet me outside," she said, untying her apron and hanging it on a hook. "This can wait. We're going to dig in the garden."

Sally taught me all about harvesting potatoes. We kneeled together in the patch lifting out plants, depositing the vegetables into a bucket. I liked the sensation of having my fingers in the dirt. It made me feel like I was doing something useful.

"You're such a helpful girl," Sally said.

"It's the least I can do, you do so much for everyone," I said, holding out the bucket to her. There was a satisfying thump as she dropped another potato in.

"Well, it's not work to me at all. It's been so lovely to have you here. I do love the rehearsal time the best. It's so much fun having you all around. And you fit right in around here. They were lucky to find you."

"Thanks, Sally. You sure you don't mind even though we eat you out of house and home? You must get tired of cooking."

Sally laughed. "Honey, I've raised five kids. If I was going to get tired of cooking it would have happened a long time ago. I'll be cooking 'til I'm in the ground, I reckon, and I don't mind that at all."

"You must have lots of grandchildren by now, do you?"

Sally used the back of a dirty hand to brush hair back from her face. "Fourteen of them, last time I checked. I reckon everyone's about done with that, though. Earl's my baby."

"What about Dorothy and Earl? When they have children, you'll have even more grandkids running around, and you'll be living with them too. That'll be nice, won't it?"

Sally was silent, her hands stilling in the dirt. "Speak of the devil, here Earl comes now."

"Hey, Mama, hey, Alice," Earl said, shoving his hands into his pockets. "Do you want me to get in there and give you a hand?"

"Look at this big bucket we've filled! We don't need help. I'm going to roast some of them up to have with supper."

"Always loved the way you do potatoes, Mom. Alice, I came out here to let you know I just got a call from Gene about your clothes. She said you can go on and pick them up any time from now."

"Oh, that's great," I said. I wished Dorothy had come to tell me. Earl and I rarely spoke to one another, even though he was the manager.

"I was relieved to hear from her. She's never let us down before, but she really took it down to the wire this time."

"I'll go and get them once I've washed up."

I scrubbed dirt from under my fingernails and changed. I was on my way toward the front door when I realized that I wasn't quite sure what to do. Dorothy had assured me I wouldn't need to pay for my dresses, but I didn't know if she'd already taken care of it. It would be horribly embarrassing if I got there and found out that she hadn't. I had no idea how much it would all cost.

I went back into the house to find Earl. He had his feet up on the table, the phone cord stretched across the room. He didn't look up when I came in. "I tell you, you're going to want to hear some of this new stuff we're doing. Are you going to be sending anyone out to see us?"

I checked the time on the clock behind him, wondering if Gene closed the shop for dinner. I didn't want to bother Dorothy with it, but I was impatient to get my clothes and make sure everything fit. If Gene needed to do alterations, there was only a short time left.

I only knew the general direction of Dorothy's bedroom. I wandered around until I came to a closed door and put my ear to it, but there was no sound. I knocked softly.

"Yes? Come in?"

I pushed the door open cautiously. Dorothy lay in her bed with the covers pulled up over her. She sat propping herself up against the pillows.

"Oh, excuse me, Alice. I thought you were Earl," she said, drawing the quilt more tightly against her chest.

"I'm sorry. I should have said who I was when I knocked," I said. I took a quick look around the room. It was decorated in earthy tones, with a brownish quilt and heavy maroon curtains. The carpet was thick and dark. A framed picture of Dorothy and her sisters sat on the dresser.

"It's not a problem," she said, smoothing her hair down and smiling. "I haven't been feeling too well. Headache."

"I'm sorry to interrupt you. It's just that Earl says my clothes are ready, and I was about to drive into town and pick them up."

The smile broadened, becoming genuine in a way that made me understand how fake it had been at first. "That's some good news. I was getting worried they wouldn't be ready. I called Gene a couple of days ago to ask her about it."

"Well, she came through. I was just wondering how I should pay for them?"

"Just charge them to my account."

"Oh. Thanks," I said, hand on the doorknob. Of course, she would have an account, I should have known that. "Can I get you anything? Anything that might help you feel better?"

"You're very kind, but I don't need anything. Just to sleep."

I was pulling the door closed when I heard her voice again. "Excuse me. What was that?"

"I was just saying, I'd like very much to see how the dresses look on you before we go on tour. Will you try them on for me when you get back?" she asked.

"Of course. I'm looking forward to trying them on myself."

"Great. You know the way to the store?"

"Sure thing," I said.

I worried my lips between my teeth the whole way into town. What if Dorothy didn't like the way the dresses looked on me? Something was troubling her, and I couldn't bear it if I contributed to her problems. When I arrived at Gene's I rushed inside.

"Hi. It's Alice, isn't it? I'm pretty sure I got everything right but try them on for me, so I can find out if I need to do a little nip and tuck here and there," Gene said, motioning toward a row of dresses on hangers.

When I tried on the first dress, I stared back at the mirror as though my reflection were a stranger. The color brought out my eyes, and I'd never worn anything cut so perfectly to my shape. The dress refined me into an hourglass figure and I turned one way and the other, trying to get used to how different I looked.

I pulled aside the curtain and stepped out in front of Gene.

"Uh-huh! We don't need to do anything. I reckon that's just about perfect. I'll get it all together for you," she said.

The entry hall at the house smelled of roasting meat. After carefully depositing the garment bags on my bed, I joined everyone at the dining table. Earl spoke about schedules and venues while Dorothy made encouraging noises, often taking a long time to reply. I wished I knew what was on her mind.

As usual I helped Sally and Dorothy with clearing the table and doing the dishes. I was carrying a stack of plates when I almost ran into Dorothy as I passed her walking toward a cupboard. She put her hands on my shoulders.

"Sorry," I said. Her hands stayed where they were for a moment, and then she squeezed me lightly.

"It's okay," she said. Her brown eyes pierced mine as we faced one another, her hands finally dropping away. "I think I'll go back to bed. Excuse me."

When the dishes were squared away, I went to my room and sat on the edge of my bed, to work on a letter to Bill. Dorothy's melancholy had spread to me, and I felt too glum to go to Sally and offer to help with afternoon chores. As I unfolded the pages and looked over the last few lines to find my place, I saw how much things had changed. The earlier paragraphs were composed when the band was still rehearsing, before the party. Those times had been so exciting that my words leapt off the page.

Maybe when we were out on the road, Dorothy would smile more often. Maybe then, she would want to spend time with me again.

There was a knock on the door. I glanced at my nightstand to make sure that my new book wasn't there after last night's re-reading. I must have shoved it back into its place under the mattress.

"Alice? May I come in?"

"Of course. I thought you were going to bed. Are you feeling any better?"

Dorothy placed a hand on her forehead. "Oh, yes, a little better, thank you. I was on my way, but then I remembered I'd been wanting to ask you how the clothes are. Are you satisfied with them?"

"I think so… Shall I try a couple of them on for you now?"

"If you don't mind."

"Sure," I said. She sat down on the mattress, noting the small stack of Steinbeck and Salinger books on my nightstand and the letter I'd been writing. I was glad that I'd folded the pages again before she'd come in, when so much of what I'd written was about her.

"Excuse me, I'll be back in a moment," I said, making my way to the washroom with the bundle of clothes in my arms. I unzipped the bag that was on the top of the pile. It was the red one, and I shimmied into it quickly. This time I tied the sash carefully in the way I'd seen Dorothy do it, wanting to make the best impression I could.

Dorothy stood by the bed. Her gaze trailed up and down my body, more overtly than it had at Gene's store. After the last two days of her looking right through me, the intensity of her stare was like having water in a wasteland. She came near to me, feathering her hands over my waist. I kept my eyes on her face, conscious of her long-fingered hands curling around me.

A moment later she met my eye. "You really do have the perfect figure for that dress. You know who you look like?"

I shook my head and stared back at her, frozen. Her hands were still splayed over my hips and I wished she'd press them down harder. If only we could be as intimate with one another as we were when we danced. I didn't care how, I just needed to feel her against me again.

"You look like Liz Taylor, if she had red hair anyway. Your eyes might not be violet like hers but they sure are pretty, and this dress brings them out more."

At last she took her hands away from me, stepping back.

"Thanks," I said. "Gene's good at her job, I guess."

Dorothy smiled. "She is. Do you think you could try on another?"

Obediently, I changed into the more casual gingham dress. Dorothy reached out again to touch the fabric, but this time she stayed in place. "It's wonderful, too."

"I guess the other thing to do is to work out my makeup and such. I assume you'll want me to wear it differently for the stage? I'll have to get shoes, maybe some cowboy boots like yours. And how should I do my hair?" I asked.

It took a long while for her to answer. "Why would you assume that? That I'd want you to change in any way?"

"I don't know. I guess I thought that I couldn't just go out there like this. Don't you want me to try something different?"

"I'm not trying to change the way you look. There's nothing wrong with you," Dorothy said, her mouth twisted in a grimace.

"I know. I just thought…"

"You can wear any kind of makeup you want to," Dorothy said. "Just do it however you want to do it, I don't care."

Everything had changed so fast. I couldn't understand why Dorothy was being this way when I was only trying to be cooperative.

"Okay…I'll make up my own mind about it then, I guess."

"Just don't do anything because you think I want you to," Dorothy said. She sat down on the bed, staring at the floor.

"Do you want me to try on another dress?" I asked, my voice small.

"If you want to. I really don't mind."

"Then if it's all the same to you, I think I might take Scout for a walk around the yard. It's a nice afternoon."

"All right. I'll see you later," she said.

I'd hoped that she'd offer to walk Scout with me. Even when she was right in front of me, I missed her.

Before she left she put her hand on the door frame, hesitating. "Thank you for showing the dresses to me. They really are very good."

"No problem," I said.

I yanked the zip down and stepped out of the dress, then found Scout and stalked outside.

Over breakfast the next morning I kept my eyes on my plate as much as possible, after forcing a hello to Dorothy. She'd missed supper the night before, and now there were dark circles under her eyes.

"What's everyone doing today?" Sally said cheerfully.

"Got lots of calls to make, some mapping out to do to make sure we can make the schedule work. That kind of thing," Earl said, taking a mouthful of coffee.

Sally looked around the table. "Anyone else doing anything today?"

I glanced across at Dorothy, but she didn't look up.

"Does anybody need anything from town? I thought I might go for a drive," I said.

"Oh? Where are you going?" Dorothy said, her voice raspy.

"Just into town like I said. I might see a movie or something."

"That sounds like fun. These few days is like vacation time for you. Enjoy it while you can, I say," Earl said, gesturing toward me with his fork.

"I'm sure I will."

My bad mood dropped away the further I got from the house and from Dorothy. I was so confused by her moodiness. And in town, I could experience something I'd rarely felt before: the freedom of total anonymity. Back home everyone knew me and my family, and I always had to be so careful about everything. The locals assessed who I was with, what I wore, and anything I said.

I got out of the car, taking in city streets I'd never imagined getting to see when I was younger. During the last month I'd been holed up at the house, locked in a bubble, but now that I wasn't busy working it was finally sinking in that I'd escaped my home.

There was no need for me to go back there at all unless I really wanted to. I'd always assumed that I'd spend the rest of my life with my folks, becoming the spinster everyone always said I would be. I'd told myself that I had my books and music and that it was better than having to marry some man. I hadn't realized how much the thought had been crushing me.

I found the drugstore in which I'd purchased my special paperback. Feeling like a kid in a candy store, I searched covers and read blurbs until I found two books I knew I'd like.

After I'd been walking around for a while my stomach rumbled, and I searched for a diner. The blonde waitress who came to serve me was pretty, her pink uniform hugging her figure. She wore a white ruffled apron over the top.

"Could I get coffee and a tuna salad sandwich, please?"

"Sure thing. You local?" she asked as she took down my order.

"I'm staying just outside of town, with some friends who have a big property out there."

"Well, that sounds nice," she said, tucking her notepad back into her apron pocket. "I'll be back in just a minute with your coffee."

While I ate I read one of my new books, breaking the spine and pressing the cover down hard against the table to conceal it. The waitress refilled my coffee cup twice while I raced through the first few chapters. It made me drunk with the pleasure of seeing characters that I shared something with.

I was just a normal person, not deranged or evil like some of the characters in these books were. Still, they gave me hope that maybe there were all kinds of girls like me. I just wished I could meet one of them in the flesh.

The waitress stood patiently at the end of my table. I covered the words on the page with my palm. "Would you like some more coffee, ma'am?"

"Thank you," I said. As she tilted the coffee pot, she smiled down at me shyly.

I picked up my cup and stared after her, taking in her long legs and the small tear in her nylons. Maybe it was time to face the fact that my feelings for women weren't restricted only to the special ones like Dorothy or to Sandra.

I liked women in general, and I liked the way it made me feel. There had never been a man who'd made me feel as good as it did when a pretty girl smiled at me. If I was able to put aside the fact that I was supposed to feel guilty, there was nothing so terrible about it. I wasn't hurting anyone.

I pushed open the door of the diner and went out onto the sidewalk. Acting on my feelings again had seemed impossible, but now that I was far from home it occurred to me, so what if I did? It could be a secret kept between me and one other person if I could find her. I'd found Sandra, even in my small town. Maybe there would be someone else.

As I strode along the sidewalk, I thought about the fact that my head always turned for a certain type of girl. I liked the tall ones, and I was attracted to strength and confidence. It was no wonder I'd developed a crush on Dorothy. Aside from the fact that I admired her singing, she had qualities I'd always secretly sought out. If I'd met Dorothy some other way, for instance if she'd been a girl at the office, the same thing might have happened to me.

Everyone was always saying the kind of feelings I had were unnatural, but I wasn't trying to feel this way. Desiring women was natural for me, so who was anybody to say that it wasn't? No matter how hard I worked to be interested in men, it didn't make any difference.

I got behind the wheel and pointed my car toward home. Maybe my life would be easier if I just accepted who I was and ceased willing it to change. My desires had caused me so much pain over the years, and I didn't want to feel that way anymore. I rolled down the window and put my arm against it, letting the breeze blow back against me.

I was on a roller coaster, poised on a curve, waiting to go over the edge. Everything in my life had changed over the past few months. I was ready, not just for what was to come with the tour, but to embrace my nature. I didn't want to be ashamed anymore.

CHAPTER EIGHT

My car was full to the brim, the backseat lined with extra blankets and bags that wouldn't fit in anyone else's trunk. On top of the jumble of things, I'd laid my guitar case. I checked that everything was secured enough to not tumble over and slammed the door shut.

All the cars had been brought out to the front lawn to pack everything up. Earl and Dorothy's slick-looking Chevy was parked next to Dirk's beat-up Dodge, as well as the dark green Oldsmobile that belonged to Errol. Jack was leaving his car behind to save gas. He was riding with Errol, whose backseat was taken up entirely by his double bass.

Earl propped himself against the hood of the Chevy. "All right. Now, Alice, the guys know this already, but so that you know, we're hoping it won't be too much longer before we can get ourselves a nice big tour bus. Until then, what we do is drive along in a kind of convoy. I drive at the front because I have all the maps and such."

"Okay," I said.

"You need to stop for anything, put your arm out of the window and lean on your horn so I know. All right, y'all, let's get ourselves out there!" Earl said. When I got into my vehicle, he slapped a hand once on its roof.

The tires crunched on the driveway as I pulled out, reaching down to turn the radio up loud because "Bye Bye Love" by the Everly Brothers was playing. As I'd been leaving my room, it was so peculiarly bare without my things in it that I'd slammed the door shut on it quickly. Now I had no base anywhere, and the next bed I slept in would be in a motel. All of my life was in this car.

This very evening, I would be on stage. The thought was so nerve-wracking that an impulse to turn the car around gripped me. I could return to my old job where I already knew how to do everything, in a place where I was competent and safe.

Just ahead I could make out Dorothy and Earl's shapes sitting next to one another, the wide brim of Earl's cowboy hat jutting out. I wondered what they were speaking about or if they were speaking at all. Was Dorothy only being remote with me?

The convoy rolled over the miles hour after hour until we reached our motel just outside of Charlotte, North Carolina. The brick building was painted lime green, a single row of rooms with car spaces out front. We got out of our vehicles and paced around while Earl checked us in. Dorothy leaned her head back and forth, stretching her neck. There was a soft pink scarf knotted over her hair, and I wished I could tell what she was looking at under her dark sunglasses.

"All right, everyone. Alice, seeing as you can't share with the guys, you get your own room," Earl said, handing me a key with a red plastic tag.

"I hope there's not a pea under the mattress, princess," Dirk said, holding his hand out toward Earl.

"Sorry, there were no twin bed rooms left. I had to book you guys a double," Earl said.

"Just great. Spare a thought for us all sharing a room, Alice. We'll be drawing straws to see who has to sleep on the floor," Jack said.

"I hope it's you, Dirk. You kick like a mule. I've still got a sore leg from the last time I slept next to you," said Errol, shoving him.

"Knock it off, guys. It's not her fault," Dorothy said flatly.

There were still two keys dangling from Earl's fingers. It didn't seem fair that Earl and Dorothy each had a room to themselves along with me. Dirk and I exchanged a look. I wished it was proper for me to share with one of the boys, but of course we couldn't do that.

I didn't feel bad for long though, not when I unlocked my door and saw where I'd be staying for the next couple of nights. It might not be fancy, but it was my space and it made me feel secure again to have somewhere to unload my things. I placed my suitcases on the bed, on top of the faded striped quilt, and hung my garment bags from the metal hangers in the closet.

There wasn't much time. I took a shower, trying to wash away the tiredness from the road. I applied my makeup in front of the cracked mirror and brushed my hair, arranging a bow in it. It wasn't until I opened the closet that I realized I didn't know what dress I was supposed to put on.

I frantically rifled through the rack of garment bags, as though it would give me a clue about what to wear. I could knock on the door of the boys' room to ask them, but they were all in there together and that made me feel shy. I picked up the telephone on the night stand to call the front desk to reach Earl, who'd given me his room number for if I had any questions.

"Hi, Earl. I'm just wondering what I'm wearing tonight?"

"Oh…I'm afraid I have no idea. Sorry, Alice. That's Dorothy's department. She's in number seven."

It was answered on the second ring. "Hello, Dorothy. It's Alice."

"Hello… Is everything all right?"

"Yes, of course. I'm very sorry to bother you, but I was just wondering which dress I should wear this evening?" I asked.

"You're not bothering me," she replied. "Wear the red one, the first one you showed me."

The line clicked and I stared at the receiver, then slowly put it back in its cradle. After I'd stepped into my dress, I pulled the zip up as far as I could. I was reaching around to try and inch it up a little further when there was a knock on my door.

I ran over to it, thinking it must be Earl coming to fetch me. Dorothy stood there with her makeup in place and her hair styled in flawless curls. There was a hand on her hip and her chin was raised. Since I'd last seen her she'd transformed into Dorothy Long, primed to hold an audience in the palm of her hand.

"I wanted to check if you needed help with anything."

"Thank you," I said, standing off to the side to let her pass and fiddling with my sash. "I was having a little trouble with my dress."

"First, can you do mine, please?" she said, turning her back to me.

"Of course."

I drew the zip up, closing it over her pale skin. I turned so that she could do the same for me and then she turned me back around in her hands, reaching for my sash.

"Here, let me do this again for you. It's a little crooked. Hard to do on yourself," she said, tongue sticking from the corner of her mouth as she tied a perfect bow.

She rested her hands on my shoulders and searched my face, settling on my eyes. "You look just lovely."

"Thank you. So do you," I said quietly.

"I scrub up all right, I guess," Dorothy said with a half-smile. "How are you feeling? Are you very nervous?"

"I'm okay. No, that's not true. I'm terrified."

We laughed, the tension between us breaking easily as Dorothy rubbed her hands up and down my arms. Though my fear hadn't dissipated, it suddenly felt like something I could manage if she was standing up there with me.

"You are going to be just fine. Let's get on out there and break a leg."

I slipped on the cowboy boots that she'd given me, a pair she'd bought that were too small for her. They were butter soft with a small heel.

I travelled with Dirk in his car, grateful for the distraction as he described the time he'd spent with his family. Now and then while he spoke I'd picture Dorothy's hands on me and the way we'd laughed together.

The show was at a honky-tonk that didn't look so different from the one at home. Like Merle's it was a freestanding rough timber building, though I could tell right away that it was going to be much larger inside. An American flag waved from the roof, above a sign that said Baxter's Inn. The sign was surrounded by advertisements for liquor, and a makeshift sign hanging by the door said Dorothy's name. We drove around to the back so the boys and some men from the bar could unload equipment from our cars. They placed the guitar cases and the double bass by the back door, leaning them carelessly against the wall, eager to have the work done.

They stood in a circle, smoking cigarettes, and one of the guys escorted Dorothy and me inside. My mouth was so pasty it was as though I'd swallowed glue, and there was a sense of unreality I couldn't shake as we made our way to the backstage area.

A black curtain separated us from the crowd, the stage protruding from it, though at the sides I could make out the movement of bodies. It was a noisy joint, the hall filled with the sounds of voices and a jukebox playing. Dorothy walked over to the curtain and bent a little, twitching it the tiniest fraction across so that she could peek out.

"Looks like a good crowd for your first show. They'll be an energetic bunch. They won't just leave you standing there."

"Now I know you're lying to me. How can you tell it's going to be good just by looking at them?"

"A girl gets a sense after being in this game for a while. Big pack of live wires. Trust me," she said. When I looked at her with narrowed eyes, she shrugged. "You caught me. We've played here before. It's a jumping joint if I remember right."

We stood next to one another a few feet back from the curtain, and Dorothy reached down to take my hand. My palms were sweaty, and I hoped she didn't find it unpleasant to touch me.

"'Scuse me," Earl said, walking past us with my guitar. The rest of the guys followed, jostling against us as they lugged out the heavy equipment, pushing through the gap in the curtains. Dorothy guided me to stand to the side where nobody would catch a glimpse of us. When the instruments were being set up there was a change in the room, the anticipation of the crowd ratcheting up.

"They'll be ready for us to come on in about five minutes. We have to make a grand entrance, you see?"

"*You* have to, you mean. Shouldn't I just go out there with the rest of the band?"

When Dorothy turned toward me her eyes stunned me, their beauty always a shock. "You're not just another band member, Alice. They need to know how special you are."

She clutched my hand, and I swallowed thickly. After a moment she loosened her grip and draped an arm around my shoulders instead. How I'd longed for this tenderness from her again, and I softened against her, immersing myself in it.

"You okay, honey?" she said, our heads leaned together.

"I will be. Just nervous. Sorry."

"Don't be sorry. I threw up the first few times I went on stage. You're doing just fine," she said, tightening her arm around me and patting my shoulder.

Standing side by side, we listened as they set up and tested the microphones. Then Dorothy took my hand to shepherd me toward the curtain, and we stood at the front of the stage with the crowd before us.

I'd never realized how hot the lights on the stage would be. The packed house stomped and clapped for us, and I sought a cue from Dorothy. I copied the broad smile on her face and the sweep of her hand as she waved.

Dorothy adjusted her microphone, lowering it to her mouth. She posed with one hand around the stand while the other rested at her waist.

"Well, hello. It's lovely to see y'all tonight," she drawled. "This is one of my favorite towns to play in. I couldn't wait to come back. Was anyone at our last show here?"

The crowd cheered, and she let them run on before she dipped her head close to the mic again. "Then we've already met, so you know me and my band. But there's someone you haven't met yet, that you really should. Tonight, I'd like to introduce you to this lady right here, Alice Johnson. Are you all going to make her nice and welcome?"

This time when the audience cheered it was for me.

"Alice is our newest member, and I wanted y'all to know that she wrote all our new songs. I think you're going to enjoy her on the guitar too. This girl is going places."

I smiled and nodded to Dorothy before moving to take my place. The solidity of my guitar under my fingers helped me to stop shaking so much.

When we started I played mechanically, hitting the notes correctly but without much energy. The first song was a blur I was just trying to get through. Afterward Dorothy approached and placed a hand on my forearm, leaning close to whisper into my ear.

"You're doing great. Just remember to have fun. Play it to me," she said, moving her hand to my cheek. I looked into her eyes, letting their dark warmth calm me.

When she walked away, I loosened my grip on the neck of my guitar, and for the next song I tried to imagine we were in our rehearsal space. I focused on Dorothy's voice, letting the faces of the crowd melt into the background. I looked around at the guys in the band, each of them grinning at me when I caught their eye. The chemistry clicked into place, a current that ran across the stage and through the five of us like a wire.

The realization that I was up here doing exactly what I loved hit me, and I began to enjoy myself. I fed from the energy thrown up at us by the audience, reveling in the way they danced and stomped along the floorboards in time to our beat or stared raptly up at Dorothy when we were performing ballads. In the gaps between songs Dorothy turned to me, smiling or winking.

When we played "In My Heart" I searched the crowd and took in their upturned faces. There were expressions that conveyed to me that people understood it and that they had felt some of the same things I felt. It was as though for a moment, we all felt less alone.

We played two encores, then exited the stage to rapturous applause.

Dorothy and I stood back as our equipment was packed into the cars. I bounced up and down on the balls of my feet and Dorothy caught my hand, rubbing her thumb over the back of it. "You were wonderful tonight."

"Thank you," I said. "They liked my songs!"

Dorothy tugged on my hand. "They loved them. Just like I knew they would."

On the ride home I stared out the window biting my thumb, but I was no longer anxious. Now that the first show was over I felt powerful, sure that I would only keep getting better. I could stop worrying about my place in the band. I'd earned it tonight.

At the motel I began to lift my guitar from the backseat to take it to my room.

"You put that down, Alice Johnson. That's not part of your job!" Dorothy said, closing her car door.

"There's nobody around to see. I can help."

"No, you can't. Why don't you come with me and have some warm cocoa? It's what I always do to wind down before bed."

"Okay. Good night, guys," I said.

When Dorothy opened her door, I furtively searched for signs that I might be wrong about Earl having his own room. There was one suitcase at the end of the bed, and Dorothy's robe hung from the handle of the closet door. Perhaps Dirk was right about a few things.

Dorothy filled an electric jug with milk and set it to boil.

"I take this thing on the road with me everywhere I go. A bit of an extravagance, I know," she said, bustling around and tipping powdered chocolate into plastic cups. "I can never sleep if I don't have a cocoa before bed, it's one of my rituals for the road. It's those little things that keep me going when I think it's all going to wear me out."

There was a faded brown armchair next to the window. The only other place to sit was the bed, so I walked over to the chair. Dorothy approached me holding the cups, and I took the steaming drink in my hands. She arranged herself on the ground near the armchair.

"Do you want to sit down?" I asked, starting to move from the seat.

"No, no. You stay right there. I don't mind the floor one bit."

It was quiet for a moment, then we both moved to speak at once.

"Please, you first," I said.

"What did you think of the show? Did you have a good time tonight?"

"Of course, I did. It was… Well, it was magical."

"It felt like that, didn't it?" Dorothy said, nose crinkling as she smiled.

"For you, too? Is it always like that?"

"Oh, I wish I could tell you that it is. Some nights there's just no spark, and you can't get it if you try. But when there is, there's nothing like it, is there?"

"There sure isn't. Not as far as I know."

Dorothy edged closer to my chair. Though her red dress was modest, looking down on her meant I could see the shadow of cleavage where the neckline dipped. It made me think of one of my paperbacks. A cover would have us painted just like this, her leaning toward me. Only she would be putting her hands on my knees, and I'd have my hands on her too.

I gripped my cup. Sometimes I feared that I might lose control of my senses and reach for her.

"Tell me what it felt like to you," she said, resting against the arm of my chair.

"Why?" I asked, our gazes locked.

Picking at the carpet with her fingers, Dorothy shrugged. "You'll think I'm real strange, if I say."

"I could never think you were strange."

I moved to sit on the ground next to her, leaning my back against the chair.

"Okay then, I'll say it. Having you up there with us, it made me catch what you had. I felt like you and I were connected and then that connected me to everyone else on the stage and in the crowd, too. So, I guess I wonder if it was like that to you as well or if it was all in my head."

I couldn't look at her for a moment. "Of course. I always feel connected to you when we play. But it was even better with the audience there. It was really special."

Dorothy lifted her hand toward me, setting off butterflies in my stomach. She pushed hair back from my face, then cupped my cheek again like she had during the show. "I'm so very glad you feel that way. I hope it's like that every night."

"It will be," I said. "I know it. Now, can I ask you something?"

"Anything you like," she said, hand moving back to her cup.

"Why did you get mad at me, over the makeup?"

"Oh. That. We don't need to talk about that, do we? I was being very silly. I'm sorry."

"How can I know how to not make you mad, if I don't know what I did wrong in the first place?"

"Alice," she said, her eyes soft. "It's not for you to worry about making me mad. That was my fault. I just wanted you to know you're good enough as you are, and there's no need for you to change. I'm sorry if it came across badly to you. Listen, I have my moods, and you just can't pay any attention to me when I'm like that."

"Okay, I won't," I said.

"You must think it's strange that Earl's not here. Don't you?"

Had she noticed the way I'd looked around the room when I came in? "I figure you must need your sleep or something."

"Earl and I have a marriage that's not typical. But it works out just fine for us."

"Well, I figure it's nobody's business but yours what your marriage is like. Is it?"

Dorothy held out her empty cup, tapping it against mine. "Nobody's but ours. That's what I like to think even if the rest of the world doesn't always agree."

"Well, I should go in to bed. Thanks for the cocoa," I said.

"You're very welcome. You can join me for cocoa every evening. If you'd like to?"

"Of course, I'd like to very much. It's helped me to feel tired. I didn't think I would."

Dorothy walked me to the door. Without giving myself time to think about whether it was wise, I put my arms around her. She had changed my life into something I'd never thought possible and gifted me with the feeling that there were people in this world who could understand and appreciate me. Dorothy leaned into my embrace, and I was glad I'd taken this chance.

We stood holding one another for a long time. My hands were on her back, her hair tickling my skin. It smelled of her shampoo, so good that I wished I could bury my face in it. I filled my lungs, wanting to remember.

"I just wanted to say thank you, for everything," I said, releasing her.

"You're very welcome," she said.

"I'll see you tomorrow."

The following night we played a second show in Charlotte, in a theater with a high, arched ceiling and beautiful carved pillars, to another appreciative crowd. Now that our first performance was over my confidence swelled, and I improvised a solo with Dirk's encouragement. When Dorothy invited me to, I even said a few words into the microphone.

Earl had decided that because the next evening's show was so far away, we should put in a couple of hours of travel after the show to get a head start before we stopped in at a motel. I drank bitter black coffee from a thermos, Errol at my side to help keep me awake while we followed Earl and Dorothy's car.

It was after midnight when we pulled into a motel just off the highway. When Earl came out of the manager's office he scowled under the neon light. There was a vacancy sign, and I wondered if they'd forgotten to change it over.

"What gives? Are you gonna tell us we have to sleep in the cars again?" Jack asked.

"Not quite. It's just that they only have two rooms left," Earl said, rubbing his hand over his stubbled chin. "Sorry, gang. I thought it'd be okay. I should have called ahead. Didn't think I needed to."

Jack cursed and kicked a tire.

"Let's take a vote. Stop here or keep driving? Maybe we can find another place on down the road," Earl said.

"Who knows how long that would take? And if the desk would be manned? I don't see what the big hubbub is about. We'll separate up, the guys take a room and the girls take another. I'm not sleeping in the car again. We got extra blankets. C'mon," Dirk said, already unloading cases from his trunk.

"Everyone all right with that?" Earl asked. When nobody said anything, he went back to the office to check us in.

I cut my eyes across to Dorothy, trying to figure out if she was annoyed that we had to share, but her back was to me. For whatever reason she didn't even sleep in the same room as her husband. I couldn't imagine that she'd be happy about being in one with me.

When we were inside, I warily took in the double bed. I unpacked my toiletries and nightgown, putting them next to my suitcase on the floor. I looked hopelessly at the plain white of my nightgown, thinking it worn and childish.

Dorothy disappeared into the washroom for a moment and when she came out, I could feel her eyes on me. "What's wrong with you? You're awful quiet."

"Nothing's wrong, I'm just tired is all. It was hard to drive after the show," I said, picking up my nightgown.

"Are you bent out of shape about sharing? In case you couldn't tell, we've had to sleep in our cars before. All part of the glamour of touring, just like I warned you about. This is not that bad, trust me," Dorothy said, yawning as she took off her earrings. She removed her wedding band and there was a light clatter as she dropped it onto the nightstand.

"I know. I'm not mad or anything like that. I don't mind sleeping on the floor. You can take the bed."

"Don't be silly. The bed's big enough for the both of us. Shall I make you some cocoa?" she said, setting the kettle on the floor where she could plug it in.

"Yes, please. I'm going to take a shower."

I stepped into the shower recess, my mind racing. What if I did something in my sleep? I might dream of her and roll over to touch her. I should get into bed as soon as I could and pretend to be asleep, but I'd stay awake as much as possible to avoid doing anything stupid.

"You know what, I don't think I feel like my cocoa tonight. I'm so tired I don't need it," I said as I walked back into the room.

"Okay, suit yourself," Dorothy said.

I stood by the bed uncertainly and she smiled at me in my nightgown. I'd left my bra on for the sake of modesty, and I wondered if she could tell and thought it strange. I pulled away from her gaze and slipped into the bed. I shifted onto my side, hearing her rinsing out her cup in the basin. The washroom door closed, and I guessed that she'd gone in to wash up.

Finally, the mattress shifted when she crawled in beside me. I didn't know how long I'd been laying there, still and scared, when she whispered my name.

"Yes?"

"I'm not all that tired. Are you?" Dorothy said.

I turned toward her, moving the pillow under my head. My eyes had adjusted to the dark so that I could see her face. "Not really."

"I want to know more about you. You never talk about yourself."

I laughed and moved again, onto my back. It was easier if I wasn't looking at her. "I'm not very interesting. What do you want to know?"

"That's not true. I find you interesting. Tell me about where you grew up."

"Now, that's *really* not interesting. It's just a small town."

"Gave you something to write about, though, didn't it?"

"Ha, ha."

I inched my hand toward the body near me. It stopped short of her, but it allowed me to dream more vividly of what it would be like to touch her. I had never talked in bed with anyone like this. I could only imagine what it would be like to curl up against her, for us to hold one another here like we had when we were dancing.

"Tell me about how you first got into music," Dorothy said, her voice lilting. She pulled the quilt snugly around us.

"It was at church when my folks would take me. I'd drift off during the service, but when the hymns came around I loved it. Made me understand why people like going to church in the first place."

"I think I'd like to hear you sing a hymn. It would sound beautiful."

"Not really."

Dorothy rested her hand on my arm. "I know it would."

"Did your parents take you to church as well?"

"No, they didn't. I don't know them that much. They live in California. They were young when they had us all and left. We were raised by my grandparents, but they both died a few years back."

"Oh, I'm sorry," I said. "What did your parents go to California for? I mean, is there a reason why they're there?"

"They thought they were going to make their fortune. They write scripts together, a little team who call themselves artists. But they ended up grinding out B-grade nonsense. They're pretty awful people, really. Terribly self-absorbed."

"I'm sorry."

"That's all right. Can't be a country singer without a few stories to tell, huh?"

I asked Dorothy about her sisters and what it had been like to play in a band with them. Dorothy's initiation into the industry had been so different to mine. She'd been sent to charm school to learn how to act onstage, along with the other Stellars.

"What kind of house did you live in with your grandparents when you were little? I mean, what was your childhood like?" I asked.

"Poor. Our little shack didn't have running water or electricity, and there was no land to speak of. Jill and Ginnie and I had to sing, just for something to do! My grandparents were wonderful people who took good care of us and gave us a lot of love. But we never had much. I guess that's why I always wanted to live somewhere like I do now."

"You must be very happy with the house, then?" I said, thinking of its size and warmth and how lovingly it had been decorated.

"Of course. I remember, Earl came running into the studio one day, telling me how he'd found the most perfect place just outside of town. I fell in love with it as soon as I saw it. It's my little slice of paradise."

At Earl's name, I ran my hand through my hair, pushing it back from my forehead. "Where did you meet Earl, anyway?"

"We were introduced at a show I was playing with my sisters, actually. He was a pretty big-time booking agent around Nashville. Others had tried to get me to split from the group before, but he was especially persuasive."

"Oh?" I said. "He talked you into it?"

"You might say that, yes. I'd been thinking about it for quite a while, though."

"What's it like being married?"

"Why, are you planning on getting married yourself sometime soon?" she said, nudging my foot with hers.

"I don't think so."

"Why not? Plenty of men would want to marry you, I bet."

"Maybe they would. I just don't want to marry them."

I wanted her to understand me, even if it was only this little piece.

"What do you mean?"

"Nothing. I just don't want to get married, is all. I want to have adventures and run around and do whatever I want. I don't want children, either."

It was the first time I'd declared myself and named what it was that I wanted from my life. To me it sounded wonderful, but Dorothy didn't reply at first. When she spoke again, I couldn't read her tone. "Well, good for you."

In the morning, I couldn't remember either of us deciding to go to sleep. I only recalled the way our conversation had ebbed, becoming strange and slow as we'd slipped out of wakefulness. My plan to stay alert came to nothing. It was a deep sleep, and I woke up well rested despite having talked until so late.

I slid my hand across the sheet, feeling the warmth that was left behind from Dorothy's body. I grabbed her pillow and pulled it close, breathing in the faint scent of her hair.

It was her voice that had awoken me. I smiled to myself at the sound of her belting out one of my songs in the shower. I watched the bathroom door as it swung open.

"Good morning," Dorothy said, beaming at me. She sat on the bed, toweling her hair. "We've got to be getting on the road before too long."

"I guess I'll have a shower and get myself ready, then," I said, sitting up to stretch my arms over my head.

"I'm going to go to the office and get a cup of coffee before we check out. Want one?"

"I'd love one, thank you."

Dorothy smiled at me again, her face lighting up. She dropped her towel onto her lap. "That was fun, talking last night, wasn't it?"

"It was," I said. I'd loved it so much that I felt gloomy now, to think that it had only been an accident.

"You know, I have a crazy idea... Maybe I shouldn't say it, but..." she said, biting her lip.

"Go on, what is it?"

Dorothy turned all the way around, her knee bent as she sat on one of her feet. "I was just thinking that we could save the tour a lot of money if we were to share a room. Plus, I liked the company. I don't normally sleep so well."

"I don't normally sleep very well either," I said, hope ballooning in me. I'd never wanted anything more than to know that she liked to have me near her. And I'd never wanted anything more than to be with her at night and to wake up with her in the morning, just like this.

"I don't want you to feel obliged. It wouldn't have to be all the time. Just when we feel like it," she said. Her gaze dropped down, outlining my body under the sheet.

"I wouldn't mind at all. I know the boys have been sharing a room. I did feel a little funny having one all to myself, to tell you the truth. So, it's fine with me."

"All right then, it's settled. I'll have a talk to Earl about it. He's always happy to save a buck or two," she said. She ran a hand through her damp hair, and then she was tugging on the sheet, pulling it from me and laughing while I tried to snatch it back from her.

"Time to get up, lazy bones!" she said.

When I got into the shower, I sang to myself too.

CHAPTER NINE

That afternoon when the sun was just starting to dip we arrived at our double-story motel, red brick against the blue sky. When Earl emerged from the office he handed me a brass room key. Then he passed by Dorothy to hand another to Dirk.

Dirk put it in his shirt pocket, then shook his head. "Gee, bad luck to get a room shortage again."

"It's not that. Alice and I decided to share," Dorothy said, her arms crossed.

Dirk shrugged. "All right. Makes no difference to me, does it? Hey, Alice, let me get that guitar for you."

I walked on air at the show that night, at a tavern in Tallahassee. The crowd danced in front of us, slopping beer out of their glasses. The show was wonderful, and I couldn't wait to be alone with Dorothy again. We'd spent the afternoon wandering around the lush state park, Dorothy looping her arm through mine while she pointed out flowers that she liked.

At the motel, there was a double room rather than twin beds once more. It was possible that Dorothy might only want to sleep this time instead of talking to me, but it made me deliriously happy to know that she was going to be at my side. We wouldn't have to part after we'd had our cocoa together.

While Dorothy was in the washroom, I remained on my back, my toes curled in anticipation of the hours that lay before us. When Dorothy came out, steam rose in a cloud from the open door.

"Hello," she said, carrying her discarded clothes in a bundle and grinning brightly at me.

"Hey."

Dorothy perched on the edge of the mattress with her back to me and slipped the robe from her shoulders, folding it and laying it on the ground next to the bed. Above the silk of her nightgown, pale skin contrasted with the dark of her hair. Muscle and bone shifted under flawless skin as she took her ring from her finger and dropped it on the nightstand before picking up a small tub of lavender-scented cream.

She looked back over her shoulder, not seeming to mind that I was watching. "Want some?"

I dipped my fingers into the tub. She twisted the lid closed as I rubbed cream into my hands. "So, this is why your hands are always so soft, huh?"

"One of my secrets," she said, putting a finger to her lips.

Dorothy turned off her lamp, plunging the room into darkness. She drew back the light quilt and pulled it over us, patting it down. It didn't take long for her voice to drift toward me.

"Now, tell me about your brothers and sisters. You know a little about my sisters. I'd love to know about yours."

It would be like last night. By tacit agreement, we each edged closer to the center of the mattress.

"They're mostly a pain in the neck. That's why I spend more time with my aunt than any of them. You must think I'm being awful," I said.

"I don't think that at all!" she said, a bare leg brushing against mine. "But what is it they do that bothers you?"

"I'm the youngest, and I guess I just hate being treated like the baby. They don't care what I say or what I think about anything."

"It's awful that it's that way. What about your parents? Is it different with them?" she asked. Light slanted through the curtains, from a bulb outside our room meant to guide the way for late night travelers. She lay on her side watching me, resting her head on her hands.

"Sometimes. Mama's okay. Daddy and I used to have some awful arguments, but things are a little better now."

"What kinds of things did you argue about?"

"We just didn't get along when I was a teenager. I'm not quite the kind of daughter he wanted. He hated it when I got the job at the cannery, said it wasn't any place for a girl. Flipped his lid and said all kinds of terrible things."

Dorothy found my hand and brought it up to her mouth, pressing her lips to it. I shivered, fidgeting against the mattress.

"I think it's wonderful that you've worked. You know how to take care of yourself," she said. When she dropped my hand, I let it rest near her.

"Did you get along well with your grandparents?" I asked.

"I did. My pop was a great man, a real eccentric type of fellow. He made his own way in the world and taught us to do the same even though we're girls. I like people who are different, you know?"

I slept heavily again, Dorothy's warm body at my side, the two of us sinking into slumber close to one another. When I awoke before her, I measured her breath in the rise and fall of her chest, wishing that she might dream of me. Her eyelashes were dark against her cheek, her hair fanned out across the pillow.

Without further discussion we shared a room every night. Dorothy had a gift for remembering exactly what we were speaking about at the time we fell asleep. The conversations were like a book that she opened to the correct page as soon as the light had been put out the following night. Aside from the thrill of being on stage, the days were only obstructions to the dialogue that flowed between us. A week passed that way, and I never wanted the tour to end.

Our fifth night together was especially humid, and Dorothy had thrown the sheet back. The fan overhead stirred warm air over us. The show that night in Tuscaloosa had been a particularly good one; the club manager said that it was one of the best he'd ever seen.

"Tell me about what you were like at school. Did you have good friends when you were there? Were you popular?" Dorothy asked.

"It was okay. I wouldn't say I was popular but, yes, I did have some close friends. A lot of them are married now," I said.

"Who was your dearest friend?"

"A girl called Sandra. She lived around the corner from us, so we spent an awful lot of time together. I stayed at her house often."

"And are you still close?"

An image of Sandra came to me, her gold-colored hair and hazel eyes frozen in time. She hadn't said goodbye before she'd left town. "No."

"Did you go steady with many boys when you were in school?"

My stomach dropped. Dorothy understood so many things about me, yet she was oblivious to how much I hated talking about that. "A few. You know, you never did tell me. What's it like, being married?"

Dorothy paused, and then there was the low rumble of her laughter. "You've been thinking on that, haven't you? It's nothing really."

"What do you mean, it's nothing?"

"It's just not the be-all and end-all of life. You might feel differently about it yourself when you do it, but it's really not that important."

"I won't feel anything about it. Like I told you, I'm not getting married. I haven't changed my mind in the last few days," I said, keeping my voice even despite my rising temper.

She sighed, close enough for me to feel breath on my cheek. "You can't know that just yet. You're still young enough to change your mind. I thought I wouldn't get married either, but look at me now."

I wished I'd never told her. Like everyone else, Dorothy thought there was something wrong with me. "But there's just no reason for me to get married. I'm going to make enough money to look after myself. I've been thinking about it a lot. I know what I want."

"What about love, though?"

"I don't need it. Sometimes I don't think marriage is that much about love anyway. I mean, how much do you love Earl?" I said. I knew how rude the question was, but I was angry enough to want to hurt her back.

"Don't ask me questions like that. You're talking like you're cynical but you're not. You're idealistic. It's probably what makes you such a great songwriter," Dorothy said, staring up at the ceiling. It seemed that she could ask me whatever she wanted, but when the conversation turned to her I met a wall.

"I'm not idealistic. I'm realistic. I'm not some weak person who's going to marry someone I don't want to just to please everyone else."

My words were sharper than I'd meant them to be, threaded with anger at all the pressure from my family.

Dorothy breathed out harshly. "Is that what you think? That I'm weak because I may have compromised on a few things in my life?"

"I didn't say that. I'm not even talking about you. I'm only talking about myself," I said.

"I'm tired," she said. When she rolled away, the space between was like a mile. I reached for her, my hand landing uselessly between us. She would shake it off if I tried to touch her, I was sure of it.

In the morning when the bed was empty I checked the washroom, but Dorothy was already gone. We'd all agreed to meet for breakfast in the motel restaurant, and I rushed to get dressed and pack up some of my things.

The aqua and white booths were filled with travelers, sitting on cracked and worn leather. Dorothy was against the wall with Earl at her side, Jack and Dirk in the booth across from them. I stood by their table on my way past to get to Errol. He was on his own a couple of tables away.

"Good morning, everyone," I said.

Dorothy didn't look up from cutting into scrambled eggs and toast. The boys all said hello, but they were busy eating and I felt strange standing there while nobody said anything further. I sat down across from Errol and ordered a bowl of Special K. Dorothy was in my line of sight and though I stared, willing her to see me, she never did.

I worked on a speech for Dorothy, even mouthing the words to myself as I drove. "I'm sorry if I said anything to offend you. I didn't mean anything by it…"

I'd stepped on a landmine with her, and it was difficult to find the right words when I wasn't quite sure what I was apologizing for. What if she got so sick of me she sent me away? She could decide this wasn't working out anytime she liked.

That night at the hall in Hattiesburg, Mississippi I sought an opportunity for some privacy, but we were running late. Earl led the convoy directly to our show rather than checking us into a motel. Dorothy and I dressed hurriedly in the back of the bar, the wall of a restroom cubicle separating me from her, lights flickering overhead. When I asked for help, she tugged my zip up briskly.

We stood next to one another at the mirror. When Dorothy's reflection made eye contact with me I smiled timidly. I wanted to say something about how we were playing not so far from my hometown, but I could see she didn't want to talk. She opened a tube of mascara, blinking as she painted her lashes.

"Shit," she muttered.

"Can I help with anything?" I said.

"No," she said sharply. A moment later, her tone was apologetic. "It's nothing, it's just these lights. Makes it hard to see what I'm doing. C'mon, we should get out there. Nothing worse than a riled-up crowd because you're late."

As I followed her to the stage, I realized that she hadn't stopped to give me the usual pep talk. At the start of the performance Dorothy introduced me to the crowd in the same way she always did, crediting me with songwriting and inviting them to cheer for me. Nobody in the audience would notice her coldness and how she kept her distance from me. It was Errol and Dirk whom she favored with her attention, singing into their microphones with them. It was the first show that I didn't enjoy playing.

I gripped the wheel while Earl was in the motel office, only stepping out of the car as he came toward us. Dorothy and I would be laughing about the misunderstanding soon or at least I hoped so. I couldn't wait to huddle up with her again and for this sick sadness to be gone.

Earl walked over and handed a key to Dorothy and then to Jack. When he began to approach me, my gaze flicked across to Dorothy, who toyed with her key and didn't look back. I grudgingly put my hand out to take the key from him.

At my questioning look, Earl shrugged and leaned close to me. "Dorothy needs some time to herself this evening."

I kept my expression smooth and untroubled. "Of course."

Dorothy was by the Chevy, talking to Dirk. There was nothing in the way she stood to show it, but I had the feeling that she was watching me from the corner of her eye. At my door I fumbled the key into the lock, while Dorothy did the same at the room next to me. She was inside with her door closed before I could get mine open.

After I'd washed up, I sat, wondering what Dorothy was doing on the other side of the wall. My whole heart was in her hands, and she could ruin my night with one decision. I recalled the way Earl shrugged when he handed me the keys. The idea of them talking about me turned my stomach.

There was no way of knowing if Dorothy and I would ever share a room again. Though I'd always found Dorothy's moods to be unpredictable, the betrayal was worse now that we had grown closer. How could she treat me this way after all our time together? Had she only been talking to me to amuse herself?

The night was too long. I pulled on the terrycloth robe that hung in the closet and went to her door, looking down the row of rooms. There was nobody around, though I could see a chair outside Dirk's room where he must have dragged it to smoke. When I rapped on it, the door flew open. Dorothy waved me in urgently.

When I was inside, she placed her palm against the closed door for a moment, frowning. She was wearing only her black nightgown, the bottom edge trimmed with lace. "What do you think you were doing? Someone might have heard that racket and come looking."

Dorothy gestured toward the bed, sitting down next to me on the maroon quilt so that we were both facing forward. It was stupid of me to come here, and my bravado had evaporated as soon as I saw her face. My speech was forgotten. I hunched forward, brushing hair behind my ear.

Dorothy sighed. "I'm really very tired, Alice. I was just about to go to bed."

I moistened my lips. If I walked away now, I might not have the courage to try and approach her again. "I just think that...I just think that if you wanted to change our sleeping arrangements, the polite thing to do would be to talk to me about it."

"Excuse me?" she said, placing her hands on the bed beside her. "I told you it would only be when we felt like the company, and I didn't feel like the company tonight."

I pushed my hair behind my ear again. I didn't even recognize this version of her. "I don't understand what I did to upset you so much."

"I would never have suggested sharing a room if I'd known you were going to make me feel like this," she said, her nostrils flaring. "You're being childish."

"Don't call me childish," I said. "You know how I don't like that. You're using my words against me."

"Then don't act childishly."

"I don't understand any of this. Why are you being so mean?"

"You think I'm being mean to you? You weren't being very nice at all last night, the way you were speaking. I don't know what I've done to you to make you speak to me that way," she said.

I entreated her, hands outstretched. "I just wanted you to stop judging me about not getting married. That's all. That's the only reason I said what I did."

"I don't know what you mean by that. How have I ever judged you? What have I ever done but tried to help you?" she said, whispering hoarsely, her face near to mine now that we'd turned fully toward one another.

"To help me? Dorothy, when you say it like that it makes me feel like you think I'm a charity case."

"If that's how you feel, I won't try to help you anymore at all," she said, sneering.

I jumped up, standing in front of her. It seemed that everything I said was wrong and that she had been determined to argue from the moment I'd come in. It scared me how out of control I was, how much I felt like yelling or grabbing at her. Even more alarming was the fact that I wanted to kiss her, to crush her to me. It was as though I was boiling over, with a confusing blend of desire and anger I'd never felt before.

"I don't know why I annoy you so much. Are you going to ask me to leave? Is that what's going to happen, if it keeps going this way?" I said. My eyes welled up and I swallowed, trying to pull myself together. "Actually, I'm not going to wait for it. I'll just leave. I'd rather get it over with."

In the silence that followed, the tendons in Dorothy's neck ceased to stand out and her body slackened.

"Alice," she said, stretching her arms up to clutch my hands, pulling me down so I was sitting by her again. "Wait... You wouldn't really go, would you?"

"Well...I don't want to! But don't you see that you're making me feel like you don't want me here? You're making me feel like I *should* go."

"How could you think I don't want you here? After everything, after I sought you out and brought you to us? I

told you how carefully I chose the people in this band, but I
didn't choose anyone more carefully than I did you," she said. As
she talked she ran her thumbs over my hands, then tentatively
cupped my cheek.

I closed my eyes, leaning into her hand. "Why do you treat
me like you don't care, then?"

"Because…"

I watched the working of her mouth, but no words came.

I gazed at her lips, tracing their full red softness as they
parted slightly. I lifted my stare to see that she was looking at my
mouth too, unforeseen longing in her dark eyes. Her hand was
on the back of my neck, gently pulling me to her. As improbable
as it was, I was certain that she wanted the same thing as I did.

I could never have found the courage if she wasn't looking
at me the way she was. Leaning forward slowly, I waited for
the yearning in her face to reveal itself as something else, but
it remained steady. Her hand was insistent on the back of my
neck, and I closed the space between us.

When our lips connected I found that mine had a thousand
points of sensation in them and that Dorothy could wake up
each one. The kiss was achingly sweet as her mouth pressed
lightly against mine. Her hands came to either side of my face,
holding me still as she tasted my lips. To steady myself, I circled
her wrists with my fingers.

It had always been clear that Dorothy cared for me, but I'd
never allowed myself to dream that she wanted me like this. Yet
when her mouth was on mine there was an inexplicable sense of
rightness, as though it was always meant to happen.

When we pulled apart at last, she leaned her forehead
against mine. My eyes were wide with shock, her breath shaky
against my lips.

"Alice. Is it all right?"

I had the compulsion to laugh, that she would ask me that.
I tilted my head to brush my lips against her cheek, hearing her
sigh at my touch.

I was shaking, and I moved to turn off the light, thinking
that the dark might calm me. I was more terrified than I'd been

when I'd auditioned for Dorothy at her hotel room and even more than I'd been the first time I'd performed. As I walked back toward her, there was a rustling as she shifted onto the bed. I unbelted my robe, pushing it off my shoulders.

I climbed into bed and she moved over to me. We sought out one another's lips again. When she came closer, our lips moving steadily against one another's, I breathed in the scent of her hair. She was halfway on top of me, her hand resting on my waist. I leaned my head up eagerly to meet her.

Dorothy tilted my chin with her fingers and slipped her tongue into my mouth. I put my hand to the back of her head, closing my eyes and losing myself.

This was how it was supposed to be. The times I'd kissed men, and even Sandra, I'd experienced a remove that led me to wonder what all the fuss was about. With Dorothy every caress enthralled me, made me feel like I could go crazy with it.

After a long time, she drew back. She ran her finger over my bottom lip, our bodies still pressed together.

"Well," she said. "I wasn't expecting this. Are you sure you're all right?"

I pulled her back down toward me, opening my mouth to her once more.

We became bolder. Dorothy shifted to kiss my neck and my head dropped back. I'd never known how sensitive I was there, nor could I have imagined how it would feel when she kissed the flesh just above my nightgown. My breath raced when her lips played over it, her hands on my sides and spread just below my breasts.

At last she stopped, placing her hand lightly on my throat. "As much as I don't want to, we'd better stop and go to sleep. If we're going to be any good at all tomorrow, that is."

"It's Sunday, we're not playing tomorrow…"

"I know," she said. "But you're going to have to drive to the next stop in Louisiana in the morning, and I don't want to be responsible for you having an accident."

"You're right," I said, pressing my lips to hers one last time. "I'll go."

"Don't go. Stay in here with me? Let's just sleep."

She curled up into me, helping me move onto my back so that she could lay her head on my chest. Her eyelashes fluttered against my skin. I wanted to speak, but the union felt delicate somehow, like if we spoke we might break the spell that had been cast between us tonight.

I kissed the top of her head, so overjoyed that my throat was thick with tears.

The next morning, I awoke to her lips on my cheek. "Alice? I think you'd better go back to your room now. I'll see you at breakfast in an hour or so. Okay?"

"Of course," I said as I sat up. I found my robe, knotting it around my waist hastily.

Dorothy walked me to the door, putting her arms around me. I tipped my head back, our mouths joining. I loved to have her kissing me in the daylight, the morning sun bright around us.

She held the door for me and I poked my head out to make sure I wouldn't be seen. I crept back on bare feet to my own room. I stood staring at the untouched bed, with my whole world changed.

When it was time I walked to the diner across the street from the motel. The band was sitting around a large round table, strewn with coffee mugs and menus. I sat across from Dorothy, watching as her bow-shaped lips curved into a smile.

How strange it was to have to sit here and act like nothing had happened. If I could, I'd take her hand. I'd lean across and kiss her forehead, to wish her good morning again.

I was still thinking about it when Dorothy winked at me. I coughed and turned my attention to the menu, trying to suppress a smile. I was starving, and I ordered toast with bacon and eggs.

"Hey, how far is the drive today? Did Earl tell you?" Dirk said to Jack.

"Not sure. I think he said we'd be there by this afternoon though, so not too far."

"Oh, now that sounds good. I'm going to have an afternoon nap," Dirk said. "I'm so glad we don't have a show tonight."

"Good morning, everyone!" Earl said, sitting down next to Dorothy. He scooped up a piece of toast from her plate and stole a large bite from it. I pushed my unfinished plate away.

"Hey, guys, I'm going to head back to my room to pack."

When we were loading our things into the cars, Dorothy strode toward me. The top button of her dress was undone, the swell of her breasts beneath it.

When I looked up, Dorothy was smiling knowingly at me. "How do you do this morning, Alice?"

"I'm a little tired, but I'm good. And how are you doing, Dorothy?"

"Good, good." Dorothy trailed the toe of her shoe across the dirt. "I thought you might like some company for the drive today?"

"If you want to, that sounds fine."

I grinned as I settled into my seat. I had so many questions, but I wanted to wait to see what she was going to say first.

"You're staring. What?" I asked.

"Nothing. I was just thinking. I was never sure about you. Until last night."

"What do you mean?"

"Like I said last night, I wasn't expecting it," she said. In the rearview mirror, I saw her stretch her arm out, resting it close behind me on the seat.

"I wasn't expecting it either," I said. "From you."

"I wasn't sure if you just had friendly feelings for me or what. These things can be kind of hard to figure out."

"Well, I think we've got it pretty well figured out now, don't you reckon?"

Dorothy laughed loudly, and after a moment I joined her.

"I always think you're shy, it's one of the things I like about you. But I'm starting to think you're not shy at all. Not where it counts," she said.

"I don't know, I still feel pretty shy. What happened last night… It's not something I do all the time."

She grabbed a handful of my hair at the back, tugging on it lightly. "And are you okay about it? You don't feel funny today or anything like that?"

"I don't feel funny, and I especially don't feel sorry. I feel happy."

She didn't say anything for a while, and then I could hear the smile in her voice. "I'm glad."

"There is one thing I've been wondering about, though. Earl."

Her hand was on my thigh, dragging just up under the hemline of my dress until I squirmed. "Oh, Alice. Haven't you figured out by now that Earl and I aren't really married? It's an arrangement. A deal we made. That's why I got so upset when we were talking about marriage in the first place."

"A business arrangement? What do you mean?"

"Earl is a good friend of mine, and we're married because it works out well for both of us."

"Huh." I adjusted the rearview mirror to have something to do with my hands.

"Is it a problem?" Dorothy asked.

"I guess I just find it pretty strange. How do you even come to a decision like that? I mean, how did that all come about?"

She stared out the window, her hands folded in her lap again. "There were all kinds of rumors about me. People thought I was sleeping with Dirk and all kinds of things! I only told you, so you'd know I wasn't doing the wrong thing by Earl. Maybe I shouldn't have mentioned it."

We'd covered miles by the time I spoke again. "If we're not playing a show tonight, what will we be doing? I mean, what do you all usually do on nights when there's not a show?'

Dorothy ran her finger along the ridge of the open window. "I don't know. Rest, I guess."

"We'll be sharing a room, though, won't we?"

Her head rested back against the seat, and she was biting her lip. "Are you trying to say you want to?"

"Why wouldn't I want to? I was hoping maybe we could go to dinner or something. Just you and me, I mean. Tell everyone we want some girl time."

She brushed her knuckles over my thigh. "I think that's a wonderful idea."

It was such a beautiful day, the puffy white clouds against blue sky framed by the windscreen. It felt like the day was just for us to enjoy, made for us to spend laughing and passing sandwiches or sodas back and forth.

"That's cheating! You can't say my car, not when we're in it," I said.

"I can see it, though, so it's fair game."

"I still say you're a cheater."

"Hey. You won't tell anyone what I've told you, will you?" Dorothy asked.

"Tell people what?" I said, still thinking about our game of I Spy.

"About Earl and me. We could never risk something like that getting out. Nobody knows except for us. And Sally," she said, sitting ramrod straight.

"Sally knows?" I asked. Sally had never given anything away all those times we talked, and she loved Dorothy like a daughter.

"Just tell me you're not going to tell anyone, please. It's very important."

"Of course I'm not going to tell anyone. Why would I do a thing like that?" I took her hand and clasped it while I drove. "I promise. Nobody knows about me either, you know. Not even Aunt May or Bill."

"Who's Bill?"

"My friend. The guy I brought with me, the first time I met you."

"Oh, I remember him. Okay, then. Thanks."

At the motel Dorothy drew the faded yellow curtains. It was like every other room we'd stayed in, a single framed picture on the wall, cheap lamps, and a plain quilt. There were twin beds, when I'd been looking forward to snuggling up with her all day.

We took turns changing our clothes to go out to dinner. I tucked my green blouse into my skirt. When Dorothy passed me to pick up her handbag, I wished I could take her in my arms. It was suddenly absurd that I would do anything like that, as though we'd only been pretending all day.

"That outfit is so gorgeous on you, Dorothy," I said. Her blue blouse perfectly matched her plaid blue and yellow skirt, which hung to just below her knee.

"Thank you," she said, more shyly than I'd ever heard her say anything.

We strolled past the row of closed stores in the small town, unable to find anywhere to go. This town reminded me of Greenville. I'd come to find myself preferring the large cities we'd been travelling to, the bright lights, and all the different kinds of people that you could meet, but I felt at home here. Eventually we came across a diner with an open sign hanging on the glass. It was almost empty, only one grizzled older man at the counter looking up from his burger when we came in.

When our grilled cheese sandwiches and shakes arrived, I inched my leg further under the table until my skin touched Dorothy's. She hooked her leg around mine, keeping her eyes on her plate, though the corner of her mouth tugged upward.

"So. You know your friend Bill that you mentioned earlier?" she said.

"Yes?" I said, sipping from my chocolate milkshake, the thick sweetness rolling over my tongue.

"Did you ever sleep with him?"

I almost spat out my mouthful. "Sleep with him? You mean… Have sex with him?"

"Yes," Dorothy said, a blush creeping across her skin. "You seemed close, so I was just wondering."

"No, I haven't slept with him. I haven't slept with any man."

Dorothy swirled her straw in her shake. "You mean you haven't slept with anyone?"

I'd never told a soul about Sandra and me. Sandra had always been so ashamed that it had infected me too, poisoning any pleasure I might have found. And it was so very long ago now. I stared down at the table.

"You have!" she said.

"It was nothing really, though. Only a handful of times."

"Well. I guess I'm a little jealous."

"But you have too, haven't you?"

"Yes," she said. "But it seems like nothing, as well. Now that I've met you."

Each of us beamed and her leg pressed harder against mine. "So, you don't like men at all in that way then?"

I shook my head deliberately. "Not that way, no. Do you?"

"Good. Me neither," she said. She reached over to wipe a crumb from below my mouth, catching my lip with her thumb. I'd never thought of my difference as being in any way positive, but Dorothy actually liked who I was. It thrilled me that she was the same.

"I just wish…" I trailed off. The curly-haired waitress approached to take our plates away, and when she left I leaned closer, my elbows on the table. "I wish we'd found a nice restaurant. I wanted to take you out for a proper dinner."

Dorothy kicked me under the table. "Don't worry about it. I like spending time with you. I don't care where it is."

Darkness was falling as we walked back to the motel, and Dorothy threaded an arm through mine. I put my hand on hers, where it rested on my forearm.

"When we get back, I've got to go to see Earl to work out a few things about tomorrow's show," she said.

In the motel room I took my guitar from its case, my elation bleeding into the way I struck the strings. I was still playing when Dorothy came back, leaning against the door once she'd closed it.

"I love hearing you play. Keep going while I make the cocoa?"

Dorothy placed my cup on the nightstand and pressed a lingering kiss to my cheek. I turned my head so that our mouths met. Her plump lips seemed to fit perfectly to mine, and she teased her tongue over my lower lip before she drew away. She removed her shoes and lay on the bed opposite me, propped on her side with her head on her hand. She rubbed her feet together, sipping from her cup.

"You are so lovely," Dorothy said.

I sang her words back to her, along with the chord pattern I'd been playing. Dorothy's head fell back as she laughed.

"You said you wanted us to write together, well, we just did. I'd been wondering anyway, why it is that we've never talked about writing together again?" I asked.

"I don't know. I guess it makes me too nervous. I don't think I'd be all that good at it. Maybe one day I'd be willing to try, but your songs are all we need for right now. Don't you think so?"

I shook my head, rising from the bed to find my notebook. "I'm going to prove you wrong. We're going to write a duet together. A sweet little ditty about two people who really like one another."

"Wherever would you get an idea like that?" Dorothy said, winking.

We crafted lines and ideas for a while, and Dorothy was a great deal better than she'd given herself credit for. She never opted for the obvious choice, and I was certain listeners would get a kick out of her unexpected phrases.

"See? You're a great lyricist. Much better than me. I think this song is going to be really interesting and different from anything else we have," I said.

"I like the way it sounds a lot. Problem is, we can't sing this together," Dorothy said, chewing on her thumbnail. "Not unless we want to get ourselves arrested."

"So we just change a few words around and you'll sing it with Errol or somebody?"

"No, Dirk. He has a much better voice, don't you think?"

"You're right. Your voices will sound great together," I said.

Within an hour we had the bones of a song worked out. As with many of my favorite compositions, the creativity flowed without effort, inspiration seeming to come from a place outside of ourselves. I loved that it was about the two of us. Dorothy even slipped in a line about two hearts being just the same, so that nobody would know what we meant.

"That's enough work for tonight, don't you reckon?" she said.

She crooked a finger to beckon me. I'd never seen anything as inviting as the sight of her stretched out on the bed, her legs bent beside her and her head tipped back as she waited for me to kiss her. I slowed my footsteps, drawing the moment out.

I scooted onto the bed and took her face in my hands. Her heavy-lidded eyes were on mine, breath hot against my mouth as her lips parted. Even without lipstick coloring them, they were so rich and enticing. As I leaned down she pushed her hands into my hair. We kissed leisurely, drinking one another in.

"I've wanted to kiss you all day," she said.

"Oh, so have I."

We kissed again, hungry mouths opening. Dorothy untucked my blouse, gliding her hands along my lower back. Her tongue entered my mouth just the right amount, only enough to make me chase it with mine. Dorothy rolled onto her back, taking me with her until I was on top of her. She splayed her hands over my back, her thumbs stroking the sensitive skin of my waist.

Dorothy's head moved back, exposing her throat. When I kissed it, she arched against me so that her breasts were pressed against mine.

Even after last night it was unfathomable that we were like this, that she was dragging me upward desperately to kiss my lips. She needed me like I needed her. Heat bloomed as we shifted against one another, Dorothy moaning into my mouth.

She wrapped her leg around me and it made me kiss her more greedily, our tongues sliding against one another's. I pushed my hand slowly up her stomach under her blouse, loving the way she strained against me, lifting herself up against my body. The flesh of her abdomen was so delicately supple as I ran my fingers over it. I slid my hand up further along her ribcage, and at last I cupped her breast.

My forehead was pressed to hers, her brown eyes looking hotly up at me. She exhaled sharply at my touch and pushed herself against my hand. I kissed her neck while I held the weight of her breast in my hand, caressing it over her bra.

After a few moments she stiffened. I pulled my mouth away, my hand falling from her.

"Is everything okay?" I asked.

"Of course. More than okay," she said, kissing my cheek sweetly and stroking my hair as I withdrew my hand from under her blouse. "It's just that I think we should probably get some sleep?"

"Oh. Sure," I said.

Dorothy gathered her nightgown from under the pillow and took it into the washroom. I flopped onto my back, my forehead hot under my fingers. I'd groped her like a teenager. At first it had seemed that she was enjoying it too, but it was clear that my eagerness had repelled her. I was so unused to wanting like this; I was rendered weak and stupid by it.

I hung a dress in the closet for the following day and turned down one of the beds. After Dorothy, I went into the washroom to change. The mirror was steamed over, and I cleared it with a palm while I brushed my teeth. We'd passed one another without making eye contact.

The lights overhead had been turned off when I came out of the washroom. By the glow of the lamp I could see the outline of her body, under the quilt of the bed I hadn't turned down.

I got into the other bed. If I strained I could hear her steady breathing. I kicked off the sheets, sighing.

CHAPTER TEN

I woke up slowly, so that it took a few beats for the boiling shame from the night before to seep in. Harsh light cut across my face as the door opened. I hadn't heard her leave. I rolled to face the wall and saw the dirty handprints of strangers on the paint beside me.

The mattress shifted under her weight, and she slid a hand down my back. "Alice, sweetheart? I've brought you some coffee."

I faced her and tried to smile. Dorothy rested the coffee on the nightstand and bent to me, kissing my forehead and then my lips. She tasted of mint.

"I haven't brushed my teeth!" I said, pulling away.

"Silly. I don't care about a thing like that," she replied, lacing our fingers together. My coffee grew cold as her tongue slid into my mouth.

That day she got into the passenger seat of my car again. While I focused on the road, Dorothy took a notebook from her handbag, the pages covered in Earl's small hand. She traced words with her finger. He wrote down lists to go along with maps, cities and landmarks to guide the way. "You know, we're going to cross Lake Pontchartrain before the day's out. You've never seen it, have you?"

"Sure haven't. Never been anywhere near it."

"Well, I have, but seeing it with you makes it all new. I can't wait to see your face when we get there."

"Sounds great," I said, checking the fuel gauge. We'd have to stop for gas soon.

Dorothy closed the notebook, stowing it away in the glove compartment. "Is that all? You're quiet today. What's eating you?"

"Nothing's eating me."

"I thought I was the one who had moods," she said, touching my leg to make me smile.

"Sorry. That really does sound wonderful."

That afternoon we drove over the endless causeway. The water stretched as far as my eye could see, and I gazed around at it while I drove, full of how many sights I'd seen this trip that I never would have seen otherwise. Dorothy put a hand on my knee, watching me with her head propped on an elbow.

In the evening I got right into bed after I'd washed up. It had been a long day, and though I'd never say it to her I wished Dorothy could share the driving with me. Dorothy was kind and sweet to me during the trip, but I couldn't stop thinking about the way she'd reacted to my touch. It was like Sandra all over again. Why couldn't I find someone who could enjoy it like me?

Dorothy crawled into my bed, her warm body pressing into me from behind.

"Are you still awake?" she whispered.

I turned in her arms so fast that the quilt fell from the bed. Dorothy dropped kisses along my jawline. I moaned at the way she gently took my lower lip between her teeth, then kissed me full on the mouth.

"You are so beautiful," she said, feathering kisses along the column of my throat. "Do you know that?"

When she held her face against mine, her eyelashes fluttered against my skin.

Having her like this excited me beyond reason. My nipples were drawn tight and between my legs was slick with need for her. I tried to ignore my desire for more and focus only on enjoying Dorothy's mouth and the subtle pressure of her body on top of mine. She shifted rhythmically against me while we kissed, grinding herself into me.

She tipped my head back, kissing my neck again. When she moved up to kiss my lips, her leg came between my thighs. I forced myself to stay still, to not move against her to try to relieve the pleasant ache of it.

Dorothy moved her hands up and down my torso, grazing them lightly over my chest then away, as though their owner had suddenly remembered where they shouldn't be.

I couldn't imagine asking her what she wanted from this or why she was holding back. Instead I lay with words caught in my throat while her tongue danced with mine. I mustn't let my hunger overtake me. My fantasies had already come to life; it was greedy to not be satisfied with it. Dorothy was so close to me, all over me in the dark.

Two weeks passed, our days a merry-go-round of diners, motels, and crowds as we crisscrossed over the Southern states. I became practiced at living out of my suitcases, at packing and unpacking with no fuss. I figured out how to plan my outfits so that I had enough to last until we had time to get to a laundromat, and Dorothy showed me how to operate the new coin-operated machines. I learned to apply makeup in the car, holding my elbow steady with my hand, and dressed for shows at lightning speed.

I acquired other, more vital skills.

While Dorothy stood at the mirror at night after washing her face, I put my arms around her from behind to hear her sigh. I brushed my body against hers in the mornings, listening to her beg me for one more kiss before we had to rise. We woke in the middle of the night and edged toward one another, unable to resist kissing and touching no matter how sleepy we were. Dorothy loved it when I took charge, when I lay on top of her and kissed her fiercely. She'd wriggle and strain against me while I held her down. It excited her when I was beneath her too, lying back languidly and sighing as she ran her hands over me.

We shared a room every night and rode together in my car almost every day. If we were tired from staying up late we'd share easy silences, Dorothy's hand resting on my knee or passing me beef jerky and bottles of soda. I loved driving just knowing that she was next to me, sitting with a scarf tied over her head and her fingers dragging out of the window in the wind.

I glanced over at Dorothy while I was steering on a winding dirt road on our way to Birmingham. She was resting her feet on the dashboard, her red polish gleaming under the sun.

"Are you quite comfortable there?"

"I sure am, teddy bear," she said, gazing out of the windscreen.

"What are you thinking about?"

"My grandma. It's her birthday today."

"Oh, I'm so sorry," I said, grabbing her hand. "I didn't know."

"Thanks. You know, sometimes I think I can still feel her presence. I can't explain it. It's real strong on days like today."

"Do you believe in all that? Ghosts, I mean?"

"I don't think so. But you know, sometimes I wonder. I go back and forth."

"My sister Francine says that she woke up one night and saw our grandfather on Daddy's side, standing at the end of her bed. Looking down at her."

Dorothy screwed up her face. "Oh no, don't even say things like that!"

"Sorry, but she insists that it's true."

Dorothy was laughing now. "What if I wake up tonight and someone's standing at the end of our bed? I can just imagine ol' Grandpa tickling my foot like he used to do when I was a kid. Yikes!"

"I'm going to pull on your foot while you're sleeping!"

"You'd better not!"

We settled down from our laughing. Dorothy leaned over and brushed hair behind my ear. "I love watching you drive. You always have the cutest little serious expression when you're doing it."

I drew my eyebrows together and hunched over the steering wheel, exaggerating my look of concentration. "Like this?"

"Just like that."

"Hey, what are you calling our duet, Dorothy? We never did give it a name."

"Hmm," she said, humming a line. "I think keep it simple. 'The Two of Us.' What do you think?"

"I like it," I said. When she'd said the name, she'd looked at me so hopefully my chest squeezed with tenderness for her. We'd been working on the song when we had time, sometimes putting down ideas when we were on the road.

"We should think about adding it to the set, don't you think?" she said.

"Of course, I'd love to!"

"We'll play it for them this afternoon. We should have time before the show."

Soon after we arrived at the motel we rounded everyone up and crammed into the room Dorothy and I were sharing. We'd been careful to put our things separately at the end of each twin bed. Now I sat on one of the beds with my guitar resting on my knees, Dorothy next to me. Earl, Errol, Dirk, and Jack were on the other bed opposite us, so close together it was comical to see them lined up in a row.

By now I had none of the nerves I'd experienced the last time I'd played something new for them. Still, I couldn't look at Dorothy while I sang the "male" part, focusing my gaze on the wall behind the guys. When we were done, Errol let out a low whistle while each of the guys clapped.

"I keep saying it, but, Alice, you are going to be such a little hit factory," Earl said, shaking his head at me.

"Well, Dorothy wrote just as much of the song as I did!"

"Good work to both of you, then. What do you all think?" Earl looked down the line at the band. "Who's going to sing the part Alice was singing?"

"We were thinking it'd fit best with Dirk's range," Dorothy said.

Dirk held up a fist in triumph. "Yes! Thanks, guys. It'd be an honor to sing that song."

"You know what, this should be our next single, I'm sure of it. We'll do 'In My Heart' for the B-side. Let's record as soon as we can. It'd be good timing to drop some off to stations while we're driving around, if we can swing it somehow," Earl said.

"My sisters are recording in Houston soon. We'll be over there in a couple of weeks. They'd let us have the space for a few hours, I reckon," Dorothy said. She turned to me. "Ginnie's husband Ed is their producer. He has his own studio, and I bet he wouldn't even charge us for the time."

Earl clicked his fingers. "Hey, maybe we can get your sisters to do some backing vocals? Might sweeten the deal when we're trying to get it on the radio. Would you be okay with that?"

"Of course! That sounds like a mighty fine idea to me," Dorothy said. "Let's do it."

Later that night, after the show, Dorothy and I lay face-to-face. We'd pushed the twin beds together as soon as the guys left, and now our hands were clasped in one another's. With her other hand, Dorothy ran her fingers down my arm.

"I can't believe I'll get to meet your sisters," I said. "The Stellar Sisters."

"Not only that, you'll get to sing with them."

"I can't wait. Do you think they'll like me okay?"

"Are you kidding? They'll adore you. Especially Ginnie. Jill is a little pricklier, but you'll win her over once she hears your music," she said. She drew a thumb over my lower lip and I kissed it.

"I hope so," I said.

"I can't wait to play our duet for them," Dorothy said. "You know, they never paid any attention to me when I'd try to put forward my ideas. I got lost in the shuffle. It was all Jill and Ginnie. I felt like I was just tagging along."

"Really? No disrespect to your sisters, but you were the one who made that group. You're what stuck out, everyone thinks so. And it's not just your voice. Your ideas are so good, I don't know why they wouldn't listen to you," I said, playing with her hair.

"You make me better. Hey, listen, you'd better not give them any of your songs now, you hear?"

"My songs are only for us."

"Lucky me."

Dorothy leaned in, her velvety lips touching mine. After a few minutes she shifted so that she was lying on top of me. Our kisses were deep, Dorothy cradling me in her arms. The hem of her silky nightgown trailed against my legs, her bare lower leg rubbing against my shin.

I always got so worked up, and Dorothy was the one who said when it was time to stop. Yet when we were kissing like this she was more than enthusiastic. For the past couple of nights she'd been putting her thigh between my legs firmly like this, rubbing herself against me as we kissed. Sometimes feared I might go crazy from it.

I felt so close to her, her tongue in my mouth and her weight anchoring me down. She writhed against me, her hips driving into me so that I felt myself on the edge of something I'd only ever experienced alone. I wanted her to take me over that edge, was desperate for it.

Dorothy placed a hand between my breasts and brushed it down my stomach, her fingers dipping agonizingly low.

"Sorry," she said, her palm now flat beside me on the mattress.

My words came out ragged. "No, it's okay. You can do that if you want to."

"I don't know…" she said.

I took her hand and put it on my chest, just below my breast. When she put it back beside me I twisted away from her onto the other bed, turning my back. I wanted to be invisible.

"Alice?" Dorothy said, brushing my arm with her fingers again. "I've upset you."

"It's nothing."

"I don't think it's nothing."

"I'm fine."

I angrily brushed a tear from my cheek. Dorothy put her hand on my face, and her fingers must have come away damp.

"Please…"

"Can we just leave it?"

She moved away and I lay still, sleep far out of reach. After a few minutes she spoke again. "Can you talk to me?"

"I don't even know how to. Talk about it. I don't know what to say."

"I suppose I don't either. I mean, I think I know what this is all about. I just didn't know how to raise the subject."

I breathed out slowly. Fear bit at my ankles at times like this, whispering in my ear that things just weren't right between us. It was so scary to hear her talk about it, after all this time of wishing that she would.

"It's funny. You're always saying you're a straight shooter and everything. But we can't talk about this."

I turned toward her, and she placed her fingertips on my collarbone. "I know. I'm sorry I upset you, but I care about you so much."

"I do too," I said. "It's why I want more with you."

Dorothy smiled sadly at me. "There, see? You're a lot braver than I am. Of course I want more with you, as well. I just don't think that it would be a good idea."

"Why not?"

She gripped my shoulder. "Because I care. This has gone pretty far. Once we do…that, there's no going back. We can't undo it."

"Why would we want to undo it?"

"Alice, I've made my choices in life. Marrying Earl means that I'm never going to have a real husband, and I'm never going to have a family. That's all done for me. You could still have all that if you wanted, and I don't want to be the person that makes you think you can't."

I turned my back, rolling onto my own bed. I yanked the pillow under my head, hollowed out with disappointment. She didn't understand anything. "You've no right to say that. I told you from the very beginning I knew what kind of life I wanted."

After a long while, I drifted off to sleep and when I woke up my anger hadn't subsided. Dorothy studied me with her eyebrows drawn together. I rubbed my face, hating that her brown-eyed gaze got to me so much. Her eyes were puffy, and I hated that I'd made her cry too. I wanted to kiss her even now.

"Alice…I really hate to quarrel with you. I know you don't like it either. I'm sorry I didn't speak to you about all this earlier, but I'm not sorry about the rest of it."

"That's nice!" I said, starting to move from the bed. She moved toward me, but I kept myself out of her reach.

"Stop, wait. I don't want to spend the day like this, fighting all the way to the next city. Can't we just work this out now?"

"Don't worry about it. You can ride with someone else today."

"Please don't be this way with me," she said, her voice low.

My gaze trailed over her shapely legs under her nightgown, and I let her see that I was doing it. If I were a man, she'd never lie around half-naked like she did in front of me. "You know, it's your choice. I'd never want you to do anything you didn't want to. But it's not fair to start with me and then stop like you do. You don't take me seriously enough."

Dorothy pulled the sheets up to her chin, clutching the white cotton in her fists. "Don't talk to me like that."

"You're acting like you'd corrupt me if we slept together or something."

Dorothy's eyes widened. "Well, I would be. What did you think I was trying to tell you last night?"

"Because I'm like some pure virgin, is that what you think? Even though I told you I'd done it before?"

She shook her head, pursing her lips. "You told me it wasn't all that often."

"What does that have to do with what I feel about you? You talk about some kind of a normal life. I don't want a normal life! Don't you understand? I've wanted you since we met," I said.

Dorothy grabbed my hand and yanked me toward her.

In a heartbeat Dorothy was on top of me, her hands braced next to my shoulders, her mouth clashing against mine. Our teeth knocked together and I leaned my head up to kiss her, my hands making fists in her hair. As we kissed we strained against one another, her hips rocking against mine.

I dug my fingers into her waist, holding her tightly. She dipped her pelvis down into me.

Dorothy's breath was hot on my lips. "If you're sure this is what you want…"

I dragged her toward me and ran my hands over her back. We were kissing open-mouthed and hungrily, her tongue stabbing into my mouth.

I pushed my fingers up her thigh, under her nightgown, just like I'd always wanted to do. Her legs wrapped more firmly around me and I put my hands on her behind, grasping her close so that we both moaned.

She made enough space between us to move her hand up my chest. She looked into my eyes, a promise in them. When her fingers settled over my breast she bit her lip.

Dorothy's touch was only light for a moment, until she caressed my breast through my nightgown, still staring down at me. Then both of her hands were on my chest and we kissed while she touched me.

"You know it wasn't because I didn't want to, don't you?" she said, palming my breasts and putting her thigh between mine like she had the night before, settling against me. "I've been wanting to do this, so much…"

Our kiss was searing, my heart racing at what was about to happen.

We jumped apart at the tapping on the door.

"Girls?"

"What is it?" Dorothy said, her words strained.

"We were supposed to leave fifteen minutes ago!" Earl said, pounding on the door one last time before he walked away. Dorothy rested her head against mine.

"I'll kill that man someday," she said, and we laughed.

Each of us were lost in our thoughts as we passed over flat country. I knew next to nothing about sex between two women, and I was sure that my time with Sandra hadn't prepared me for being with someone like Dorothy. I trusted her enough by now to be sure that she wouldn't laugh at me, but her pity would be so much worse than that.

I tried to get swept away at the show that night in Jackson. We were playing in Duling Hall, which Earl kept saying we were lucky to get, but I couldn't stop thinking about what was going to happen when we were alone. Once I glanced at Dorothy onstage to see her staring at me, biting her lip with a certain look in her eye, and it gave me strength again.

When we were safely in our room Dorothy made cocoa for us as usual, yawning as she mixed the milk and powder together. "Great show tonight, wasn't it? I love watching folks sitting around those tables having a good time."

"It really was. I guess I'll go and shower."

I ran the water so hot that my skin reddened, scrubbing every inch of my body. What if Dorothy had changed her mind? What if she was so tired that she only wanted to go to sleep and to put it off for another night? I carefully cleaned my teeth, powdered my skin, and dressed in my nightgown.

We'd pushed the twin beds together as soon as we'd checked in this afternoon. While Dorothy was in the shower I pulled the quilt down, running my hand over the sheets. They were cheap and rough, and I wished we had something better.

I gathered up Dorothy's silver earrings and ring from the night stand and set them on the dresser with my own jewelry. I sat and listened until the rushing of the water in the bathroom stopped. Dorothy emerged from the bathroom and sat next to me. She kissed my temple, putting an arm around my shoulders.

"Are you all right, darling?"

"I'm okay. Just a little nervous."

"Don't worry. You're not the only one," she said, taking my hand and placing it in the center of her chest. Under my fingers, there was a fast pounding that mirrored my own. "We don't have to do this tonight if you're not sure, Alice. We can take our time."

"I still want to."

Dorothy kissed me until we were breathless, and we moved to lie down. Before long I was as aroused as I'd been this morning, hot from her touch. Dorothy lazily ran her hand over my front, for once not stopping when she reached my chest. She cupped my breasts, and I exhaled sharply. Her fingers were firm, stroking me while her tongue darted into my mouth.

At the top of my nightgown, she loosened the buttons from their eyes and slipped a hand inside. I bent against the mattress while she rolled my nipple between her fingers, crying out when she touched me. She lay open-mouthed above me, looking down as though this was affecting her as much as it was me.

Soon she moved away from me and motioned for me to sit up. Together we pulled my nightgown over my head.

I sat mostly naked in front of her. Dorothy's hand was behind my neck, and soon her gaze dropped. I pushed my hair over my shoulder, part of me wanting to hide but loving the hunger written on her face.

"Alice," she sighed. She pushed me until I was lying down again, exploring my body eagerly. Warm hands traced my stomach, my ribs, the underside of my breasts. I shuddered under her palms, kissing her with my arms around her neck.

Dorothy's eyebrows lifted, and I nodded. It was like being on stage, when we didn't need to speak to one another. We pulled my underwear down my legs and I lay before her. She ran her hand over my body again, and I tugged at the bottom of her nightgown until she stood up and undressed.

I couldn't stop looking at her.

When her hand came between my legs I clung to her, trusting her completely. As nervous as I was, it didn't seem to matter in the face of my excitement. Dorothy looked down at me intently as though mapping every change in my expression. I felt achingly close to her; she was holding all of me in her hands.

"All right?" she asked.

"Yes," I whispered. "Please keep going."

Her bare skin was soft and warm against me, her fingers skillful and sure. Now and then she kissed me, and I clung to her. She was inside of me, her thumb stroking me at the same time, her hips pushing into the back of her hand. Once more I looked up and into her eyes, the window into her, seeing how much she wanted me.

When I reached my peak I cried out again, so overcome that I forgot myself and almost told Dorothy that I loved her. She held me and the weight of her comforted me as it always had, pressing down and keeping me safe.

"Are you okay?" she whispered into my ear.

"Of course, I'm okay. More than okay," I said. Our kisses were slow and leisurely now.

I rolled so that Dorothy was beneath me. Now her hands came around my neck. I touched her body experimentally, my hands sliding over her hips, wanting so much to make her feel what I'd felt but not sure that I could.

"Alice," Dorothy said, a warning in her voice.

"What?"

"You look afraid. We're not doing this if you don't want to. I'll be okay," she said.

"I do want to! I'm just nervous."

"Oh," she said, kissing me gently. "You're not going to do anything wrong, sweetheart. Just touch me."

Propping myself up on an elbow, I looked down at her. Her breasts were high and firm, her belly slightly rounded. Her thighs were shapely, and I shyly looked at what lay between them, at the dark hair there. I watched as she sucked in a breath when I lay a hand on her stomach. Bathed in the dim light from the nightstand, she looked like a sculpture or a classic painting, the model of what beauty could be.

Nobody had ever looked at me the way she was looking at me right now, like there was something that she needed from me so much that she'd die if she couldn't have it. I skimmed my hand over her chest, caressing her breasts so that she bucked against me.

For a while now I'd felt confident about kissing her, and so I began with that. I kissed her lips, then her neck, and then I moved downward. Fingers tangling in my hair, she held me close. I kissed her for so long, tasting her soft skin under my mouth.

When I reached the peak of her breast I swirled my tongue around it, and it hardened even more under my attention. Her hand was at the back of my head, cradling me.

I moved up to kiss her lips again and slid my fingers down her stomach. She covered my hand with her own and guided me until I was touching her, my fingers sliding through her, gathering slickness and warmth. I closed my eyes, sighing. It wasn't like touching myself. It wasn't like anything I'd ever felt.

I loved looking down at her, her arm curled around my body, holding me as I stroked her. She stared up at me enraptured. It gave me a feeling of power that I already knew was going to be addictive, but it was power shared between us and that made it even more special.

When she climaxed she bent toward me, burying her face in my neck. We held one another, and she stroked my hair while I tried to reconcile what had just happened.

All the weeks of unspent tension were used up that night, all of it concentrating into touch and taste.

Finally, we curled up together in warm bliss, bodies pressed together. I wanted to know what the future held, what would happen after the tour. I contented myself with being wrapped up in her arms, her hand brushing softly through my hair.

Dorothy kissed the side of my face, her lips on my temple and jawline and mouth, until we both grew too excited to not begin again. She moved on top of me, a thigh between my legs.

I woke up first that next morning. Though I wanted to kiss her awake, I lay on my side, keeping myself back from her. Her plump lips fell open slightly. The sheets covered her breasts, and I studied the angles of her collarbone and her slight shoulders.

Finally, I got out from under the covers and went into the washroom. As I stepped into the shower I looked down. Everything was different now than Dorothy had seen my nakedness; she'd touched and explored me so thoroughly. My body wasn't something that I'd ever given a lot of thought to, but now it was as though I could still feel everything we'd done together, like it had stayed alive inside of me.

Dorothy rose, and we went about the mundane tasks of getting ready and packing up the car without saying much. She tapped my shoulder as she passed me to open the door to Earl, and we shared a smile.

Now she gazed out of the window with her elbow resting on the edge. Along the side of the road the grass was high, and there were mountains off in the distance ahead of us. Though her face was angled away from me I could trace the outline of her profile, her lips, and nose and chin. Her forehead was slightly crinkled as she squinted into the sun.

By now I'd viewed her from every angle. When she hadn't had enough sleep, she could seem drunk with it, sometimes jovial and sometimes grumpy. She was a person who let herself feel everything. Once we'd hit a bird with the car after it had flown into the windscreen. She cried brokenly, saying that even birds had families and someone might be missing it. And only hours ago I'd seen her unclothed, the light smattering of freckles on her back and the stunning shape of her. I thought of the butter soft skin on her stomach and the shifting of it under my hand.

It hadn't been so long, but I was convinced that I knew her better than anyone. Some time during the last weeks I'd stopped thinking of her as a star, because she'd made herself my equal.

"Dorothy?" I said, so that she twisted toward me expectantly. "No regrets or anything?"

"Not if you don't?" she said, eyebrows raised.

"Are you kidding? No way."

"Then everything is okay. More than okay."

This time, when she rested her hand on my knee, I understood that it was an oath. That night on stage Dorothy's attention fell on me as I played, contemplating my fingers on the frets of my guitar, our gazes locking a moment later. I was edgy to get to the motel, the need for her rising inexorably in me.

We began undressing one another as soon as we were inside, unzipping one another's dresses, a reversal of all the times we'd helped one another get ready for shows. When our kisses grew so intense that our legs buckled, Dorothy sank to the floor and I followed her. The carpet was rough against my back as Dorothy reached between my legs, stroking me furiously, licking and biting my earlobe. Before long, her hand was placed on my stomach, her head between my legs.

Over the next two weeks we made love as often as we could, no matter how tired we were after driving and playing shows. Afternoons before shows were spent in bed, bodies tangled in the sheets. During the rare mornings that we didn't have to get up early we lazily woke one another up with caresses, hot mouths, and desperate hands.

There was an unbroken chain of discoveries. There was the first time I tasted her, aroused beyond reason by the way that she smelled and how she moved under my tongue. There was the first time we showered together, kissing as the water flowed over us. I pushed her up against the tile, sinking my fingers into the heat of her.

For those days there was nothing but pleasure, Dorothy's skin and lips and tongue.

If I hadn't known it before, I did now. I loved Dorothy Long.

CHAPTER ELEVEN

The visit to Houston snuck up on us. I was distracted enough by being with Dorothy that I'd barely thought any more about what it would be like to meet her sisters.

"Do you really think they'll like me?" I asked as we entered the drive, butterflies beating their wings in my stomach. The house was an eccentric shade of teal with white edging on the windowsills, which were also adorned with flower boxes. Ginnie or her husband must have a green thumb. The yard was bursting with color from flowers, reds and pinks dotting the bushes.

"Sweetheart, they'll love you. You don't have to worry about a thing, okay?"

"Thanks. They're your family, you know?"

The front door was flung open at the sound of our engine. We met Jill and Ginnie just outside, and I hovered behind Dorothy as they all hugged one another. There was a straw welcome mat at my feet and a sign on the wall instructing visitors to wipe their shoes. When Dorothy turned to the side, pulling me forward by the wrist, her sisters gazed curiously at me.

Ginnie and Jill shared Dorothy's full lips and pale skin. Ginnie, the eldest of the three, was almost as tall as Dorothy, though she was a little thicker around the waist. Jill was closer to my height and struck me as being scrappy; there was something hungry about the lines of her face.

Jill's eyes narrowed. I was smiling tightly at her when Ginnie grabbed me, enveloping me in a full-bodied hug. Jill stepped forward after a moment and hugged me too, stiffly patting my back.

"We've heard an awful lot about you. Dorothy has been mentioning you in her letters," Ginnie said.

"I've heard a lot about you too," I said.

"Not to mention, word gets around. We've heard about this little upstart stealing the show left, right, and center," Jill said, wiggling her finger in front of my face.

"Oh...I don't..."

"Can it, Jill. She's just joking, sweetie. Don't worry about her," Ginnie said as the band came up behind us. I edged further back into the yard to make room for them while they exchanged loud greetings. "Hey, boys! I sure am glad to see you!"

Jill posed with hands on hips, looking Errol up and down. "Well, would you just look at what the cat dragged in?"

"Come here, you floozy," he said. "How 'bout a hug?"

We set about bringing our things in, because we were all staying at the house. Even Jill, who lived close by, was sticking around so she could spend more time with everyone. Ginnie introduced me to her husband Ed, a curly-haired man with a receding hairline and deep-set brown eyes. He didn't crack a smile, but his gaze was warm when he looked down at me.

After a big supper of spaghetti, we crowded into the living room. I found a floral-patterned armchair, sitting far forward in the seat to accommodate my guitar.

Dorothy was on the other side of the room, sitting cross-legged on the rust-colored carpet. I tried to catch her eye, but she was talking to Dirk, who nodded and plucked out a couple of notes. They must be talking about the duet.

After a few minutes Dorothy clapped her hands together. When the buzz of conversation didn't die off, Dirk stuck his fingers in his mouth to whistle so that everyone froze.

"All right," Dorothy said. "We're going to play you the two songs we want to record. The A-side is going to be called 'The Two of Us.' The B-side is a ballad called 'In My Heart.'"

Jack counted us in, though he hadn't set up his kit. While Dorothy sang, Dirk and I played the two songs back-to-back, with barely a pause between them. Jill and Ginnie were mirror images of one another, listening with their heads tilted. Their focus bounced back and forth between Dorothy, Dirk, and me.

During the duet, Dirk and Dorothy's voices complimented one another perfectly. My chest ached with how mournful "In My Heart" sounded, stripped back and full with longing. After the last notes there was dead air for a beat, before the room erupted.

"Wow! These songs are dynamite," Ginnie said.

"They really are very good. I like what you've done here," Ed said, our eyes meeting.

"Are these all songs written by Alice?" Jill asked. "All your new songs like this?"

"Dorothy and I wrote the duet," I said, raising my voice over the noise.

"Well, Alice, we're going to steal you away, so you can write songs for us instead," Jill said. "Aren't we, Ginnie?"

"Like hell you will," Dorothy said.

"Oh, look at her, she's getting sassy," Ginnie said, leaning toward Jill and laughing behind her hand.

Dorothy smacked Ginnie's arm. "Cut it out, you pair, or you can't sing with us."

"Oh no! How could we ever cope with that?" Ginnie replied.

When it was time to retire, Dorothy guided me toward the spare room. I took down a family picture from the shelf that jutted over the bed. Dorothy hadn't changed so much since being a teenager, though her face had become slimmer and her hair was cut differently now. I wished I'd known her then, that she could have been a girl sitting next to me in class or living round the way in the neighborhood. I'd been so lonely.

Dorothy stood at my back. I set the photo down, pulling her arms more tightly around me.

"Thank you for tonight. You sounded great in there," she said. "You always make me better."

"You sound amazing, with or without me."

Dorothy kissed my neck softly, then trailed her tongue along my skin.

"Are you sure they don't think it's strange that we're sleeping in here together?" I asked, pushing back against her. "I mean, won't they think it's strange that Earl's not in here with you?"

"They're used to us not sleeping in the same room. We've stayed with them before," she said, pushing her hand under the waistband of my skirt. She slid her fingers over my stomach, her lips pressing to the side of my face.

"Didn't they ask you then?" I said.

She stilled her hand. "Alice. They're my sisters. We don't talk about it, but they have a pretty good idea of why we wouldn't be sleeping in the same room. They don't need to ask me."

"Oh," I said.

Did they suspect anything about us? My greatest wish was that other people could be proud of my position in Dorothy's life. I wanted people to say all the nice things they usually did about couples, for instance that we looked good together or that we were well-matched. But people didn't say things like that about two girls.

I smiled because Dorothy was smelling my hair, my sad thoughts dropping away as she dipped a finger below the top of my underwear. I turned my head and she put a hand to my throat, kissing me deeply.

"Turn around," she said, slowly backing me up against the door. There was a light thud as my back was pressed against it.

"We can be quiet, can't we?" she asked. Then her hands were in my hair, grabbing it in fistfuls to push it back from my face.

I loved the way things were between Dorothy and me, how either of us took the lead depending on our moods. There were nights where we spent hours teasing one another for as long as we could stand it. On nights like tonight, though, we couldn't wait. After the distance between us earlier, when she felt so far away over the other side of the room, I was impatient for her.

She held my wrists over my head against the door, flicking her tongue over my neck and kissing me. She released me so that she could palm my chest roughly over my bra and blouse. She bent down and worked her tongue over my breast, dampening the fabric.

I tried to pull her up toward me so that she could kiss me again. I wanted her everywhere at once, and at last her lips were on mine again. Dorothy's hand stayed at my breast, rubbing her fingers over me so that I moaned into her open mouth.

I wrapped a leg around her waist and she clasped my thigh, clutching at it to pull me into her.

Dorothy reached under my skirt, slipping her hand between my legs. She pushed my underwear out of the way so that she could move inside me. When she touched me, the relief was so intense I struggled to stay upright, my head thrown back against the door. She curled her fingers in the most delicious way and I gasped, my hips moving against her. I bit my lip as she thrust firmly into me, her arm around my back to hold me up.

Where her caress below my waist was hard and fast, her lips were tender against my mouth. I put my arms around her, pressing my face into her neck. It didn't take long for my mouth to open in a soundless cry.

Afterward, we lay together on the single bed. She kissed my shoulder. "I love being with you."

"I love it too, I just…"

"You just what?" Dorothy said, a hand on my thigh under my skirt.

"I've been thinking tonight. I wonder what other people think of us."

"In what way? Are you worried about people finding out?" she said, withdrawing her hand, still holding me at the hip.

"No, that's not it. I guess I just wonder what this means to you," I said. Sometimes I feared that we didn't talk about the things that were important. We skirted them, our conversations a delicate, fragile thing.

"You're my girl, Alice," Dorothy said, tugging at me until I rolled over toward her.

I loved the way it sounded. Her *girl.*

"And am I yours?" she prompted.

"Of course," I said. She bent down toward me, kissing me tenderly.

"You know, you act like I'm supposed to know so much more than you. You wait for me," Dorothy said, trailing her fingers down my cheek.

"I guess I do that. Maybe it's because I'm really only good at my music. There's not so much else I feel confident about."

Dorothy arched a brow. "Well, honey, it's really not the only thing you're good at…"

I laughed, then sobered quickly. "You know what I mean. I don't feel that I know what I'm doing."

"You do know what you're doing. And you need to remember, this is all a first for me too, you know. It's the first time I've been in love with someone."

I squeezed my eyes shut tight. I'd waited so long to hear those words. "I love you too."

A week later we were in Austin and I held the vinyl disc, turning it over so that I could reread the labels on either side. My surname was enclosed in brackets under the song titles, crediting me with writing them. On one of the sides my surname was next to Dorothy's, and I liked that even better.

"I wish they'd put your name first on the duet," I said.

"Don't you think that'd be a bad idea? Then it would say Long Johnson," Dorothy replied, giggling.

I had loved being part of the recording session and couldn't wait until it was time to do it again. It was fascinating to see how all the parts were made to fit together. If I had nothing to do, Ed let me sit next to him in the control room. With intense focus, he hunched over toward the glass separating him from the musicians. I observed him pushing buttons up and down, adjusting levels until he liked what he heard. Now and then I'd ask him a question.

Ed contemplated me with his fist in front of his mouth. "You really like this stuff, don't you?"

"Of course! It's so interesting."

"You ever want to know the ropes, I'm happy to teach you. You could be producing your own tracks one day."

When I told Dorothy, she said that just because there weren't many female producers out there, it didn't mean that I couldn't do it. I smiled to myself, lifting the needle on Dirk's portable player so I could listen to the record again. I lay on my back on the motel room floor, staring up at the cracked paint on the ceiling. If I tried hard enough I could hear my own voice in the mix.

"You're going to wear that thing out," Dorothy said. She was on the bed on her stomach, paging through the latest issue of *Life* magazine. Mamie Eisenhower was on the cover this week. Janice loved Mamie; she often wore pink because the First Lady did.

"I just can't believe it's really us! It sounds so good. Don't you think?"

"I can believe it. I knew how good it'd sound. Just imagine what it's going to sound like when we cut an LP. I've already got a ton of ideas for the cover."

I rolled onto my side and stared up at her. "I can't wait to hear all about them."

"For now, though, we've plenty of work to do."

"Oh yeah?" I said, scooting over to her on my knees. She leaned over the side of the bed and kissed me.

"As much as I'd like to kiss you all day, yes, we do. I want to write notes to go with every single one of those records, for the disc jockeys. We want to stand out with these guys or we'll never get anywhere. Let's get to work, sweetheart."

A few days later we were driving through barren-looking country, the landscape flat and featureless before us. We'd agreed that we needed to stop somewhere soon for a break, but it felt like we were never going to reach civilization. I yawned as Dorothy twirled the knob on the radio, searching for music. She paused to listen when Elvis's voice came over the airwaves, nodding along.

"I love Elvis. Did you see his haircut? He sure looks like a military man now."

I nodded and she twirled the knob again. At the same time, we squealed.

"They're playing us!" I said.

Dorothy bounced on the seat, grabbing my hand as we listened. As soon as the disc jockey announced "The Two of Us," adding that he'd gotten tons of requests since he'd first spun it, Dorothy restlessly scanned again. After twenty minutes, familiar notes rang out.

"I knew this was going to be a hit!" she said. "Listen to how much it's getting played already!"

"It's really us! It's just so strange!"

"Then I like strange," she said, grinning at me and twirling through static. "Well, this is certainly waking me up. Can you believe that we only have another few weeks of shows? It's been a wonderful tour, my favorite tour ever, but I can't wait to sleep in my own bed again."

"I can't wait to sleep in. First chance I get, I'm going to sleep all day long."

"That sounds like heaven. I keep thinking about home cooking. I'm going to ask Sally to cook about ten fried chickens the first night."

"You should ask her to bake a thousand biscuits too," I said, my mouth watering at the thought of them, buttered and soaked with gravy.

"Now that's an idea. Nobody makes biscuits like Sally's."

It was quiet, save for white noise and the occasional voice breaking through. "Dorothy? I've actually been wondering. About what I'm going to do right after the tour."

"Oh yeah?" she put her hand behind my neck and rubbed it. "I assumed you'd be going home to see your folks and May. I'm going to miss you something awful. I'd put off Sally's cooking forever if it meant I got to spend more time with you."

"That's just the thing, see. I do miss my family, but I'm not so sure if I want to go back there just yet."

"You're not?" Dorothy said. Was that a note of hope in her voice?

"No, not really. I mean, of course I know I have to go back there sometime, but I don't think I'm ready for it right now. They're so funny about all of this when I call. I think they still need some time to adjust to this new life I'm living. To be honest, there's just not that much for me to go back to."

"I'm sorry it's like that for you. I wish they were as proud of you as I am."

A few beats passed while I waited. "So...I guess I'll get myself a room in town. That way I'll be ready for when we record, and I won't have to do so much driving back and forth. Just the thought of that tires me out, after all the driving I've been doing!"

"Why don't you just stay with me?" Dorothy asked, beaming. She shuffled closer to me on the seat, checking around to see how far away the other cars were, and kissed my cheek when she saw that it was safe.

"You're sure you won't get sick of me or anything like that?"

Dorothy leaned back over and kissed my earlobe, making me draw my shoulders up and shiver. "Are you kidding? I was just trying to be supportive when I said I expected you to go home. I didn't want to be selfish, but I'd be counting the days if you were away from me just now. I don't think I could stand it."

"Then I'll stay with you."

For the next hour, Dorothy abandoned the hunt for our song.

"I think it'd be really nice to go into town and see a picture when we get back," I said. This time I'd hold her hand while we watched, and we'd be on a real date.

"I couldn't agree more. And I want to spend some long, lazy days at the house. Know what I mean? We could read out on the porch, just talk and snuggle."

"That sounds so lovely."

"And of course, you can move into my room. There'll be

plenty of time in bed. Sleeping and…not sleeping."

"Sounds pretty damn good to me."

Her room at the house was so much bigger than mine, deep and dark and lovely. There would be no more worrying about having to sleep on twin beds.

"I might go back sometime and see my folks, though. I probably should. They'd have my hide if they knew we'd passed by so close and I didn't visit. Maybe you could even come with me?" I asked.

"Are you kidding? I'd love to meet your family."

It struck me now, as Dorothy stroked my knee, how thoroughly she had woven herself into the fabric of my life. Didn't we love one another as much as any man and wife did? There was nothing about us being two women that diminished that love, no matter what anyone else might think. That made her my family, too.

As the tour wound down, and we worked our way through our last dates, we noted the impact of the radio play on our audiences.

One morning at breakfast, Earl banged his knife and fork against the table, so hard that it made our dishes rattle. "Did you guys see how it was, last night? They were turning folks away at the door."

"Couldn't miss it, the place was packed! They were a great crowd, too," Dorothy said.

"Do you know how much bigger the next run of shows is going to be? It's all coming together," Earl said. "And soon we're going to be able to relax with all the touring and take it a little easier."

"You reckon we're going to be able to bring on some more people soon then?" Dirk said eagerly. "Folks to help us with our equipment?"

"Only a matter of time. We'll be able to get a bus and all kinds of things. We'll be touring the new record when we go out again, I hope, and it's going to be a winner."

The very next day we woke up to pounding on our door. I leapt out of bed and ran for the bathroom with my nightgown in hand, while Dorothy frantically reached for her robe.

"What is it, Earl? I thought we didn't have to be on the road until eight!" Dorothy yelled.

When I came out of the washroom, Earl was standing by the unmade bed, brandishing a newspaper. "Do you see this, girls? Do you see it?"

"Where's the fire? Is there another war starting or something? Just spit it out," Dorothy said.

Earl slapped the paper down on the bed. "We've got ourselves our first number one single on the country charts, that's what's happening! *And* we've cracked the pop charts, too. The record's crossing over."

"You don't say! I must remember this moment. I hope you bought up a whole bunch of those papers," Dorothy said, her hands pressed to her cheeks.

"Of course, I did. And ladies, that's not even the half of it. I already called our guy at the label. Woke him up," he said, puffing his chest out. "But get a load of this. They want to put us on the main label."

Dorothy shrieked and hugged him, but she reserved her longest embrace for me. As she shifted back she kissed my cheek, and when I looked at Earl he was staring at the floor, red-faced.

We played a matinee show that day. When we returned to the motel I pulled my cowgirl boots off, rubbing my tired feet. I wished there was a bath at the motel. I was going to take so many baths, the first chance I got.

There was one last show, planned for the following night. I wasn't sure if I wanted this tour to end or if I wanted it to go on forever. My complicated thoughts were eased by knowing how much time I was going to spend with Dorothy. And I couldn't wait to record the whole album in Nashville. Earl told us that the label was giving us a new producer, and I hoped that whoever he was he'd be happy to teach me like Ed was.

"I'm so excited to get some rest. I've been wanting an early night like this," I said to Dorothy as she started to rub my feet.

"Oh wait, wait, wait. I forgot you didn't know about our last show ritual," Dorothy said.

"What are you talking about?"

"Well, the night before our last show we go out and get rip-roaring drunk."

"That seems like a crazy thing to do. Won't we all be feeling pretty rough for our last show, then?"

Dorothy pulled on a toe and shrugged, as if to say, "Oh well, what can you do?"

"Do I have to?" I asked.

"You don't *have* to, nobody's going to make you. But we did it by accident one time and now it's bad luck if we don't. You might catch hell from the boys if you sit this one out," she said, sliding her palm up and down my calf.

Rolling my eyes, I said, "Y'all think everything's bad luck. All right. I guess I'll join in."

Dorothy's hand was reaching still further, up my thigh. "Good, I was hoping you'd come around. In the meantime, however…"

There was a bar close enough to walk to from the motel, and we piled into it. A handful of couples clung to one another on the small dance floor, swaying to "Honky Tonk World," the Bonnie Sloan song playing on the jukebox in the corner. Errol and Jack went over to the pool table while Dorothy, Earl, Dirk, and I sat around a table with a surface sticky from spilled liquor. We lined up a row of glasses in front of us, cheap beer and whiskey that I feared would make me sick.

"What are you most looking forward to, Dirk?" Earl said. "I bet you're looking forward to seeing the missus."

"Of course, and the kids. I can't wait to play with them, hear about how things have been going. Winnie's promised me my first night back she's going to cook us some big old steaks. What about you?"

"I want to head out on the lake to go fishing. That's my number one priority," Earl said, rubbing the stubble on his chin. "What's so funny, Alice?"

"It's just that you all sound like you're getting out of jail or something."

"Oh, no, it's just a holiday is all! What are you doing, anyhow? Will you be going back home to see the family?" Dirk asked.

"No, actually. I'm going to be sticking around, staying at the house."

"Oh, you are?" Earl said, pulling on his beer. "Well, that'll be real nice. It'll be good to have you for a little longer."

"Thanks, Earl. I just thought it'd be easier to stay rather than go driving back and forth," I said. I was surprised that Dorothy hadn't told him by now.

Dorothy squeezed my thigh under the table. "Well, like Earl said, it'll be great to have you around. Now, I think this party is moving a little slow. Bottoms up?"

The next morning my head thudded, and a dull ache spread over my eye. Dorothy sat up next to me in bed, a glass of water in her hand.

"Ugh, I feel terrible," I said, covering my eyes against the light.

"Me too. But that was the plan," she said, sipping from her glass. "I got you some water. It's on your nightstand."

"Thanks, but I don't think I can stomach it just yet. I still don't understand this ritual."

"Look at you, sweetheart. You've still got your makeup on from yesterday afternoon. You look like a raccoon."

"Don't laugh at me!" I said, covering my face with my pillow. Dorothy pulled it away and kissed me.

"Don't ever hide your face. You always look beautiful."

"Even when I look like a raccoon?"

"Especially when you look like a raccoon," Dorothy said, cuddling up against my side. The warmth of her body soothed me, and she dropped another kiss on my neck.

"Gosh, I was so drunk I can't hardly remember the end of the night at all. We must have all walked back here together, did we?" I said, looking around the dingy room. My clothes were strewn across the floor, my handbag dropped just inside. I'd have to check how much cash I'd burnt through.

"We did. Dirk and Errol were going to keep on drinking in their room. But I put you to bed, then went to Earl's room to talk to him. He was having a temper tantrum on the walk back here."

"What about?"

My heart raced while I waited. Though I couldn't say why, I was afraid of the blank spaces in my memory.

"It's nothing to worry about. It's just that you and I were doing a little two-step to the jukebox, and Earl said it wasn't right to do that in front of the boys and everyone."

"Oh. Was it my fault?"

Dorothy squeezed me tight. "Of course it wasn't your fault. We were just dancing. The boys were all playing games, and we got to fooling around."

"I didn't do anything, did I? Like, try to kiss you or anything?"

"No! There was nothing wrong with it. It's just Earl being paranoid, which is what I told him. He's never spoken to me like that before. He usually stays right out of my business. I guess he was pretty drunk. Don't you worry about it one bit, okay?"

"Okay. Can I sleep a little longer?"

"Just half an hour or so. I'll get you up when it's time."

That day at breakfast I avoided looking at Earl, while everyone complained about their sore heads. I leaned away from Jack, who was sipping from his flask, the smell of whiskey making me feel ill.

"Hair of the dog," he said.

"I don't know how you can do it," I said. I ordered hash and eggs, and the coffee relieved my headache.

Dirk offered to help me drive while Errol took his car. It had been a while since I'd been separated from Dorothy for the drive, and she winked at me as she got into the passenger seat of the Chevy alongside Earl. I guessed they would have plenty of time to patch up their differences on the road.

It was curious that since Dorothy told me about her arrangement with Earl we'd never talked much more about it. With that conversation he'd ceased to be important, and I'd allowed myself to forget about the level of influence he had.

I figured they might have discussed what was going on with Dorothy and me, but preferring to not think about it, I never asked.

Dirk and I barely talked as we drove. His voice was raspy from too many cigarettes the night before, and he was worried he was coming down with something. We listened to the radio and stopped plenty of times to pick up coffee or soda.

My hangover created a dreamy state of mind, and I watched the road while I thought about my plans for the break. I hadn't done much songwriting in the past couple of weeks, and ideas had been bubbling up in me as though eager to get out and find a form. Dorothy and I could write together all the time, sitting close on the porch. The leaves from the tree out front would rustle over us, and Scout might lie at our feet.

We arrived at the venue at dusk, with no time to check into a motel.

"Thanks for helping with the driving, Dirk. I might have fallen asleep if I'd had to drive on my own today."

"Not a problem. Jesus," Dirk said, putting his hand on his throat. "I still sound like shit. I'm going to have to sit out the singing tonight."

I gaped at him. "Are you sure? Who's going to sing the duet with Dorothy?"

"One of the other boys can do it. It's just one show. I'll talk to Dorothy before we go on. She'll work it out."

In the flurry of changing my clothes, I forgot about the song altogether. I rubbed my bleary eyes, gratefully accepting a bottle of cola Dorothy handed to me while we waited for another act to finish playing. I'd only had time to take a couple of sips when the announcer said our name, and the crowd roared.

When we stood onstage, I blinked back tears. There'd be other tours, but the first could never happen again. My life had altered so completely, and every person who came to see us had their part to play in it.

The fans started to request the duet early in the show, cupping their hands around their mouths and calling out. I looked over at Dorothy, wondering if it might be better to just drop it from the set. We hadn't rehearsed a change, and I didn't like the thought of doing it cold with a different singer.

"Well, ladies and gentlemen, I can hear you asking for 'The Two of Us,' but we've got ourselves a little problem," Dorothy said, pacing the stage while she confided in the audience. She'd chosen my favorite red dress tonight, the one she'd been wearing the first time I saw her. "You see, Dirk here is a little under the weather. He'd love to sing it for you, but he just can't tonight."

The crowd booed, stomping their feet. Dorothy put a hand to her ear and leaned forward until they jeered even louder. "Well, it sounds like you think we should do it anyway. Wouldn't you say that's what you're all thinking... That's what I thought. There's a person on stage who knows the song better than anyone, because she and I wrote it."

I didn't know what she was up to, but she teased me onstage like this from time to time. I shook my head, adjusting my guitar strap over my shoulder and smiling, waiting for her to move on.

"Alice Johnson. She's going to sing the song with me. What do you all say?"

I covered my microphone with my palm. "What are you talking about, Dorothy? I haven't rehearsed that song!"

Instead of covering hers too, she let the whole room hear her. "What are you talking about? You don't need to rehearse! You wrote it, remember?"

The crowd egged her on, calling out my name.

What the hell, it was our last show. When the band struck up the song I threw myself into it, high on singing the words I'd heard Dirk belting out every night. The audience stamped on the floor and sang along, not seeming to mind that it was me and not Dirk. They just liked the song. At the chorus Dorothy flung an arm around me and I leaned toward her, fluttering my eyelashes. The crowd laughed and cheered for us.

At the end of the show I wiped a tear from my eye, bowing alongside the band again and again. We'd already played two encores, and it was time for it to finally be over. Right now, I wasn't thinking about the fact that we'd be back. It just felt like the end.

That night I went straight to bed as soon as we got back to the motel, slipping my clothes off and letting Dorothy pull the sheets over me. I didn't think I'd ever been this emotionally exhausted.

Dorothy kissed my forehead, then undressed and got in next to me, putting her head on my chest.

"I can't believe that was the last one..." I said, my eyes drooping shut. "The end. It didn't really feel like the end, did it?"

"That's because it wasn't," Dorothy said, arm around my waist as she nuzzled into me. "My darling, it's only the beginning."

CHAPTER TWELVE

The next morning I woke up alone, the mattress still warm beside me. Dorothy must have gone out to get us coffee. I loved that she was so sweet that way, that she took pride in taking care of me.

For once we didn't have to rush away and we hadn't made breakfast plans. If we left before too long and didn't stop too often, we could be back at the house by early evening. The thought was so satisfying that I hummed "The Two of Us" to myself, stretching my arms over my head. I rose to pack up the few things I'd had time to take out of my case the night before, then drew the curtains so the sunlight spilled in.

Dorothy still wasn't back by the time I was done, so I got back into bed and dozed.

When the door opened it woke me up again, and I rolled over, ready to welcome her back. I hoped that she'd join me in bed for a little while. As soon as I saw her I bolted upright. Dorothy's eyes were red, and she covered her mouth, her wedding ring gleaming. She sat down heavily on the bed beside me.

"What's happened? Is somebody hurt?"

"No, I'm sorry. It was nothing like that. I just had an argument with Earl. He's very mad at me."

"Because of me, again?"

Dorothy took my hand and rubbed her thumb over my knuckles. "It's not your fault, it's mine. I guess I knew it was going to annoy him when I asked you to sing with me. I wanted you to. It's our song, goddamn him! But I was thumbing my nose at him, too."

"I don't understand. The crowd loved it. They thought we were just joking around."

Dorothy shook her head. "He said it doesn't matter. We could be putting the idea in people's heads."

It was quiet for a long time. I wanted to hold her, but the way she was staring at the wall stopped me cold. I'd seen her upset before, but never like this. It was as though she'd been sapped of all life and movement.

Finally, I reached out and touched her arm lightly. "You must be exhausted. Checkout time isn't for an hour, is it? Maybe we can nap for a little while?"

"I don't think I'd be able to, darling," she said, patting my arm absently. "You go ahead, though."

I lay back down, and after a while I heard her gathering her things, trying to be quiet. I wished she'd get into bed so that we could soothe one another with kisses. I hated that Earl was talking about us and, even worse, judging us. Where once it would have shamed me, he now appeared as an obstacle looming in the way of my happiness.

"It's okay, I'm awake," I said. "Dorothy... Do you want to talk about this thing with Earl? Is it very bad, with him?"

"Yes," she said softly. "It's very bad."

"What do you mean?" I watched while she walked to the bathroom and came back out with her cosmetics bag. She slowly put it into her case, not looking at me. "Dorothy? Earl has his own thing going on, right? He sleeps with other women, so he's not jealous of us or anything like that."

Dorothy stared at me, her mouth slightly open. "Is that what you've heard?"

"I know you said not to gossip. I'm sorry. That's what Dirk thinks goes on."

Dorothy bit a knuckle, sitting down on the bed. "Well, I guess it's better folks think that than the truth. Earl likes men. That's the reason he was happy to get married. Who else would marry a woman who was never going to sleep with him? I thought you must have known this."

"How would I know? He doesn't look like a homosexual," I said.

Dorothy shook her head impatiently. "What does that mean? You think they all look like that Liberace? Do you think you're what people think of, when they think of a woman who's a homosexual? Or me?"

"Why doesn't he understand, then? Why doesn't he want to help us?"

Dorothy sighed. "I guess it's exactly why he's so scared of people finding out. You and I could blow it for everyone and especially him. I'm sorry, but I think you'd better go ahead and book that room in town you were talking about. It will give him time to calm down, and I can talk to him some more."

I reached for her arm, needing more than ever to be close to her. "Okay… If that's what you want me to do."

"It's not what I want, it's what we must do. Earl says we haven't been discreet. He says that we're risking losing everything we've worked for."

I put my hand on my queasy stomach. "Will I still see you, though? During the break?"

"I'll try. But maybe he's right about some of it. We might have to think about cooling things off. I haven't been thinking straight."

"Cooling things off?" I said, my hand falling away.

Dorothy took a deep breath. "Yes."

"This isn't fair! Why does he get to say what we should and shouldn't do?"

"Alice, he's my husband," she said.

Why was she explaining things to me like I was a child? I thought I'd proven to her that I could understand things a long time ago. "But like you always say, he's not really your husband. It's just an arrangement."

"Exactly, it's an arrangement. He and I agreed on certain things, like discretion."

"We haven't done anything! You said so yourself. We were just dancing," I said, throwing up my hands. God, I hated him.

"Earl and I agreed we were going to put everything into this band. If what's happening between you and I ruin it, then that's not very fair either, is it? It wouldn't be fair to the boys. They're depending on this band," she said, pointing her finger down sharply, pressing it into the mattress with every word.

These last few minutes had blotted out my future. Would I be sitting in a room by myself for the next month, waiting for her to visit or call? "There's nothing I can say, is there? He's called the shots and that's it. I'm not important enough to get a vote at all."

"Please try to understand. It's his house!"

"Isn't it your house too?"

"You know what I mean. Now, I made him promise that you're in the band one hundred percent. There'll be no trying to push you out or anything like that. I'd never do anything but protect you," Dorothy said, grabbing for my hand.

I kept it away from her, my face crumpling. "I'm the goose that laid the golden egg, right? You need more of my songs."

"Please, honey, don't say things like that. That's not why I want you with me."

I got up and went to the washroom, closing the door loudly behind me before turning on the faucet in the shower. I stood under the water, where she couldn't hear me cry.

Lately whenever I'd been homesick, it was Dorothy's place that I longed for. Now for the first time in a long time, I wanted to be at my real home. My parents could never know anything about this, and that comforted me. I wanted to be around May. I was desperate to speak with Bill, too, and I thought guiltily about the fact that I hadn't sent him a postcard for weeks and weeks.

When I came out of the washroom Dorothy was still sitting on the bed in the same position. Her stare followed me around the room as I buckled one of my cases and moved my guitar close to the door. I swept my keys up from the nightstand.

"You don't want to ride with me today?" Dorothy said, her voice cracking. "Don't do that. Let's be with one another today. It might be the last time we spend some any real time together for a while."

I shook my head, looking past her toward the wall. There was a painting of a bird, and I stared at the pale colors of its wings. "You can ride with Earl."

"Please don't be this way. Honey, don't you see that this hurts me, too?"

I'd thought about not even telling her. I could quietly peel off from the convoy and drive toward home. I couldn't bring myself to be that cruel. "I'll see you in a month or so when it's almost time to record."

"What do you mean?" she asked, rising to walk toward me.

"I'm going home. Tell the boys I'm sorry, but I wanted to get a head start."

I twisted away from her stunned expression and fumbled to open the door, my hands shaking violently. I heard the rustling of her dress as she walked closer.

I didn't look back at all in the time it took to walk toward my car, my arms loaded up with my things. Was she looking out the window at me as I closed the trunk?

All day while I drove, barely seeing the landscape around me, I didn't need to wonder if I'd made the right decision. She let me go without another word. She hadn't even come outside.

Two days later Mama came out onto the front step as I drove toward it. I wasn't close enough to see her face, but when she rushed toward me, my heart lurched. When I'd gotten out of my car, she hugged me. I hadn't been held by her like this since I was a child.

She stepped back, crossing her arms. "We weren't expecting you."

"Sorry I haven't called."

"Well… Supper will be ready in an hour. If you want to wash up first."

We sat around the table, and I shoved forkfuls of tuna casserole into my mouth mindlessly. I'd barely eaten all the way back, aside from candy bars and beef jerky.

Dorothy would be eating Sally's cooking tonight. With him.

"Your sister's pregnant again," Mama said, clearing plates from the table. I got up to help, my joints stiff from sitting so much.

"Oh. That's nice."

"You can come with me when I visit her tomorrow."

"Okay."

"How long are you staying?" Daddy said.

"Alice? Are you not feeling well?" Mama asked.

"Sorry. Just been a long day," I said, clearing my throat. "I'm not sure how long I'll be here."

"Well, are you going to try and get your old job back again then?"

I looked at Daddy when he asked me that, sounding like he didn't much care either way. "I'm not sure what I'm doing. I think I'll go on to bed."

My room was exactly as I'd left it. I'd never noticed how much like a teenager's room it was, with the single bed and the pile of books and records in the corner. Mama must have dusted while I was away, because everything was spotless.

My Stellar Sisters record was at the front of the crate I stored my records in, and I lifted it to look at the picture. I stared at Dorothy's face, missing her so fiercely it stole the air from my lungs. What did it say about me that I'd do anything to see her for even ten minutes right now? How could I have let that slip away? A kiss on the lips, her hand in my hair.

I crawled into bed and drifted into sleep.

We visited Francine the next day, the pine scent of the freshly scrubbed floorboards tickling my nose. I didn't know anyone who took as much pride in their home as Francine did; she seemed to want to outdo even our Mama.

"Well, if it isn't little Miss Country Music Star, gracing us with her presence," Francine said, her pinkie finger up in the air. She didn't seem to notice how puffy my eyes were, even though I'd pressed cold spoons to them this morning.

"Congratulations, Francine."

"Thanks," she said, patting her belly. "It's been an easy pregnancy so far. When did you get back, anyway?"

"Just last night."

"We heard you on the radio, you know. The one she does with the guy. That song will get stuck in your head, for sure," she said. "I couldn't hear you, though. Do you even sing on any of them?"

"Yes, I do sing on it. I'm one of the backing singers. And I played the guitar on it too. I wrote it with Dorothy."

I hated that as soon as Francine mentioned our song I wanted to impress her. Francine only nodded, quickly turning to Mama to tell her about something Janice said over dinner that had rubbed her the wrong way.

While Francine and Mama moved on to the subject of Francine's neighbors, I stared at my hands, thinking of Daddy's questions from the night before. Now that I'd left, I couldn't imagine returning to that life no matter how much it hurt to miss her. It was so far away from me I might as well have made it all up.

What Dorothy wanted from me was impossible. I couldn't imagine going back to being only bandmates with her. I was accustomed to concealing my feelings, but my broken heart would never mend if the wound was reopened every day by being around her. Hardly anyone would know how our relationship had changed, but inside it would tear me in two.

Though I hated to think of letting the band down, they'd been just fine without me before. They could get some other guitarist to play all the parts Dirk and I had worked out or do away with the second guitar all together. My greatest value to the band was as a songwriter, and that was nothing I couldn't do from here.

"Alice? Are you listening? I've got to see the doctor for a checkup tomorrow and Mama's already babysitting Buddy's kids. Can you look after John?" Francine asked.

"Just tell me what time you need me here."

On Friday night at May's there was a tiny spark of the old excitement when I mounted her front stairs. She'd pulled out all the stops for me. The dining table was covered with platters of pate and crackers, and her ice bucket had good wine in it.

Sharp and bittersweet memories returned to me. It had all started here in this house, when Dorothy's voice had enchanted me for the very first time.

I threw back wine faster than I should, May and I giggling on the porch. Though I didn't even smoke, I asked her for a cigarette. I didn't stop puffing on it when it made me lightheaded and dizzy.

"Tell me something about the tour! I want to hear about your big adventure."

I shrugged and pulled a thread of tobacco from my lip. "It was okay. How's the office doing?"

"Frank misses you," Dorothy said, putting a foot on the chair and deepening her voice in a perfect impression. "How is that sweet little girl Alice doing?"

Henry came by, climbing up on the porch with his arms outstretched toward me. The three of us sat talking and laughing like it was old times. We were so tight that we forgot to turn on Huck's show.

"So, you haven't told us nothing about your tour yet," May said, pointing her cigarette at me. "You must have a million stories and I've just been dying to hear them."

I motioned that I wanted another cigarette. "It was more boring than you'd expect. Lots of driving and stuff."

"Oh, phooey. You must have some interesting stories to tell us. Just one?"

I looked between May and Henry, whose eyebrows were up around his hairline. "Well, some of it was fun, I guess. There were lots of little parties and things like that. It's an interesting lifestyle."

"What are they like? The band, I mean?" May asked.

"They're a good bunch of people to work with, I suppose."

"What about Dorothy? Is she a bitch or anything like that?" May asked. "Like, does she put on airs and things?"

The laugh I forced out was hollow. "No. She's a nice person."

"And now for the million-dollar question, did you find yourself a man while you were out there? Were any of the guys in the band cute?"

I tapped ash from my cigarette into an empty wine glass, then stared at the burning end.

"Oh, come on now, you're looking like there's a story there. I don't see how with a whole group of men, nothing happened at all," May said.

"Well. It didn't."

"Good golly. This whole thing is wasted on you, girl. Get me out there and I'll be with some big-time star just like that," May said, clicking her fingers.

"Hey!" Henry said, but he was laughing.

"I tell you, it just ain't right. You and I should swap places, so they can see what a red-blooded woman is like, Miss Ice Queen," she said.

I glared at May. She would never know how hot my blood ran for Dorothy, how desperate I'd always been for her fingers and mouth. She'd wanted me too. I brushed a hand over my face, suddenly so tired I couldn't stand it. "You know what? I'm going to go."

May's brow furrowed. "Oh, c'mon now. I'm just kidding around."

"I know," I said. My handbag was in the hall, and I walked inside to retrieve it, searching through it unsteadily for my keys.

"Alice, you can't drive. You've had too much to drink, don't you think?" Henry said.

"I'm all right. I'll see you later," I muttered, already halfway down the stairs. May called out for me and I pretended I couldn't hear her, slamming the car door shut against her voice.

For a moment I forgot to turn on the lights and when only darkness stretched out ahead, I finally flipped them on. Because I couldn't bear the thought of going home I headed for Bill's place. I'd been meaning to drop by the record store; he didn't even know I was home yet.

I concentrated hard on the road ahead of me, realizing in a numb kind of way that Henry had been right and I really shouldn't be driving. When I arrived I could have wept to see lights on inside and the twitching of a curtain in the front window.

When we sat on Bill's sofa, I awkwardly balanced a cup of black coffee on my knee. Bill gestured toward his varnished coffee table, smiling gently at me. I put the coffee in front of us, trying to right it as it spilled onto the saucer.

"Have you had a few drinks, Alice?"

"I have. Sorry for just showing up like this. I know it's late."

"Are you kidding? I'm so happy to see you! I really have missed you. I've been wondering about how you were doing."

"I'm sorry I haven't been better at staying in touch."

Bill waved a hand. "Oh, don't worry about that. We can always pick right up where we left off. Now tell me all about it. It sounded from your letters like you were having the time of your life."

"Yes," I said, picking up my coffee again and blowing on the surface.

"I still can't believe it, you know? Like I always said, it's like something from a movie. All that time we spent listening to her music and now you're in her band. She sounded like such a great person from the way you wrote about her."

It was on me in a flash, the pain ripping through me, and what little composure I'd gained since leaving May's crumbled. Out of the corner of my eye I could see Bill staring at me.

"I'm sorry. I should go," I said, my shoulders shaking with sobs.

"No, of course not," he said, holding me and patting my back.

"I'm really sorry," I said as he released me. "I just miss...
everyone. I don't know, it's silly."

"We all get the blues sometimes. There's nothing to be
sorry about."

I wiped at my face with my sleeve and Bill disappeared,
returning with a checked handkerchief.

"Did something happen?"

I bunched the handkerchief in my fist. "I don't know."

Bill sat with his hands on his knees, looking at me expectantly.
If I breached that barrier, if I spoke about the things that I'd
hidden so carefully all my life, I didn't know what it would
mean. But when Bill smiled at me so kindly, I knew I was safe.

"It's Dorothy. We were together. And now I don't think we
are any longer."

Bill put his hand on my back, warm and firm. "You can tell
me."

When I confessed Bill just listened, patting my back now and
then. Afterward he put me to bed, kissing me on the forehead
and taking my shoes off.

"I'm going to sleep on the sofa, all right?" he said softly.

When I woke up, I squinted against the light. Bill had a solid
mahogany headboard and I gripped it and pulled myself up, as
though bracing myself for another day. I found Bill pottering
around the kitchen, toasting bread under the grill.

"Can I get you another piece?" he asked.

"No, thank you," I said, staring down at my plate. Bill's china
had a floral pattern around the rim. "How's business?"

"Booming. Dad finally gave in and agreed that I could start
trading in rock'n'roll records, so it's going well."

"That's good, Bill."

When he walked me to my car, he rested his hand on my
back again. "You'll feel better soon. I promise. You come and
see me any time."

"Thanks, Bill."

Daddy was washing his car in the drive when I got home,
eyeing me warily. It must drive him crazy that I was coming

home in the same clothes I'd been wearing the day before, but he didn't say anything. "A lady called for you last night. Said her name was Dorothy. She asked if you could call her back at home."

I nodded, watching his work-worn hands wringing out his sponge.

"Tell your friends not to call here after nine. I had to get out of bed to answer it."

"I'll tell her."

The next day, on Sunday evening when I was at home alone, there was another call. When the shrill ringing pierced the quiet, I put down my novel and walked toward the phone on the table. I stood frozen until it stopped.

Dorothy knew that on Sunday evenings my folks would be at my grandparents' place. She'd heard all about the fights when I'd stopped going with them, and she was aware that Mama still asked me every time but that I said no.

Only a few seconds after it stopped ringing, it started again. I picked up the receiver and dropped it gently. When it rang yet again, I plugged my fingers into my ears and went outside. I didn't know how long I could listen to it ring without answering it.

The next day I walked into town to visit Bill at the record store. The streets were empty for the most part, and when I passed people sitting on their porches the faces that turned toward me were closed and hard. It was strange to think that it had ever felt like home here.

When I walked into Stone Street, Bill's broad smile lifted the heaviness in me.

"Hey, there. I'm glad you came. I've got a big stack of records for us to listen to!"

While we were working through Bill's pile, a customer came to the counter, lifting off his brown cowboy hat. When he put his purchase down in front of us, I caught the sideways look Bill gave me.

"How you doing, Ray?" he asked as he rang up a copy of "The Two of Us."

"I'm good. Been meaning to buy this one for a while. Say, you always seem to know what's going on. Do you know if Dorothy Long's going to be doing an album? I really like her stuff."

"Can't tell you, friend. Hope you enjoy this one, though."

The bells chimed when Ray left the store, and Bill raised his eyebrows. "Didn't want to take advantage of your newfound fame and impress him?"

"Not today," I replied. I looked around the store, making sure there weren't any customers lingering in the stacks. "I think she tried to call me last night. A couple of times."

He put his palms on the counter in front of him. He'd been waiting to ask me about her again, I could tell. "You didn't take the call?"

"I didn't. I don't know why. I want to speak to her, but I just couldn't pick up the phone."

"You're scared. Of what she might say," he said, putting his hand on top of mine.

"I guess that's right. You know, I really appreciate you listening to me about this. You're being such a good friend."

He gazed at me warmly. "It's nothing, I'm glad you told me. But if you don't mind me saying so, you should talk to her. It sounds like things were left in the air. I know what it's like to have things broken off suddenly. It can take an awfully long time to get over it."

Bill had long eyelashes that brought a softness to his face. I hated anyone who could hurt him. "That's happened to you, hasn't it?"

"I'll tell you all about it sometime," he said, smiling once more.

"I want to ask you something… This might sound strange. But you always seem content and happy. How do you do it, when we're treated the way we are?"

When he drew himself up, straightening his back, there was a flintiness in his eye. "Because they don't want me to be happy. So, they can all go to hell. I'll be happy if I goddamn want to."

When the corner of his mouth twitched upward, we each broke. The belly laughter was as cleansing as my crying had been.

"Maybe you're right. It's going to be hard to get any privacy, but I'll call her when I can."

"Why don't you come over to my place for dinner tonight? You can have time to yourself to call her."

"I'm not sure what I'd do without you, Bill."

I drove over to his place that night and we dined at his kitchen table, on his perfectly matched white place settings with the flowers. The meat loaf was flavored with herbs that made it much better than any version I'd had before. Despite how warm and hearty it was, I pushed it around my plate.

"I'm sorry. This is really good. I'm just not that hungry."

"Don't you worry. You can take your plate home with you if you like. It was nice to have someone to cook for, anyway."

I started to move from the table. "I'll do that for sure. I'll help clean up."

"Thanks, but you really don't have to. I'll show you to the phone."

It rested on the small table in the hall, and after Bill had pointed it out he pulled the kitchen door closed behind him. I sat on the floor, taking the crumpled piece of paper from my pocket. It was the same piece she'd given me all those months ago, torn from the hotel stationery.

I dialed carefully, slowly putting my finger in the holes one after another. What if she didn't answer now that I'd gathered my courage?

The phone was snatched up within the first two rings.

"It's Alice," I said, clutching the receiver. "I heard that you'd tried to call me?"

As it came down the line, her voice was deeper than I remembered. What else had I recalled incorrectly? If I saw her again, would her face look the same? "Can you talk? I mean, is there anybody around you?"

"It's all right, we can talk. I'm at Bill's place."

"I wanted to know, how you are? I mean…I mean, are you okay?"

I twisted the cord around my finger. "I'm just fine."

"Did you really mean it? When you said that you wouldn't be back until it was time to record? Are you really not coming back until then?"

There was another long gap, stillness between us. I lightly banged my head against the wall behind me.

"Is there anything I can say that might persuade you to come back earlier? I'd very much like to see you," she said.

"I don't think that there is, Dorothy."

I cleared my throat, eyes rolling toward the ceiling. It wasn't fair to keep it from her. I didn't know when I might speak to her again. "I should tell you now, I'm not sure that I'll come back at all. I think I might stay here."

"You want to leave the band?"

"I just think it's the best thing I can do right now. I don't think I'm cut out for it."

"Please think about what you're doing. Let's talk about this," she said urgently.

"That's what I've decided," I said quickly. "Don't worry, I'll still write for you. I'll send things to you and everything. I don't want to stop doing that."

Her voice was hoarse. "I need you to be here…"

"That's just not possible," I said, my eyes welling up. "Not at the moment."

"Then when, when will you be back? Why did you tell me you'd be back, if you didn't mean it? How could you do this? You didn't even give me a chance to say goodbye!"

I covered my face with my palm. "I thought I would be. Back. I've got to go."

"Will you call me again? When can I speak to you?"

"I don't know," I said, putting my finger out to press the button, disconnecting.

I leaned against the wall, too wounded to even cry. I left the hall, to find Bill. He sat on the sofa with a book in his lap.

"How did it go?" he said.
I shook my head, chest aching.

For the next week I dragged myself from place to place. I filled my hours with cleaning the house and cooking, wandering around and going for long drives out of town. I had already grown tired of Mama asking what I was doing and where I was going. If I tried to read a book or write I'd be swiftly interrupted by Mama asking me to get up and help with this or that.

For a while I'd been so free, and now that I didn't have a moment to myself I wasn't sure that I could bear it for long. The money from the tour was enough to sustain me for a little while, but it wasn't enough for me to get a place of my own. At some point I had to think about making some cash. Maybe one day I'd be able to live off royalties, if the songs ever got big enough, but until then I'd have to work a normal job just like everyone else.

Late one afternoon I came home from Francine's place, having spent the afternoon doing the wash and helping her starch her husband's shirts. Francine said that I could never understand how much being pregnant tired you out.

Mama stood at the kitchen sink, scrubbing dirt from potatoes. "Alice, I'd like it if you set the table. Oh, and some mail came for you today. It's on the entry table."

"Okay," I said, backing away and going to the hall. I didn't need to look at it to know it was from her.

It was a postcard, a picture of the Nashville skyline and the city's name written in large letters. I turned it over. There was no return address, and she hadn't signed it. A splash of discoloration stood out against the white cardboard, her perfume bringing a thousand images with it.

"Hello, Alice. Just writing in regards to the song we were most recently discussing. If you could get back to me about the composition 'Do You Miss Me?' with any notes and additions it would be most appreciated."

The song title was underlined. I carried the postcard to my room gingerly, as though it might burn me. After I smelled her perfume again, I tucked it under my pillow.

Of course, I couldn't smell it through my thin pillow when I lay my head down. Still, it was as though just by being there it kept me caught in her memory.

I dreamed of her more than ever after the postcard. Though I could never remember much of my dreams in the morning I knew she'd come to me in the night, flashing her sad dark eyes. It made me hug my pillow, fearing that I'd never hold her again and missing her so much that I didn't know how I'd survive it.

CHAPTER THIRTEEN

On Friday night I visited May, bearing a peace offering in the form of an expensive bottle of gin. I felt bad about the way we'd left things the last time I saw her, and I hadn't returned her calls in the weeks since.

Henry's car was out front and I pulled up next to it, reluctantly unfastening my seat belt. Now that I was here, I wasn't sure that I had the stomach for it. The two of them sat on the porch on the kitchen chairs, with drinks in hand. As I got out of my car I saw them speaking to one another while they looked at me, and I hated to think about what they might be saying.

May rose and put her hand on her hip. "Well, it's about time you came around."

"Sorry," I said, looking up at her sheepishly as I climbed the stairs. "Sorry I didn't call you back either."

"I should think so! Think you're too good for us now that you've hit the big time, huh?"

I held up the brown paper bag, pulling one side down and exposing the label.

"Well, all right, I forgive you, I guess!" she said. "Why don't you go and make us all a drink? Tonic's in the fridge."

We were halfway through the bottle of gin before I knew it. May grumbled about Mama and we gossiped about the possibility that Francine's husband might have a wandering eye. Henry mostly just shook his head at us while he sat slouched in his seat, smoking. After what happened last time, May avoided the subject of my time on the road.

"How's Frank been? He must be missing me something awful," I said, having to grab onto the words before they floated away. I'd been drinking too fast.

"Oh, you just know that he is! But he's got an eye on your replacement, I reckon."

"Do you think my replacement is going to be sticking around for a while? I mean, I guess I wonder if there are any vacancies," I said, and I couldn't help it when the corners of my mouth turned down.

"Henry, why don't you go on inside? Alice and I have got to talk about a few things," May said, after staring at me for a moment.

"Huh! Come on, you can talk about things in front of me!" Henry said, leaning over the edge of the porch and spitting.

"Henry! I told you not to do that. Now scram!" May said, kicking her leg out at him.

"All right, all right," he muttered. "Guess I'll just have a little party by myself inside then."

May turned to me as soon as the door shut behind him. "What the hell is going on, Alice? I've heard your songs on the radio, so I know things are going well. Do you know how excited everyone's been for you at the office? I've been telling anyone who'll listen that you wrote that song."

I sat with my arms crossed, avoiding her eye.

"Are you going to tell me what's been eating you, or am I going to have to spend the rest of the night dragging it out of you?"

"It's nothing," I said, picking at a fingernail. I hadn't played my guitar for days and days and I'd let my nails grow long when usually I was meticulous about taking care of them. Once Dorothy had told me that I had beautiful hands, that my fingers were like parts of a perfectly crafted instrument.

May poked me, her finger digging into my arm. "Don't even try that on me. You haven't been yourself since you came back. Is it a man? Is that why you got so mad at me, last time you were here?"

I laughed. "It's *nothing*."

Each of us sipped our drinks, locked together in silence. May put her hand on my arm, softly this time. "Alice… Is it a woman, then?"

My pulse thudded. Had she finally figured it out? I fiddled with my drink, wiping condensation off the glass. I drew my shoulders up, casting a line to see what she'd say. "What if it was? Would you hate me then?"

"How could I hate you? You're my own flesh and blood, aren't you?" she said. It was quiet for a long time before she spoke again. "I'm not going to pretend I understand it. That kind of thing. Don't think I've never met one. Of course I've known of a few in my time. I never thought you'd be that way, but then you've always been a bit different."

"I can't help it," I said.

"I guess you would, if you could. It's a miserable life," she said grimly.

I opened my mouth but closed it a moment later. The only misery was in the way other people saw it, but they were imagining something false. To them it was a shadow life, like a story in one of my paperbacks. May could never understand the happiness I'd experienced with Dorothy, the sweet secret bliss of it.

I thought of Dorothy and me talking in bed at night, her arms secure around me while my head was on her chest. I summoned up the idea of us making love, the way that Dorothy could unlock wave after wave of pleasure from me. If I told May that for me it was better than being with a man she'd scoff, but nobody could take away what I knew to be true.

"So, what would you expect me to do? Be by myself forever, even though you agree I can't help it?"

May cackled, throwing her head back. "What do I know? Hey, maybe we're not so different. My love life has always gotten me into trouble! Just be careful, won't you? Don't let your mother ever find out. She'll find a way to blame me for it."

"I wasn't planning on it."

"Why do you think you're like that? I mean, did something happen to you, honey?" May said softly.

I faced her. "Nothing bad happened to me. It's not like that at all. Okay? It's just how I am."

The door creaked open and Henry poked his head out. "Hey, can I come back now? You ladies finished having your heart to heart?"

May grabbed me, hugging me for a second. Then she pushed me away, rubbing her knuckles against my head. "Okay, Henry. I think we're done. Get me a smoke, will you?"

That night I slept on May's sofa. As I drifted off I could hear music from the radio on the porch, and Henry and May's low voices mixing in with the sound. I rolled over and pushed my face into an embroidered cushion when "The Two of Us" came on. No matter what I did, even if I stopped writing music for her, I'd never be able to escape Dorothy. That voice would follow me wherever I went.

I rose before anyone else, washing my face and slipping on my shoes not long after dawn. I drove home through the quiet streets, the air crisp where it drifted through a cracked open window. As soon as I got there I climbed onto the mattress to sleep off my hangover. I had an awful gin-soaked headache, and I still couldn't believe I'd had that conversation with May. At least I wouldn't have to pretend with her anymore.

I reached under my pillow and fingered the corner of my postcard. How could it be all I had left of her? My eyes fell shut over my tears, as I sank back into sleep.

"Alice! Wake up, a car just pulled up outside. I don't know who they are," Mama said sharply. She hated it when I slept all day, and she'd probably been waiting for me to get up to help her with supper. Sun on its way to setting bathed my room, and I guessed my brothers and sister would be over soon.

"Huh?" I said, rolling over and opening an eye, looking at her groggily. Sleeping in the daytime always made me feel low.

Mama scowled down at me, a dish towel draped over her shoulder. "I said, get up. There are people out the front of the house. Go and see to them, will you? I'm in the middle of something, and your daddy's not home yet."

I got up and smoothed down my plaid dress, yawning. Mama hated dealing with salesmen or anyone she didn't know. I padded out of the room and down the hall. As I stepped out onto the front porch, I readied myself to tell them we weren't interested.

It was Dorothy standing in her pale blue sundress, like an apparition born of my own desperate desire.

She stood by the Chevy while Earl lifted a case out of the trunk. She stared up at me, shielding her eyes from the late afternoon sun with a long-fingered hand. My mouth went dry, and I looked behind me, into the hall. How was I supposed to explain this to my folks?

At that moment, Earl looked up at me too. He tipped his broad cowboy hat before turning away to get back into the car. Dorothy leaned down toward him, speaking through the open window. She was motionless while he drove away, her case at her feet with her brown-eyed stare on me.

The two of us stayed in place, me up on the porch and her down in the yard with her feet planted on the dirt driveway. She picked up her case, then put her shoulders back and walked toward me. We met in the middle on the green grass, eyes fixed on one another.

Dorothy set her case down, scrutinizing me for a moment before throwing her arms around me. I breathed in the smell of her hair, the scent of her skin.

"Oh, Alice," she whispered, crushing me against her, her palms flat on my back.

I stood stiffly with my arms at my sides. "What are you doing here?"

Dorothy drew back, arms still about my shoulders and head bent as she stared into my eyes. "You didn't think I was going to let it end like that did you? How could I?"

Dorothy put her hand on my cheek, and we jumped at the sound of the screen door opening.

"Alice? Who is that?" Mama said.

Dorothy stepped forward. "Hi, Mrs. Johnson. I'm Dorothy. Dorothy Long."

"Oh. You're the lady Alice was travelling with?" Mama said, looking her up and down. "She didn't mention you were coming."

"Oh, that's my fault," Dorothy said smoothly. "We did discuss my coming to visit, but I accidentally told Alice the wrong date. My husband was coming here to visit some friends, you see, and I thought he'd meant he was coming a couple of weeks later. I should have called when I realized my mistake, but I can be a bit forgetful like that. I hope you don't mind."

"Oh…that's all right, I guess," Mama said, glancing down at Dorothy's case. She took the dish towel from her shoulder, folding it while she spoke. "You'll stay with us, of course? Or are you staying with those friends you mentioned?"

"She can stay in Francine's old room," I said. "I'll make up the bed. Come on, Dorothy, I'll show you."

"Your father will be home soon. Everyone else should be here any minute, too. I'll put out an extra plate for you, Dorothy."

"Thank you. I appreciate you accommodating me at such short notice," Dorothy said, smiling charmingly at Mama. To my surprise, Mama gave a genuine smile back.

Dorothy trailed behind me as I walked toward Francine's old room. I ushered her inside, noticing that it had a musty smell. Mama's sewing machine took up all the space on the desk now, but it stayed closed up most of the time. I picked up clothes from the bed, where there was a pile of old things that Mama must be intending to mend. I folded a shirt and laid it on the floor.

"Sorry it's such a mess in here."

"It's not a problem."

"Saturday night, so it's family dinner soon. All my brothers and my sister will be here. I guess you are meeting my family, like we talked about," I said, with a cynical laugh.

"Alice? Are you going to look at me? I mean… Is it okay that I'm here?"

I folded a sweater, tucking the arms underneath and patting the top of it until it looked neat. "We can't really talk now. You heard her, they'll be here very soon. Maybe we could go for a drive later."

Though my back was to her, I sensed it when she stepped closer.

Dorothy fitted her warm body against my back, her curves pressing into me, her hips jutting into my waist. She moved a handful of hair from my neck, pushing it out of the way and kissing the skin she found there. I dropped the sweater, winded by her touch. I turned until she was kissing me, her mouth firm on mine.

Our kiss was measured and careful, each of us conscious of the open door nearby, but the undercurrent of heat was there. How had I survived this long without her?

Dorothy spread her hands over my waist, rubbing her thumbs over my sides. As she looked into my eyes she pulled me upward and into her hips, holding me there for the briefest moment as I rested on my tiptoes.

I was already weak at the knees, frantic with want for her.

"Well, if you're not the most beautiful sight I've ever seen," she said, honey-voiced.

Gesturing toward the door, I licked my lips, her gaze following the movement. "We really should go out there before somebody finds us."

"Of course," she said, finally releasing me. "And yes, of course I think we should go for a drive."

There was the sound of a deep voice in the hall, calling out to Mama. "Come on. That's my brother. I'll introduce you."

One by one, my siblings and their spouses said hello to Dorothy as they filed down the hall. Each of them looked at her with surprise as though they'd never quite believed she was real. Buddy's stare roamed over the pale skin of her chest, and he scowled a little at the cut of her sundress.

Daddy arrived last. When he saw Dorothy he took his hat off, leaving a red band on his forehead. "Oh. Hello, ma'am."

"Daddy, this is Dorothy Long."

"It's a pleasure to meet you, Mr. Johnson."

"Pleased to meet you. Excuse me. I should go to wash up," he said, holding up his grime-stained hands.

Dorothy was to my right at the dining table. I jogged my leg up and down, surveying her out of the corner of my eye. Mama had prepared a pot roast with all the trimmings, and I was guilty all over again that I'd been too hungover to help with things today. Food seemed to stick in my throat, and I sipped water after every swallow. My two worlds were meeting, and I had no idea how to behave.

"So, I says to the guy, you're going to have to pay for that," Gus said.

Dorothy laughed along with the rest of the table, but it was the polite one she reserved for when something wasn't really tickling her funny bone.

"I would have loved to have seen the look on his face. I really would have liked to have seen that," Buddy said.

Gus's laughter ebbed away, and he stared across the table at Dorothy. "Dorothy. You're the lady Alice was traveling with, huh?"

"That's right," Dorothy said.

"And you're some kind of famous country singer, right?"

"Not quite. Maybe one day. Alice joining the band has made it a little more likely, I'd say," she said, tipping her head toward me.

"How's that?" Gus said, leaning forward.

"Well, the songs she's written for us have been more popular than anything we've done before. Mrs. Johnson, this dinner is really lovely."

"Huh," Gus said. "Well, we'll see, I guess. Anyway, you should have heard what Gus Junior did at school yesterday. I mean, ain't nobody could forget he's my son."

When dessert was brought out, I bolted down the key lime pie. Dorothy helped us carry the dishes to the kitchen. When Mama moved to light the stove to boil water for coffee I put some mugs out, then stood at her side.

"Can you excuse us? Dorothy and I are going to go out for a drive now."

"Why? Where are you going?" she said, shaking a match until it snuffed out.

"Nowhere! It's just...Dorothy's husband is here, like she said. We're going to meet him and his friends. She's not here for long."

Mama sighed. "You haven't been here for an awful lot of these dinners you know, Alice. I just thought that when you were finally here you might think about really being here."

She bent over the counter, spooning coffee powder into mugs. Her actions were slow as though she was tired, even though it wasn't late. In all this time, she'd never once said that she missed me. I leaned over and kissed her temple, and her hand froze. "Sorry, Mama. I'll make sure I come to church with you and Daddy in the morning, okay?"

"Just don't be out late."

"We won't," I said. I looked back over my shoulder to where Dorothy stood watching us.

"I'm sorry to take her away from you, Mrs. Johnson. We won't be long," she said. "Thanks again for the wonderful meal."

"You're welcome."

I grabbed my keys and we walked down the hall, passing my brothers where they sat outside. Buddy was perched sideways on a step and he lifted his feet out of the way, so we could get through.

"See you later," I said, barely glancing at them.

"Where are you going? I thought you two might play us a show!" Gus said.

"You can pay for it like everyone else!" I said, ignoring him when he shouted after us.

My headlights illuminated the group of them, watching as I backed out. When I bought the car, it had been an object of derision, and I'd had to put up with a lot of jokes about women drivers. I revved the engine and peeled out.

Dorothy hadn't spoken a word since we were inside, and it remained that way as we drove down the street. It was impossible to not think about all the other times I'd steered with her by my side.

"Your family are nice," she said.

"We both know that's not true," I said, and she flinched at my tone.

"Well, your folks are, anyway. Where are we going?"

I rolled my window down, trying to ease the trapped heat. "I don't know. Somewhere quiet, I guess. Or we can just talk while I drive around."

"I think it would be nice to sit somewhere. Can we do that please?" she said, rubbing her hands on her knees.

"Sure," I said, heading toward somewhere I knew on the outskirts of town. It was a kind of lover's lane a boy or two had taken me to back in high school. The place was an old empty lot near a gas station that had never been open for as long as I could remember. There were two other cars parked there, but they were far away so that it felt private enough.

I turned off the ignition, looking out of the windscreen as though I was still going somewhere. "Why did you come here?"

Dorothy's hand rested on my chin, moving me to look at her. My eyes were slowly adjusting to the darkness.

"I'm sorry, Alice. I never meant for it to go the way that it did. It all happened so fast."

Both hands were on my face now, holding me. I moved nearer, as though towed toward her by a current. "Earl is with you."

"He drove me here after I talked to him."

"And now he's here with you because why…because he gave you permission?"

With her hands in my hair, she shook her head. "That's not how it is, with him and me."

"How would I ever know, when you've kept so much of it from me?" I said. I turned my head, leaning into her and kissing her palm.

"It's true that he made me feel guilty about us. He did that from the beginning. I guess he could see that I was serious about you," she said, tracing my lip with her finger. "I wasn't supposed to get serious about anyone."

I wanted to ask her. Was she truly serious about me? I sat mutely, still trying to catch up to the fact that she was here.

"I knew you were special as soon as we met. I tried so hard at first, thought I'd be able to hold back. Thought we could just be friends, and that'd be enough. It could never be enough. No. I'm no match for you, never was."

"Dorothy," I said quietly, looking into her eyes as much as I could in the dark. "But you…I never understood that I was being foolish with you. I never realized that it was never going to happen."

"It *is* going to happen, don't you understand? We're going to make it happen," she said, clasping my hand.

I didn't believe it, but she was so near to me. The fragrance that had clung to my postcard was overpowering now. Dorothy bent to me and rested her cheek on my own. Her skin was smooth against mine, sliding against me as she shifted to join our lips. Some of the hurt melted away under her mouth; she kissed me so lovingly.

"I missed you," she said. "It's been hell."

"For me too."

Dorothy gathered me in her arms, holding me to her. Then she took my lower lip between her teeth for a moment before she kissed me sweetly.

As it continued, our tenderness dropped away until we were kissing desperately, leaning across to one another, the gear shift between us. Dorothy put her hands on my arms, running them up and down, raising goose bumps.

I put my hand on Dorothy's leg, sliding it up her thigh under her dress. Her breath caught and her legs parted slightly as I caressed her. I wished we were in Dorothy's bed or one of the motel rooms we'd made our sanctuaries, anywhere but here. I wanted to feel her underneath me, for her to be looking up at me in that needful way she had.

"Is there somewhere we can go? I don't want to wait for you…" she said.

I looked around. Through the windscreen, I saw one of the cars turning on its lights and driving away. The other vehicle most likely had windows so fogged up they wouldn't be able to see anything anyway.

"Let's go in the back," I said.

I let her go first, watching over my shoulder as she swiftly got out of the car and moved into the backseat, the upholstery shifting under her weight. After a moment I looked around again and followed, opening the other door and sliding onto the backseat next to her, leaning forward all the way.

I loved nothing more than the time before we were about to make love, when my heartbeat bolted and my skin sang for her. Two nights ago I'd touched myself to memories of her, crying when it was over because I thought I'd never feel this good again.

"Come here," she said, clutching my blouse in a fistful by the front, lying back and pulling me so that I lay on top of her.

Dorothy dug her fingers into my thighs, grabbing onto me as she kissed me, her tongue in my mouth. She pushed her hands under my dress, dragging it upward so that it bunched around my waist.

We kissed feverishly. The heat she drew from me hadn't subsided, no matter how much I'd been hurt, and I pushed my hips down and into her. She wrapped her legs around me. For a while we lay fused together, kissing and sliding against one another, unbearable tension between us.

I bit lightly above her dress and then flattened my tongue, bringing it across her skin. She moaned, bending into me.

"Alice," she said. "Can you?"

There wasn't a moment's hesitation, and when she raised herself up I helped her tug her underwear down her legs. When she was laying down again I reached between us and found her, biting my lip at how willing she was.

I pushed my fingers inside her slowly, wanting her to burn sweetly with it. I watched her face as her eyebrows knitted together and her mouth fell open. I moved inside her while her hips rose up to meet my fingers, bracing myself on the seat with my other hand.

After a while she asked for more and I increased my pace. I moved my arm so that it was curled under her back, bringing her up. Her fingernails scraped over the fabric of my dress at my back as she pulled me near. We rested our foreheads against one another's.

Finally, she shuddered underneath me, softly crying my name. As I withdrew my hand she kissed me again and again on my cheeks, forehead and jaw, her arms thrown around my neck.

Now that it was over I couldn't look at her, and I leaned against her with my head on her shoulder while she rubbed my back.

I swallowed, trying to chase away the urge to cry. I buried my face in her shoulder while she cradled the back of my head with her hand.

"My darling…I wish I could make you understand how much I've missed you," she said, her breath against my hair. "Do you feel it, when you touch me? Do you know what's between us?"

I nodded against her, my limbs slack in surrender.

"Then what can I say, to make you come back?" she said.

"*How* do you want me to come back, though?" I said, my voice muffled.

"Wait a minute," she said. She sat up, still breathing rapidly, and pulled her dress down, reaching toward the floor for her underwear. I looked away while she rearranged herself, and then she took me by the shoulders, moving me so that we were facing one another again.

"I want you to come back as my love. I love you."

"I love you too," I said, fiddling with the neckline of her dress. I pressed my fingers to her collarbone. "I do. You think I want too much, though."

Dorothy's brow furrowed. "What do you mean?"

I took a deep breath. "I know what kind of a world we live in. I'm not stupid, or naïve. I'm aware that there's a lot of things we can't do."

"I've never, ever thought you were stupid. Go on."

"I just don't want Earl saying what we can and can't do. I can't see how it would work. I couldn't live like that, getting away from my parents just to have someone else calling the shots. I want you and me to be…a couple, like a man and a woman would be, I mean, where we can be together all the time."

"That's what I want, too! It's all I want," she said. She kissed my forehead once and then again. "This is just what I talked to Earl about. Things have to change. I don't think we can get divorced, not yet anyway. There's too much at stake. But he's given me his word that he'll stay out of our way. For real this time."

"But you'd still live together. Wouldn't you?" I asked. Before, when I'd thought of staying at the house with Earl and Sally it hadn't bothered me. I'd felt secure back then in our privacy, and when all the boys were staying at the house it didn't seem to matter anyway. Now that Earl had taken it upon himself to judge us, I couldn't imagine being near him.

"Not necessarily. He and I talked about this too. Alice, you and I are going to be partners, if that's what you want. You'll come first."

"That's your home. You love it there."

Her fingers tightened around mine. "Not enough to stay there without you."

I leaned my head back against the seat. She was saying everything I wanted to hear, but surely it couldn't be as simple as her coming back and offering me the world. "I can't ask you to do all this. This is impossible. I don't want you to resent me. You must have said what you said back then for a reason."

"I'm offering this to you because I want to. Listen. I was scared back then. I didn't have time to think about anything properly, and I was exhausted. I've done nothing but think about all this the last weeks."

"We've only known another for a little while, and like you said you and Earl had a deal…something you agreed upon ages ago…"

Dorothy was laughing, gripping my shoulders. "All right, stop. You were always right. Why are you trying to talk me out of it all of a sudden?"

"I don't know!" I said, pushing hair back from my face, her laughter infectious. I blew out a breath. "Okay. I guess I just think, who am I to come in and try and change everything?"

"You're not. And you ask who you are, well to me you're the woman that I love. I didn't know when I married Earl that I was going to fall in love, but I'm so happy I did."

I looked down at my hands. How could I ever do anything but go with her? "I think I could live with a few compromises…"

"I don't want you to just live with them. I want you to be happy. So… What do you say?" she said, a hopeful smile breaking across her face. "Do you want to give it a try?"

"I do."

She lifted our joined hands to her mouth and kissed the back of mine. We sat in the backseat and I put my arm around her, closing my eyes. She nuzzled into me, and I'd never felt so warm.

"Can I ask you something that might sound a little strange?"

"You can ask me anything."

"I've missed your singing. Will you do a little something for me?"

"I'll sing for you forever, if that's what you want," she said.

In the darkness of the car she sang me a melody I'd never heard before. Her precious voice surrounded me, helping to heal my broken heart.

CHAPTER FOURTEEN

I closed the buckles of my suitcase, pressing the top down and putting all my weight on it. I'd stuffed as much into it as I could fit, knowing that I might not be back for a long time. I spun around and walked into Dorothy's arms, resting my head against her shoulder.

"I can't wait until we can be alone together again," she said, her voice so close to my ear that it made me shiver. "Not that Francine's bed isn't just lovely."

For the past week, we'd been sleeping in separate rooms and stealing kisses whenever we could. It had been a pleasurable novelty to show Dorothy around Greenville. She came to church with us, and I loved seeing the heads of the locals turn at the beautiful stranger in their midst.

It had been a time for ironing out our problems and readying ourselves for what was to come. The day after she arrived, we'd gone out on the highway to meet Earl at his motel. We sat around the square formica table, Earl sipping whiskey from a mug.

Earl rubbed his stubble, a red flush painted across his neck. "I'm sorry I got involved, Alice. Dorothy and I always agreed that we wouldn't interfere with each other's business, and I guess I kind of broke that rule."

"It's okay," I said stiffly. I wondered if I was supposed to apologize too. I was still getting used to the idea of talking about these matters openly. It felt oddly civilized and at the same time just plain odd.

"I can promise you it won't happen again," Earl said. "You know, Mom is going to miss you, Dorothy. You too, Alice. I know she always liked having you around. You helped her out so much with the cooking and all that."

Dorothy's eyes met mine. "I'll need to talk to Alice about this privately, but would it be crazy to suggest that we stay for a while? At least while we're recording?"

Earl jumped in. "If she's all right with it, I will be too. It'll be nice and private, I promise, and I'm sure Mom will say the same thing."

I thought of the house, of Scout and Sally, and the chickens in the yard. I recalled the kitchen, the soft buttery light in the morning and its warm cooking smells. It would be strange to be there and have Earl and his mother know about us, but the thought was so appealing I barely considered turning it down. "I think I'd like that."

"Hell, let's do it! The boys will all be around. It's going to be a great time!" Earl said.

"Then it's settled," Dorothy said. "Earl, I'm going to drive back home with Alice, but not yet. She wants to spend some time with her family."

"Sounds good. I guess I'll get on the road early tomorrow morning then," Earl replied.

I remembered the way he'd shaken my hand again firmly before I left, then patted me on the back. I could see that he didn't quite know how to be with me and that he was treating me like a man because he didn't know what else to do. Though I felt the same way, I had a feeling that we were going to work it out eventually. Maybe one day he and I could even have a friendship. There were things that only people like us could understand about one another.

Dorothy rubbed my shoulders lightly. "I can't wait to wake up with you at the house. It's going to be so wonderful. I'll bring you coffee in the mornings."

I laughed. "No, you won't. When you're at home, you're lazy. I'll be finished cooking breakfast with Sally before you even open your eyes."

Dorothy kissed my neck. "Well, I'm not going to try and deny it."

"Either way, I can't wait either."

Dorothy pulled away, patting my shoulders. "I'll come and say goodbye to your parents, then leave you alone for a minute."

"Okay," I said. I grabbed the handle of a suitcase and looked around my bedroom. I had no idea when I'd be back, and the old homesickness was already starting to overtake me. Yet soon I'd have a different home with Dorothy, and that was a balm strong enough for any sadness.

We walked down the hall together to the kitchen. My parents had risen early, and Mama was serving up Daddy bacon and eggs with beans. Daddy sat at the breakfast bar with his elbows on the table, his hat next to his plate.

"Well, we're going to head off now," I said, a lump in my throat.

"Thank you for your hospitality this week," Dorothy said. Daddy only nodded, but he gave Dorothy a rare half-smile. Mama walked over to stand in front of her.

"You're welcome. I wish I'd been able to meet your husband, but it's nice to be sure that Alice is going to be with sensible people."

"Thank you, Mrs. Johnson. I'll go and pack up the car."

"Well. When will you be coming back to see us?" Mama said, bustling around the kitchen again, moving to pile another batch of bacon onto Daddy's plate. She stood poised with an egg flip in hand.

"I'm not sure. I'll send you some postcards, though, okay?"

"Yes. You could stand to be in touch with us a little more you know," she said, pointing the egg flip at me.

"I will, Mama. I'll try and make it back here around the time when Francine has the baby, at least."

"Good. Well, we'll be seeing you then," she said.

"Bye, Alice," Daddy said, stuffing his mouth with a piece of toast.

I fixed the image of them in my mind, Daddy wiping crumbs of bread from his chin and Mama looking at me sadly from across the kitchen counter.

When I got out to the car, Dorothy had already finished putting our cases in the trunk. She waited for me in the passenger seat. I sat next to her, my eyes watering.

"You okay?" she asked.

"I will be. Hard to say goodbye, you know?"

"Of course," she said. "I'm sorry it's hard."

"Thanks," I said, shaking my head as though to loosen the grief from me. "All right. Let's get on the road."

"Let's do it," she said.

I pulled out of the drive and we passed through the quiet morning streets. We drove through the center of town to get to the highway, and as we passed Stone Street Records, I waved to the shop front.

"Bye, Bill!" I said, even though it was too early for the store to be open.

"He's so nice. I wish I could spend more time with him," Dorothy said.

"You will, one day. Maybe he can come visit us or something."

"Sounds good to me," she replied. "Maybe he and Earl would like one another!"

We'd visited Bill on Wednesday night, when he'd invited us over for dinner. He met us at the door dressed in a checked Western shirt and blue jeans. The toothy smile he flashed as he beckoned us inside made me want to hug him.

"I'm a big fan of yours, Dorothy," he said.

"Well, that's a coincidence, because I'm a big fan of yours, too. Alice here talks about you all the time!"

He grinned at her and then at me. "I thought I'd grill us up a couple of steaks. What do you think?"

"That sounds lovely," I said.

Bill served dinner with red wine. He served the steak just how I liked it, tender without being too rare. Dorothy looked around the room, at the mahogany bookshelves standing against the walls. Her head was tilted as she read the spines of his book collection.

"Looks like you've got a lot of great stuff here!" she said.

"You should see his record collection," I said, gesturing toward him with my glass of wine in hand.

"I'd love to!"

"I'll take you into the living room for a look after we've eaten, for sure. So, what's the plan now? You're heading back to Nashville soon?" Bill asked.

"That's right. Dorothy and I are going to drive back on Monday morning, then it'll be time to start recording."

"Wow. That'll really be something."

"You helped Alice with the songs, didn't you? Transcribed them?" Dorothy asked. I loved the way she was looking at him, smiling as though she was so proud to meet him. I could see that she liked him just as much as I did.

"I did," Bill said. "We had a great old time doing that, didn't we?"

"We did have fun. You taught me a lot of stuff."

So much had happened since then. It was difficult to remember a time when I hadn't been in love with Dorothy. Perhaps even in those days, when I barely knew her, I'd been in love with her a little. Every mark on the paper, every note, had brought me closer to her. "I didn't really know what I was doing."

"Oh, that's not true. I helped with the technical stuff, but you knew exactly what you were doing. I was just trying to keep up," Bill said.

"She's so very talented, isn't she?" Dorothy reached for my hand on the table. After a glance at Bill I let her, grasping her fingers in mine.

He raised his glass to his lips. "Well, but you're both very talented, right? That's why you're so perfect together."

Dorothy and I smiled at one another, my stomach fluttering. It was an extraordinary feeling to have someone I cared about be so happy for us. I wished it was a sensation I could have more often, and I savored it.

I beamed at the memory then focused back on the road, Dorothy putting her hand on my knee as I drove. "Shall we stop soon, get ourselves something to eat?"

"Yep, sounds good," I said.

Though I'd been delighted to eat home cooking, I now found myself looking forward to one of the greasy spoon diners we typically stopped in at. It would be filled with truck drivers and travelling salesmen, world-weary waitresses and families with tired kids. Sometimes the food was rubbery or soggy, but now and then I'd order something perfect. There had been thick-cut smoky bacon, fresh baked bread, and fried green tomatoes with toppings I'd never have thought of.

"Where did you just go?" Dorothy asked.

"I was thinking about all the places we've stopped to eat on the road. It would be great to write a road song, maybe something about the people you meet out there. Something people could sing along to while they're driving. What do you think of that?"

Dorothy smiled, rubbing my knee. "I think I love to watch that brain of yours at work. It's a wonderful idea."

"Thanks. I want you to help me write it. I like your ideas too."

"I'd love to."

It was quiet for a while, Dorothy lifting her hand to my shoulder and then rubbing the back of my neck.

"Now what are you thinking about?" I asked.

"I was just thinking I want to learn how to drive, to help out with all the travel. I've always been a little scared of driving for some reason, but I think I'd like to conquer it."

"Hey, if you want to. Want me to teach you?"

"I do! You said May taught you?"

"She did. We had a lot of laughs. She told me I'd taken a few years off her life, but she was a good teacher."

"I can see how she would be. She's a character, huh?"

"She sure is," I said.

I'd introduced Dorothy and May last Friday night. When we arrived, my aunt was sitting on her front porch as usual with a glass of straight whiskey. As we got out of the car, I could feel May's eyes on us, sizing Dorothy up. When I glanced over at Dorothy, she was smoothing down her hair with her hand.

"It's okay," I said to her quietly.

"All right. I just hope she likes me," she said from the corner of her mouth.

"She'll like you," I said.

"Well, you must be Dorothy Long," May said.

"That's right. It's nice to meet you, May."

"Well, come on," May said, putting her arms out. Dorothy stepped forward and she wrapped her in a loose hug, patting her back. "Pleasure to meet you. Let me get you ladies a drink. Whiskey?"

"I won't have one," I said, gesturing over my shoulder toward the car.

May's eyebrows shot up and she shook her head at me. "This all has changed you! You'll have a drink with me at least, won't you, Dorothy?"

"Sure thing."

"I like her already," May said, pretending to whisper.

Dorothy and I walked behind May to get ourselves chairs from the kitchen. When Dorothy was stepping outside with hers, I turned to May. "Henry's not here?"

"No," May said as she took a whiskey bottle with a faded label down from the shelf. "I thought it best that he didn't come over tonight, with Dorothy here."

"Why?"

At the sink, she used a silver pick to stab a chunk of ice. "He has a few opinions about this sort of thing that you wouldn't like."

"Why on earth did you tell him?" I said, my voice rising an octave.

"Didn't mean to, I was three sheets to the wind. It just slipped out, I guess. Don't worry, though. He's not going to run around the whole town telling everyone," she said, pouring a couple of fingers of whiskey into glasses.

"You make sure he doesn't! You know how quickly it would spread around this place."

"I'll be sure of it. Henry's a bastard, but not that much of a bastard. He knows you're my favorite niece. He wouldn't want to ruin your reputation. Here, take this out to her," May said, handing me a glass of whiskey on ice.

I dragged the radio outside with us, so we could listen to Huck's show. The sound of a slide guitar played as a Patsy Cline song opened, and May leaned forward in her chair.

"Have you ever met this lady? I like her. I think she's going to go far, don't you?" May said.

"I sure do. I haven't met her myself, but a couple of the guys in my band have. I hear she's a wonderful woman," Dorothy replied.

"What about that Ernest Tubb? What's he like?"

I sat back while they talked, taking in their animated expressions and hand gestures. I loved that Dorothy's passion for music wasn't affected at all by the fact that she was a part of that world. She was still as excited about music as May was. A moment later it struck me that I'd become a part of that world, too.

"Do you reckon you two could sing me a song later?" May asked. "I don't know when you'll get around this way to play, and I'd love to have my own private show."

"We'd love to!" Dorothy said eagerly.

"I didn't bring my guitar, though," I said.

"That doesn't matter. We can do it a cappella, can't we?"

"Sure," I said, smiling at Dorothy.

"Honey, go and get us another drink, will you?" May said, holding out her empty glass toward me.

Dorothy stood up and put out her hand for May's glass. "Here, let me."

May turned to watch as she walked inside. "Well, darlin', I'll never understand it, but I suppose if you have to be with a woman you've just about picked the best one you could have found."

"I knew you'd like her if you gave her a chance."

"I was just worried, is all. You have to see it from my side, this lady coming into your life and all of a sudden you're…that way," she said.

Laughter bubbled up in me. "Oh, May, you've got to be kidding me. Deep down you must have known. She didn't turn me into anything."

May sat back in her chair, crossing her arms. "It's no laughing matter. Like I said, you're my favorite niece. I just want you to live a happy, normal life."

Her words softened me. She was wrong about so much of this, but she cared. That had to count for something. "All right, May. But trust me, I'm as happy as can be. Happier than I ever could have imagined."

"Good."

"I appreciate you trying to have an open mind," I said.

"She really is nice. And a pretty lady, too. I just don't understand how you can do it without the…you know, without the…" May lifted her little finger and wiggled it in the air.

"Oh, May! I don't want to talk about that with you, ever!" I said, looking sideways at her, then leaning close. "But for your information, there's nothing to worry about on that score. Nothing at all."

We both erupted into giggles, our heads close together. The sound of footsteps announced that Dorothy was coming back out onto the porch, holding the two glasses. "Here you go, May. What are you two laughing about?"

"Nothing," May said. While Dorothy was sitting back down in her chair, May wiggled her finger at me again and I shook my head.

I'd always remember that night, the three of us talking and laughing as the two of them got sozzled together. When I was getting so tired I had to drive us home, I watched as Dorothy and May hugged one another goodbye. The two of them swayed drunkenly, May clutching onto Dorothy.

"You be good to her, won't you? I miss her like crazy when she's not here."

"Of course, I will. We'll come and visit too. I'd love to see you again," Dorothy slurred.

My vision blurred as I remembered the way May had hugged me, too. She'd whispered in her ear that she loved me and said again how she wanted me to be happy.

I wiped my eyes.

"You okay, sweetheart?" Dorothy asked.

"I'm just a little emotional, I guess. But glad that we're heading out on another adventure."

"I'm happy too."

The road was like a ribbon unwinding before us, leading us back to Dorothy's house. When we got there, I would move my things into her room. I'd lay my toothbrush next to hers at the basin in her washroom and slip my nightgown under her pillow. In her closet, my clothes would brush up against hers.

I couldn't wait to slip into bed with Dorothy, to feel her skin against mine and the cool cloth of the sheets laid over our bodies. I wanted to be near her in the dark, to be able to trace every curve of her body with my tongue and fingers. The thought of it made me shift against the seat.

I'd written that in any small town there was a girl like me, waiting for a love like her. I was no longer sad and blue. Now when I wrote about love, my creations were infused with truth. There were so many things that I no longer needed to imagine.

I would write a thousand songs for her, songs that soared and ached with love.

We'd write them together, Dorothy and I.